YOU BELONG WITH ME
BY
KATHRYN R. BIEL

You Belong with Me

DEDICATION

This is for my parents, Philip and Mary Rose Kopach, who drove us to soccer practices, sat through soccer games, worked the soccer concession stands, bought us cleats and shin guards, melted in the heat of August and froze in the cold of October, and made it seem not at all weird to get up in the middle of the night to watch World Cup Soccer matches before they were popular.

AUTHOR'S NOTE

Dear Readers:

When I started writing the Boston Buzzards series in September 2021, we were very much still living in a pandemic society. Here in the Northeast portion of the United States, we were wearing masks, social distancing, and overall social events were limited. I included a fair amount of that in the first Boston Buzzards book, *XOXO*. However, since my books are written for escapism, I prefer to escape to a world where the pandemic didn't change our daily lives for what seemed like forever.

As such, in scenes that overlap those previously depicted in *XOXO*, there is talk of mask wearing, but it is not continued throughout this book. This is a purposeful stylistic choice rather than an error. I hope you can forgive the non-continuity.

Content Warnings: This is a fade to black romance that contains off-the-page consensual encounters. There is discussion of sexual relationships and language around that. Cursing and profanity is present.

Trigger Warnings: Hospitalization with significant illness, divorce, PTSD

CHAPTER 1: HANNAH

You know that recurring nightmare where you show up for your calculus exam except you've never taken calculus, and you start to panic because the whole page looks like it's written in Greek?

Actually, calculus *is* written in Greek, so that's not a dire enough example. No, this is much worse than that. How about the dream where you are out in public buck naked with nowhere to hide, and everything's just hanging out for the world to see?

That's how I feel right now.

No way is this happening. Not to me. Not tonight.

Heat floods my face as my hands grow cold and clammy and threaten to drop this entire tray of champagne I'm carrying. I flex my fingers because that's the last thing I need.

I can practically picture the crash, all eyes turning toward me. He'd see me, no doubt. There's no way in hell I'm letting that happen. Also, I'd probably get fired, and I don't have the energy to look for another meaningless job right now.

If I didn't know better, I'd say I was on the verge of a panic attack. Hannah LaRosa doesn't have panic attacks. She's cool, calm, and collected.

Yet, that's not how I feel at all.

Also, Hannah LaRosa totally has panic attacks. They usually have one specific trigger, and that's not what's happening now. I should *not* be panicking over this.

I need some fresh air. Or to at least be in a separate room. Yes, those two things are important. But first, I need to put this tray down before I drop it. By some small miracle, I manage to avert disaster, get the tray to a stand, and rush to the bathroom. Surely there is some exit in there through which I can escape from him.

It wouldn't be the first time.

As I approach the bathroom, I pick up speed. I may be out of shape, but my body remembers how to sprint. You'd think I was being chased by a serial killer rather than my current situation.

Which, to be clear, is: after a dozen years, I'm finally in a room with the one who got away.

Well, he didn't actually get away because it's not like I truly had him in the first place.

I need to calm down.

I will, once I'm out of the line of sight. In two seconds flat I'm inside, protected, with my back to the door.

Not that he saw me.

Or that he'd come in here after me if he did.

Or that he even remembers me.

Okay, I'm fairly certain he remembers me, but maybe he's taken so many soccer balls to the head that he has selective amnesia.

One can hope.

It's not that I want him to have a brain injury or anything, but I would rather have a toe-nail fungus from a pedicure than have him see me here tonight.

STOP. I need to stop this whirling chaos in my brain. What the hell is wrong with me?

I'm suffocating behind this stupid mask, and I can't breathe. There's not enough air to fill my lungs. I hate that the waitstaff still has to wear these, but when the booking party requests it, we comply. I rip the infernal thing off, trying to process the last three minutes. Maybe my brain is deprived of oxygen, and I hallucinated the whole thing.

That would be a stroke of luck I don't have.

There is only one man who can send me into this type of tailspin, and it's Callaghan Entay. And he's here. In my place of employment. Definitely, my worst nightmare is coming true.

I mean, other than the nightmare I actually went through because of him.

"No no no no no."

"Are you okay?" The voice makes me jump, not that it would take much to push me over the edge in my current state. I really do need to calm down. The concerned voice belongs to a woman in a sparkly white and silver dress.

"I need to get out of here. Right now. But if that's not an option, I'd settle for the earth swallowing me whole this very instant." Now that I've declared my needs, I search for a way to make it all happen. See? I can still be logical. I'm not totally panicking. My eyes lock in on the window on the other end of the room. It's a rectangle, just below ceiling height.

Jeez, it looks small.

Maybe it looks tiny because I'm so far away. I walk closer, hoping that in reality, it's the size of a sliding glass door.

There's no appreciable change in its dimensions.

Shit.

Maybe I'm just not a good judge of this. Maybe the girl in the sparkly dress has an eye for this. "Be honest, do you think I'll fit through there?"

I grasp my ample hips and then swing my hands up, trying to gauge how wide they are as compared to the window. It's a maneuver I once saw Marilyn Monroe do in an old movie.

She got stuck in that window.

My companion puts her hand on my arm. "It can't be that bad. Whatever it is, it can't be that bad. And trust me, I've done tons of embarrassing stuff in my life. This moment will pass, and trying to squeeze out of an opening the size of a vagina is not necessary."

I blink, looking at her. She's probably right, but still, maybe I should try rebirth. I mean, at least I have experience succeeding at that. It's how I came into this world.

She continues, "I mean, hell, I just married a man I barely know. But that's me, the good little wifey. Anything to support his career."

Her admission is enough to pull me out of my own head, my own tailspin screeching to a halt. I did *not* expect to hear that. Did she say she barely knew him? Hell, that's definitely worse than the man you pined after for years showing up. A wedding does explain her white dress. It looks out of place compared to the sea of skimpy black body-cons this crowd normally wears.

"You got married?"

"Yeah, like literally a few hours ago. I'm not saying it was wrong or I'd take it back, but you know, like, we all do questionable things sometimes. You'll live."

Her nonchalance about being a screwup brings me back to the situation at hand. Wait a minute, what if she married *him*? I mean, it's not like I have any claim on him or anything, but if she married him, I am totally diving out the window.

I don't even care that it's on the second floor. The trip in the ambulance would be worth it.

It wouldn't be the first time I fled from Callaghan Entay and ended up in the hospital.

I have to know. "Did you marry one of these guys? One of the Buzzards?" Because of course, I know Callaghan Entay plays for the Boston Buzzards. Because of course, I've followed his career.

I'm a masochist like that.

In my defense, I follow all sports, not just his. Occupational—if I'd ever followed through on my career plans—hazard.

She shrugs. "It's complicated, but sort of. Why? Does your escape plan have anything to do with someone on the Buzzards?"

This will be totally awkward if I have to tell her I slept with her husband, but then again, she said she barely knew him, so it's not like she can hold it against me. It was a long time ago.

I'll leave out the part about being in love with him back in college.

I'd better fess up. She's been nice. "Yeah, it does. I haven't seen him in a few years, but of all the banquet venues in all of Boston, he has to walk into mine."

Seriously, why didn't I pay attention to what the event was tonight? Oh right, because it doesn't matter. I need the money and working at a catering facility is good pay these days. They're desperate for help, especially good staff, so they make it worth our while.

Since the odds of me becoming a professional sportscaster are only slightly better than of me being a professional athlete, I've got to do something to pay the bills. And this is about as good of a thing as any.

"Did you dump a drink on him? Spit in his food? Accidentally lick him?"

My eyes grow wide. How did she know? About the licking? Although to be honest, he did much more of the licking. And it was no accident. I mean, it was, because I should never have been with him in the first place because he didn't feel about me the way I felt about him, but it wasn't like I tripped and accidentally trailed my mouth down to his nether regions out in the middle of the dance floor.

"No, nothing like that. Just, well, I … he … well, we hooked up. Like way back in college. So yes, there was licking." My face flames at the memory of him between my thighs. "It was a long time ago, but the licking was quite purposeful. And consensual. I was a soccer player too, at least I tried to be, and now he's one of the best in the USSL, and I'm serving canapés."

There it is. My villain origin story. Not that I'm a villain. I think I'm a pretty decent person. Maybe a bit boring, but super reliable. But that night is where my downward spiral started. I don't need to get into those gory details with a complete stranger.

More gory details. Sharing information about licking was quite enough.

"Well, I don't know your deal, but you're here doing honest work. Nothing to be ashamed of unless something happened during your time together." The woman smiles.

Our time together? You mean countless hours in the gym where he saw me as one of the guys. Studying for tests together. Our platonic fist bumps that he called his good luck charm. Scrimmage matches and practice sessions where he'd talk about all the women he slept with. Until that one night, I told him I thought his brags and boasts were a lie, and that he needed to put his money where his mouth was.

Oh, boy, did he go for the money shot.

It still sends tingles down my spine.

But then, he got called to try out for the Nevada Renegades and I ... well, I ended up on a different path.

What a long, strange trip it's been.

I sigh, slightly pulling myself back together. "No, it was fantastic. But there's a chance I might have freaked out and run away in the morning. I wish I hadn't, but then when I tried to contact him again, he was a big star, and I didn't want to seem like a cleat chaser."

Plus, so much happened in between that I wasn't about to dump it on him at the start of his career. It wasn't his fault I was secretly in love with him and then almost died.

That's a lot of baggage that he was in no place to unpack.

The bride shrugs. "I say you just get out there, do your job, and if he approaches you, be candid and honest with him. That's all you can really do, right?"

I guess she's right. I do a quick mirror check and swipe my fingers under my eyes to catch some errant eyeliner. I guess I'd better get back out there before I get fired. I pull my mask back up and wash my hands. Even if I weren't in food service, I'm a freak about germs. This pandemic didn't help.

Time to face the music.

I look up to see the bride smiling at me. "I'm Ophelia, by the way. Ophelia ... Henry."

Thank God she didn't say Entay.

"Hannah LaRosa."

Ophelia opens the door for me, which I totally should do for her because she's a guest here. "You ready, Hannah LaRosa?"

At this moment, I forget why I'm even nervous. I pull my mask down and mouth "thanks" as I head back out into the reception area.

Candid and honest. Candid and honest.

I can do that.

But as I spy Callaghan Entay across the room, I'm wishing I'd taken a chance on the vagina window.

CHAPTER 2: CALLAGHAN

I'm counting the minutes until I can leave this stupid event. We're in training. We have the biggest two games of the season ahead of us. We should be resting and watching videos, planning our strategies. Not attending a fancy cocktail party, eating all sorts of crap food, and drinking heavily.

Proper rest is significantly underrated.

In my head, I say that in the poshest voice, my time spent playing soccer in the British Football League allows me to.

In reality, I'm from New Jersey, and we all know there's no cure for Jersey. My ex-wife told me that as she was storming out for the final time. I love that she used that as an excuse when we all know that my affinity for pork roll has nothing to do with why she left me.

Good riddance to bad rubbish.

Another saying from across the pond that I can't quite pull off.

Not that I need a fancy accent to help me out. I do alright.

I scan the room looking for someone who might have the potential to get me through the night. Just something quick and uncomplicated. It's been a while. With the Global Games in Paris a mere eight months away, I've been in such a zone that I've neglected this need.

Frankly, I've neglected every single person in my life who's not on the soccer field. It's an occupational hazard. What it takes to succeed at the top level.

I look for someone who might want to hang out for a bit tonight, but it seems as if most of the women here are with dates. My gaze falls on a woman in a sparkly white dress walking across the room. She's alone.

No wait, she's with … Is that Xavier Henry? What's he doing here?

There's absolutely no reason for him to be at a publicity event for the Boston Buzzards, yet here he is. Word on the street is that he's getting benched from the Baltimore Terrors.

They're a bunch of assholes.

Henry's not bad, despite the rumors. Our paths overlapped slightly when I played in the BFL, but then there was that thing with Phaedra Jones, and Henry was history. He showed up in the US a year or so later, playing for Baltimore.

I never really liked Phaedra or Edmund Jones for that matter, but still, what Xavier did was a shit move. I haven't heard a negative word about him since, though, so he's either cleaned up his act or has the best agent in the world.

He's a killer defender. I only wish we could get him on the team for the championship game. No matter the outcome of the game next week, Henry would be an asset to the team.

I finish off my whiskey. I'd bet a deal is already in the works. That's how things are done. It'd be the only reason why he's here tonight. I make a mental note to call my agent, Justice, to see if he's heard anything. Only so I'm prepared if HQ is shaking up the roster.

Shit. What if they are shaking up the roster? What if they're looking at another major revamp for next season and there's no longer a place for me?

It wouldn't be the first time.

I swallow the enormous lump that's formed in my throat. Miller's never given any indication that he's displeased with me, but I'm not getting any younger. I'll be thirty-five by the start of the next season and the Global Games next summer.

It's practically ancient in the soccer world. I might as well have Justice book my next endorsement for AARP or Prevagen since I'll be their target demographic.

That's a long way off, and it will do me no good to think about that now. I need to focus on the next thing. The next practice. The next game.

No need to think about things too far into the future.

I have no future.

Hard as I try, I can't picture a world beyond the Global Games.

And I don't want to.

I consider the road mapped out in front of me.

Tomorrow the Boston Buzzards leave for Indianapolis. We've got a semifinal game on Tuesday. Depending on how that game goes, we'll either be in the finals on Saturday or doing the most epic walk of shame back to Boston. Actually, it'd be a flight of shame, but that doesn't have the same ring to it. I can't think about that now. I have to focus on the positive. If we can win the next two games, I'm a strong contender for the US National Team. It's especially important heading into a year in which the Global Games are being held. Eight months from now, I could be in Paris, repping the US.

I only have to get there.

And I need the Buzzards' success to guarantee a place for me. There are a lot of talented goalkeepers out there. A little competition is good for the soul.

A lot is bad for morale.

I glance around the room, trying to assess if my teammates are behaving themselves. You'd think that they all know how important this is.

Of course, not everyone has a shot at the National Team.

It's a long shot still, but this is the closest I've ever been. And like Alexander Hamilton says, I'm not throwing it away.

Yes, I can quote Hamilton the Musical. My ex insisted on seeing it. But also, the music is pretty catchy, so I listen to it while I run. Don't judge me.

Maybe I should abandon my idea of finding a hookup and just go home. Our flight to Indianapolis leaves at ten a.m., so I don't think anyone will be surprised if I make an Irish exit. I'm only about 10 percent Irish, but this is Boston, and my first name is Callaghan. No one's going to question it.

My gaze falls back on Henry and his date. They're dancing in the middle of the floor as if they're the only ones in the room.

He's so in love, it's not even funny. Gak.

Maybe that woman is who set him on the straight and narrow, as if falling in love can actually change a person.

Though my ex did change me. Or at least my bank account.

I should grab one more drink and then leave. If I'm not going home with someone to tire me out, perhaps another whiskey will do the trick.

I'm in my own world as I wait at the mahogany bar for my drink, planning out what the upcoming week will hold for me. I'm grateful that the semifinals and finals are in Indianapolis. Lucas Field is a dome, so we won't have to deal with the potential weather extremes that playing soccer in mid-November can bring.

Not to mention it gives me some home-field advantage.

Indiana University, class of 2009, baby. Or I would have been, had I not been recruited and eventually drafted by the Nevada Renegades, missing out on my last semester. Go Hoosiers.

Shit, that was a long time ago.

Suddenly I feel more than my age. My muscles are tight and my bones ache, and I wonder if I can hang on for eight more months.

I have to. There's nothing else for me.

Soccer is all I have.

And it's all I want, so that works out nicely for me.

Except with every game, every season, every year, the possibility of life without soccer looms closer on the horizon like a dark cloud.

I look at my half-full drink, pondering if I should quit for the night. It would be easy to dive headfirst into a pity party in the same way I dive to block a shot on goal. That mental state, plus an open bar and early morning, are a recipe for disaster.

"Yo, Cal, you see Henry here?" TJ Doyle elbows me as I turn away from the bar.

I nod. He tends to get under my skin at times, mostly because he's a social media whore. He'll put anything and everything up for the world to see. He's always got his phone in his hand, even on the side of the field. He's one of those players who has a huge following but doesn't necessarily have the playing chops to back it up.

He's okay.

I mean, he's on a professional soccer team in the United States Soccer League, but he definitely has no chance of making the US National Team. I'm sure his agent will land him a lucrative deal, nonetheless.

"They just got married. That's random." TJ's still talking. It takes me a minute to realize that he's referring to Xavier Henry and the woman in white, who, now that I think about it, does look more bridal than cocktail party. "It was on his Insta."

Naturally, TJ would find it there. I scan the room, looking for an excuse to leave. Not just for the conversation but for the night.

"Um, okay. Good for them, I guess."

Xavier Henry's personal business is just that. Personal. Unless it affects his performance on the field, I don't care who he's married to. And until he officially gets traded to the Buzzards, none of it matters to me.

Across the room, through a sea of black suits, black dresses, and black waitstaff uniforms, something catches my eye.

Someone. A feeling of déjà vu.

I shake my head and blink, but then it's gone. I check the room again, but nothing. I can't even put my finger on who or what it was. Just … something from the past. Suddenly, I'm thinking about college again. When the hallucinations start, it's time to go.

"TJ, I'm out. You might want to think about it too. We've got to be at Logan by eight, and there's nothing worse than flying hungover."

We've all had that experience at one time or another. Zero out of ten, do not recommend.

I head to the coat check and give the girl my ticket. As I'm waiting for my coat, Xavier Henry and his bride approach.

My curiosity gets the best of me, and I have to know if they're in talks for him to join us. "Taking off so soon?"

"Yes, well, I didn't want the focus on us. It's your night. You should be celebrating. Best of luck to you next week," Henry answers.

That gives me nothing. Nothing except a little bit of respect for the man. He's definitely not a spotlight grabber. He's humble and hardworking. He would be an asset to the Buzzards. I should play it cool, but I have to know. "Are you really coming to us?"

Xavier shrugs. "Tryin' to. I'd be happy to play for Janssen again."

That's right. He did play for Janssen before the pandemic shutdown. My gaze drifts to Henry's companion. His wife.

He's a lucky man.

"I hear congratulations are in order."

If I'm not mistaken, Henry glares at me. "Yes, well, we're going to go off and finish our celebration, if you don't mind."

I laugh. He's a very lucky man, with a very lucky night ahead of him. "Yeah, big night. See you soon."

My coat is ready, so I hand the girl a tip and head out into the cold November night. I consider ordering an Uber, but it's only a three-block walk down Stuart Street to get to the Westin in Copley Square, where I'm staying for the night before we fly out in the morning.

It sure beats driving all the way back to Foxborough and then back up to Logan during the morning rush.

Not to mention the walk might help to clear my head. Something's not sitting right with me, and I just can't put my finger on it. I should be excited and exhilarated for the week that's to come. I should have my eye on the prize—the literal national championship—and the doors that will open for me.

If we can win, then it's practically a done deal for me. I'll have everything I've ever wanted.

And then what?

CHAPTER 3: HANNAH

Listen, Han, you need to quit your job."

Funny, after last night's close encounter with my past, I was thinking the same exact thing. Not like The Tower is a bar that I expect Callaghan Entay frequents, but I don't want to take the chance that he'll be back. It took me long enough to get over him the first time around. I can't afford to get trapped in his orbit again.

On the other hand, I can't let my roommate Carlos know he's onto something. He already thinks he's God's gift to the male species. I can't stroke that ego any more by letting him think he's a career counselor too.

But also, I'm curious. He was still out when I got home around midnight, so I didn't get to tell him about my near run-in with the best—and worst—hookup I've ever had.

The one that derailed my life.

Not that I'm bitter or anything.

"What's prompting this pep talk so early?" It's after ten, but we're both night owls, so that's not saying much.

"You're never going to get anywhere doing catering."

"I'm going to get a paycheck. I'm going to pay rent and they let us eat the leftovers, so I get my fill of lamb chops. That's all that matters."

That, and the health insurance.

If my parents hadn't had good health insurance, my medical debt would have ruined them. I may take crappy jobs, but they all at least have medical coverage.

That will always be the number one priority for me. Once you don't have your health, you realize how little everything else matters.

Carlos rolls his eyes. I'm so used to him in his makeup that to see his eyes without liner and shadow and a set of lashes is a little bit disconcerting. "Girl, you're pushing thirty."

"Carlos, I'm thirty-two."

He looks me up and down and shakes his head. "The fact that you admit that is a problem. But look at you. You're still working the same type of jobs you've been doing for the past decade. You move from one to another without settling down. I thought you moved out here to make something of yourself."

We have this talk about once a month. He means well, but damn if it isn't starting to grate. I'm going to ignore him, just like I did last month.

"I'm fine with who I am. Serving food is an honorable profession." I believe I heard that somewhere. Maybe from that girl in the bathroom last night.

"I'm not sayin' it isn't, but is it really your life's dream? Before you go lyin' to me, tellin' me you're content, tellin' me you're *fine*, ask yourself, is this what you dreamed of when you were a little girl?"

I stand up, practically slamming my coffee mug on the counter. "That's not fair. You know ... you know it wasn't." I want to storm out of the room and pout like a spoiled teenager. Except it seems oddly coincidental, and I'm not a person who puts a lot of stock in coincidence. First seeing him last night, and then Carlos bringing it up today.

I tend not to dwell too much on the past, especially since it took me so long to move past it. If you can call leaving home and going from job to job for a decade without ever pursuing my passion moving past it.

My life and mental health just work better if I stuff everything into boxes and put them way at the back of my brain closet. As long as they stay sealed and buried, I'm good to go. However, that also means I pretty much gave up on myself and my career.

Even my parents have given up on the "but you worked so hard for your degree" crap. I had a plan once, and that plan went immediately to shit with one night of impulsive behavior. I think my parents understand, at least a little. Hell, it took me years to figure out why I gave up on myself. Once I did, the panic attacks stopped and the insomnia even went away, for the most part. The only one who still rides me about not chasing my dream is Carlos.

Which is rich, considering he wants a career as a professional makeup artist, yet he's teaching art at the senior center.

He comes over and pulls me into a hug. I've got two inches and about fifty pounds on him, so it's not the comforting embrace I desire. But, still, it's the thought that counts, and I'll take it.

"I've got a plan for us, Han. For both of us. But it's going to take time and dedication and a lot of hard work. If we put in the work, I think we can both get what we want at the end of this. All you have to do is quit your job."

I roll my eyes. "Are you covering my rent? Are you buying my food? Are you making me lamb chops?" *Are you paying my medical bills in the event of a catastrophic complication?*

Carlos flops down on the couch. "I'm going to do you one better. I'm going to make us famous."

Un-huh.

"How do you plan on doing that?" I sit down next to him.

"How many followers do you have on ClikClak?"

I pull out my phone and check. "Um, eighty."

Carlos's mouth falls open. "Excuse me? Did you mean eight *thousand*?"

I laugh. "No, I mean eighty. Eight-zero. I don't post any videos, and I recently made my profile private. I'm not even sure how I got the eighty to begin with. Why? What does ClikClak have to do with your plan?"

"I want us to be content creators. Do you know how much money content creators make? We could be famous and rolling in it."

"Famous for what? What am I supposed to create?" I understand what Carlos would do there. He wants to be a makeup artist. From the precision with which he can do an eyeliner wing, I would say he's got the skills. Me on the other hand ...

"You know, do your thing."

"My thing? I don't have a thing. I'm like the world's most thing-less person."

Carlos throws up his arms in exasperation. "Han, when you were little, what did you want to be when you grew up?"

The answer is swift. "I wanted to be the next Lesley Visser."

"I have no idea who that is."

"Lesley Visser was the first female NFL analyst on TV. She's the only sportscaster in history who has worked on a Final Four, the NBA finals, the World Series, the Triple Crown, Monday Night Football, the Olympics, the World Figure Skating Championships, the US Open, and the Super Bowl. And she's a woman." I rattle her stats off as easily as Bobby Flay rattles off his recipe for shrimp and roasted garlic tamale. "Did you know that, to this day, she's the only woman to preside over the presentation of the Super Bowl trophy? That was in 1992 when Washington defeated the Buffalo Bills 37–24."

"And that's your thing. Boring sports statistics."

I huff. "They're not boring."

"To a lot of people, they are, but I bet there are a lot of people on ClikClak who would eat that shit up."

I shrug. "If you say so. But what does that have to do with anything?"

"It's a back door, but—"

I raise my hand up and get off the couch. "Stop right there. Don't ever—*ever*—refer to me and the back door again. Got it?"

This time I actually throw my coffee cup before I storm out of the room. Lucky for me, it's empty, so I don't stain the living room rug. Also that it lands with a soft thud on the arm chair. Damn, I'm still on the edge from last night. Some rational part of me knows it's not Carlos's fault, but I don't care. Those words hurt too much, instantly bringing me back to the worst time in my life. There's no way he could possibly know. But still …

It's like the universe is definitely sending me a sign, if I believed in those things, and they're all pointing at *him*.

I collapse onto my bed, burying my face into my pillows. It was a long time ago. I should be over it. I should be over him. It wasn't anyone's fault, not really. Just a bunch of stupid mistakes and stupid coincidences that created the perfect storm to totally tank all my hopes and dreams.

Not to mention almost kill me.

No big whoop.

Suddenly, the boxes at the back of my mental closet are in the front of my mind. They're threatening to spill open.

"Okay, seriously, what was that? You stormed out like a diva having a meltdown. And there's only room for one diva in this apartment, and we both agreed that would be me."

I groan and roll over, trying to remember that this has absolutely nothing to do with Carlos. I take a big breath and let it out slowly. "I would never dream of taking your title. You hit a nerve, that's all."

Carlos folds his arms over his chest and cocks an eyebrow high in a way that makes me totally jealous. I wish I had that kind of control over my appendages—if eyebrows are considered appendages.

"Let's just put it this way, it's never a good thing to get saddled with the nickname of 'Back Door Girl.'" My cheeks flame with embarrassment saying the words aloud. I cover my face with my pillow and for the second time in just over twelve hours wish I could dive out of the window to save my dignity, not that there's much left.

Sitting down on the corner of my bed, Carlos lets out a low whistle. "Well, I always figured you for straight vanilla sex. I had no idea you had a wild side."

Now I scream into my pillow. "Do you know what it was like to have *that* rumor spreading around college? The best thing that ever happened to me was the collapse of MySpace. If it hadn't imploded, I was going to have to delete my profile."

"So I take it you are not as adventurous as the name implies? You had to get it somehow." He lifts a perfectly sculpted eyebrow again.

I hug the pillow to my chest, still staring at the ceiling. I don't like this story, and I never tell it unless

I have to. Unfortunately, from my previous admissions, I don't have much of a choice but to spill the beans now.

I don't make eye contact and start rattling off the story, not making sure Carlos is even listening. I just have to say it as quickly as I can, and then I can pack everything up and put it out of my mind for another dozen years.

"Okay, so I went to Indiana University. I played soccer. We were a decent team. My freshman year we were ranked something like twenty-fifth in the country. The men's team was even better, ranked in the top ten. We used the same facilities and worked around each other's schedules, like for field time and time in the weight room and with the trainers and whatnot. So we all knew each other. There was a bit of rivalry between the two programs, but the men's team was definitely better."

I steal a glance at Carlos. He looks like he's going to fall asleep.

"So anyway, I was pretty shy. I didn't date a lot or talk to a lot of guys."

"So basically nothing's changed since then."

I throw my pillow at him and continue. "And it wasn't like I had a line of guys banging down my door. I was in great shape, but I definitely had what you'd call an athletic build. I was never the cute and perky co-ed that most guys seemed attracted to. And I wasn't confident enough in myself to pursue anyone either. Many of my teammates were legendary in their conquests. I ... I didn't know how to talk to anyone without resorting to random sports facts that probably didn't have anything to do with anything."

"So again, nothing's changed."

The only other pillow I have to throw is currently supporting my head, so I gently kick Carlos instead. But he's not wrong.

"But, you know, there was this one guy on the men's team. The goalie. He was fairly attractive. Okay, he was super hot. Anyway, it was right after the end of the season. There was a party for both the men's and the women's teams, and since we finally didn't have to be on the field at oh God o'clock in the morning, I decided to let loose a little."

Basically, I drank my face off.

"And somehow, I ended up talking with him for most of the night. We had had a class together the year before and were friends-ish. Okay, we were friends. He used to give me fist bumps all the time."

"Totally friend zone."

I nod. "Yup, I know. And I was totally in love with him."

"Did he know?"

I shake my head. No one knew. They'd have laughed at me if I ever so much as tried to bat my eyelashes at him. Mostly because I couldn't flirt to save my life. Like Carlos said, nothing's changed.

"But that night, it was different. I went home with him." To this day, I still can't quite figure out how it happened. "Totally out of character for me. I'm pretty sure it was the standard operating procedure for him. He wasn't the biggest ho on the team, but I don't think he was saving himself for marriage, if you know what I mean."

Memories of that night flash into my brain, and I feel my face grow flush. Let's put it this way: when you have two rock-hard athletes in peak physical condition, you can get quite creative.

Plus, I loved the fact that at 6'4", he made me feel small and feminine. Being 5'9" with an athletic build didn't often afford me that feeling with the few guys I did date. No one else had ever been able to lift me up and throw me around quite like that. It was spectacular.

There was a lot I loved about Callaghan Entay.

I fan myself at the memory.

"But in the morning, as I sobered up, I started to get self-conscious. I knew all his roommates. They were all on the team. I'd have to see them around campus and on the field. They were going to label me as another cleat chaser or something equally demeaning. They wouldn't give him shit for hooking up, but they would have to me."

"Damn double standards," Carlos murmurs.

I was also afraid that they'd make fun of him for being with me. Like I wasn't worthy because I wasn't pretty enough or girly enough. My ego couldn't handle that. At least not where Callaghan was concerned.

"For real. Joking around, I said to him that I didn't want to do the walk of shame out in front of all his roommates. He winked and pointed to another door and told me that it was another exit. I felt like the gods were smiling down on me, and I got dressed and left without even using the bathroom."

I can still remember that feeling of relief, that I wouldn't have to face the jeers and taunts about being another conquest. I wouldn't have to hear them make fun of Callaghan for sleeping with me.

Had I known what was coming for me, I would have peed first.

"Okay," Carlos says. "What's so bad about that? And you know I want more details about the hookup."

This is where it gets embarrassing. "Apparently, I was not the first girl to use the second egress. And you could totally see the sidewalk from the living room. Every single one of his roommates watched me sneak out on my walk of shame. And one of them decided that I was to be known as the 'Back Door Girl' from then on out. That's what they called me."

Even a dozen years later, I still want to die when I think about that. The sad thing is that it was just the beginning of my life falling apart. Going through college with a nickname that severely misled people about my sexual prowess seemed like the worst thing that could happen at the time. I had no idea that, within a week or two, things would be infinitely worse.

"Girl, that's awful, but nothing we all haven't had to deal with."

I glance at my friend, knowing that he's heard all the comments—and much worse. Giving him a thin smile, I continue, "Yeah, well, even before I knew what they were calling me, I had already started to freak out. I mean, he was the hottest guy on the team. I was totally in love with him, and until that night, I didn't think he saw me as anything but a friend. He was the team captain and was going places.

Like literally. I didn't even have to figure out how to avoid him, because he got called up by the Nevada Renegades and left. He was gone like the next day."

"So that was it then?"

I shake my head. I don't want to unpack the rest of it right now. "No, but that was the last time I saw him."

"What happened to him? Did he become professional? Did you follow his career?"

I level a stare at Carlos. "Are you really asking me if I know his sports stats?"

Carlos holds up his hands. "Please don't talk sports at me again. You know that's not the kind of ball play I'm into."

"You watch games with me all the time."

"Yeah, because they're fine specimens in tight pants with rock-hard abs. Also, why I'm not into baseball, other than it being so boring. Too much variability in the tightness of pants and the physique of the players. Shallow, I know."

I can't fault him for any of that. It's why any number of my female friends over the years have tolerated watching game after game with me.

"He plays for the Boston Buzzards. He's their goalie. They're heading to the playoffs in Indianapolis this week."

"And you haven't had any contact with him or seen him since the morning you snuck out of his room?"

I let out a sigh and begrudgingly stand up. I've got to get into the shower, as I'm working another event at The Tower tonight. I work for Longwood

Venues, which owns five elegant, high-end facilities in Boston and Rhode Island. My favorite is Alden Castle in Brookline, but I'm usually at The Tower.

"Contact, no."

Carlos jumps to his feet. "What's that mean? That's pretty cryptic." My damn roommate doesn't miss a beat.

I take my robe off the hook on the back of the door. "The event last night was for the Buzzards. He was there."

In a freakin' tuxedo. Hotter than ever. My mouth goes dry remembering how he looked last night. He's aged like a fine wine. I didn't think it was possible for him to look better than he had a dozen years ago, but achievement unlocked.

"And?"

"And nothing. I avoided him and thought about jumping out a window so I didn't accidentally make contact."

"Why?" Carlos puts his hands on his hips. "Why didn't you reconnect? Maybe you could have gotten a little action. Don't take this the wrong way, but you could probably use some."

I look down. While I'm not ashamed of what I do for a living, it's not like I've done anything remarkable. I'm no longer an athlete. Nor do I have an athlete's body. Normally it doesn't bother me, but when the other person is literal physical perfection, one can't help but be a smidge self-conscious.

Not that he was going to see me and immediately pull me back to bed. Not that he'd want to. I'm not sure why we hooked up in the first place, other than copious amounts of Fireball.

A dozen years later, and I still can't handle the smell of cinnamon.

"Let's face it, I'm not even sure if he'd remember me. It was a long time ago. I'm sure I wasn't the sentinel event for him that he was for me." He wasn't the one with feelings there. Not to mention, he didn't have to deal with the repercussions for years to come. "What was I supposed to say to him? It was a one-and-done, and it's in the past. No need to make things awkward."

Like crawling out of a second-story bathroom window wouldn't have been awkward.

I shake my head, trying to get thoughts of Callaghan Entay out of it. He's taken up entirely too much mental—and emotional—space in my life, and I don't need to let him back in. "Plus, I hate him."

The look on Carlos's face could only be described as dubious. "Right. Of course, you do."

"Okay, hate might not be the right word. It's definitely complicated. Way too complicated for right now. Plus, you have a diabolical plan for making all my dreams come true."

I don't hold out much hope that one of Carlos's plans might actually come to fruition, but if it will get him off the topic of Callaghan Entay, then I'll welcome the reprieve.

"Right, so you need to start a ClikClak series. About your sports stuff or whatever. Really drill down on your niche. And take off, getting a huge following. Apparently, that's how the media hires now. They go for people who have their own platform. It's your in to ESPN. All you have to do is go viral."

"With my eighty followers, I'm sure it'll be a cinch. I'll probably be hired in time to report from the Rose Bowl on New Year's Day."

"Start a new account. The algorithm will push you out right when you start. Put out tons of content, all with your sports reporting. Like you're auditioning with each video."

It's my turn to raise my eyebrow. Except I can't do it, and I'm sure I just look constipated. I'll have to work on that. "This is your most harebrained scheme yet."

Carlos raises his eyebrow, trumping my own's failure, and then winks. "That doesn't mean it won't work."

CHAPTER 4: HANNAH

Carlos's plan is actually sort of genius, really. If I can get my face out there, then I'll have something to bring to the networks. Something other than a terminated internship, gaps in my college career, and a decade of jobs that have nothing to do with sportscasting.

Luckily, I do have degrees in not only journalism but sports management. It took me a long time to get them, and even longer to use them, but now it looks as if they might pay off.

I take a day and explore SEO strategies, which is the big way that ClikClak is predicted to shift in the new year. They want to become a search engine to rival Google.

I do a quick scrub of my social media, removing anything that might give too much away or add negatively to my image. Not that I expect this to go anywhere, but one can never be too careful in this day and age.

I brainstorm content ideas. I even buy a new notebook, writing down topics and subjects. Then, it's time for the real research to begin.

I have to watch ClikClak for hours on end.

With paper and pen in hand, I make notes while scrolling through videos. I'm still doing this on my old profile, so as not to mess up the algorithm for my new account, which is a hack I learned while spending hours scrolling the infernal app. Before I would have felt guilty for wasting so many hours of my life, but Carlos promises me this is the key to bigger and better things. I watch as often as I can. On the T, going to and from work. Lying in bed at night. While I'm making my breakfast.

I consume and study and process. What's popular? What makes a video go viral? What are the features that viral videos have in common? Sometimes, it's easy to see, like that girl who flew out to surprise her boyfriend, only to find he was cheating on her.

Wait—that's the girl from The Tower. The one in the bathroom who had just gotten married. I look at the profile. *@LovelyLia.* That doesn't sound familiar, but I swear it's her.

I scroll through her videos. It's definitely her.

Because that's definitely Xavier Henry, in her kitchen, making a smoothie. He plays for the Baltimore Terrors, which makes me wonder why he was at an event for the Boston Buzzards the other night.

She's pretty ClikClak famous. I jot her name down and give her a follow. Maybe, if I get stuck, I can reach out to her.

After about three days, I finally have some ideas. I also have a day off, as does Carlos, which is perfect. It's time for phase one.

"I'm just going to use my name, Hannah LaRosa," I announce as Carlos is applying some makeup goop to my face. He's integral in phase one—making me look attractive. Attractive people definitely get more views. At least that's how it seems to me. Plus, I never really learned how to do makeup, and since I live with an aspiring artist, it seems foolish not to take advantage of his talent.

He's also going to photograph every look for his Instagram profile, so we're both getting content here, in addition to the transition videos he's filming. That's part of his plan.

"Why not jazz it up a little? Try something memorable. Like … Hannah Storm."

I dip my chin and roll my eyes at Carlos, causing his brush to slip.

"What is that look for? Keep your chin up."

"There's already a Hannah Storm. She's on *SportsCenter*."

"And I would know this how? You know I'm not watching any females during sporting events."

I'm tempted to roll my eyes again, but I don't want Carlos to take my attitude out on my face. He won't let me look in the mirror until he's done. I know he's talented—I see how he transforms himself for nights out on the town—but I doubt there's much he can do for me. I'll still have a square jaw, fair complexion, boring brown hair, and tobacco-brown eyes. Nothing exciting here.

And no matter what camera angles we use, I'll still have the body of someone who used to be athletic but has let herself go and carries the weight to prove it.

I'm fine with my body. She went through a lot, and I'm not going to punish her. I also realize life is too short not to enjoy carbohydrates.

The TV industry, however, does not seem to realize this. Females are expected to be thin, regardless of age. For men, it seems, there's a lot more leeway. I remember being at my parents' house and watching their local news during the year I was recuperating. The male "star" anchor had to weigh well over three hundred pounds, while his female co-host was undoubtedly a size 4. I doubt she would have kept her job had the roles been reversed.

That was years ago. Maybe we're heading into a time of growth. That all bodies are worthy of love and acceptance, and my clothing size does not impact my ability to discuss and analyze what's going on in the sporting world.

Based on the current physiques of the top female sports reporters, like Erin Andrews, Lindsay Czarniak, Cari Champion, and Rachel Nichols, I still don't think the decision-makers in the industry have received that message of acceptance and inclusion.

Maybe I'll change all that.

"Did you figure out what you're going to wear?"

I shrug, trying to pretend that he's not putting eyeliner on my water line. I didn't even know that the very inside rim of your eye was called the water line until about ten seconds ago. I'm pretty sure it's named that because my eye is watering something fierce. I'm also pretty sure that you aren't meant to paint that part of your body.

"I knew you wouldn't take this seriously. We're putting a lot of work in here. You have to commit to the part. Like, all the way."

Carlos pulls back and walks over to his closet. "Voila!" he exclaims, pulling a bright red suit out of 1988.

I mean, his closet.

"What the hell is that?" I can see the shoulder pads from across the room. "No. No way, no how."

He lays it carefully on the bed as if it were some expensive couture gown by some famous designer. Clothes have never been my thing.

"I can see it all planned out. It's part of the gimmick. You're doing these super serious reports of ridiculous information in '80s and '90s power suits. It's going to be a look. When you do your 'This Day in Sports' videos, you can go for a more contemporary style. Trust me, you've got to do something to make yourself stand out. And we can see which videos do better, but either way, you'll have a body of work and a following."

While there's a non-zero chance that Carlos is right, I don't want to look like an ass either. Next thing you know he'll be asking me to dance for my videos.

There's a reason why I was a soccer player and not a cheerleader. I'm athletic and fluid with a ball. That's about the only time. Rhythm is a stranger who wants nothing to do with me.

I pick up the suit. "I'm not dancing."

Carlos laughs. "Girl, I don't dislike anyone enough to make them suffer through that. We want people to hire you, not run screaming."

The suit fits like it was made for me. The skirt hugs my hips and thighs and lands somewhere in the mid-calf region. The jacket part has almost puffy sleeves that gather around my forearm as if I pushed the sleeves up to get down to business. There are large black buttons on the sleeves and four on the front of the blazer that somehow makes my waist look snatched.

I know this because Carlos tells me, "Damn, your waist is snatched in that."

He pulls out large black plastic earrings that complete the '80s vibe. If nothing else, I'll have a kick-ass Halloween costume next year. I tug on the skirt and then the fitted jacket.

I stare at my reflection in the mirror. My dark hair is pulled into a low bun thing, but it still has some volume and waves around my face. It doesn't even look like me. I had no idea I could look so soft and feminine yet still fierce at the same time.

Now I know why people hire makeup artists.

If this harebrained scheme works, I should make ESPN hire Carlos as my personal makeup person. I doubt anyone will ever be able to make me look this good ever again.

He must be a magician.

It's time to get this ball rolling.

With my Vans on my feet and patent leather pumps in a bag, Carlos and I head over to the dog park.

That was my brilliant idea. To visit different dog parks and report on their playing as if I were calling a game. I'm not actually a dog person. After a neighbor's pit bull tackled me when I was about nine, I've never been super comfortable around them.

But dogs equal views and clicks.

We've timed it well, as the park is crowded. There are at least three golden retrievers, a labradoodle, a few muttish-looking dogs, and a much smaller dog that is barking its head off as if it owns the place. I zoom in with my Google lens to find out that it's a corgi. Apparently, it's the kind that Queen Elizabeth had. I know even less about the royal family than I do about dog breeds, so I file that fact away. I do a quick search of the other dogs, just to make sure I'm somewhat believable and so that I don't look like an idiot.

More of an idiot.

It's hard to take yourself seriously when you look like an extra from the *Working Girl* set while you are using a kitchen spatula as your pretend microphone and talking about the athletic prowess of a walking baked potato.

"You ready?" Carlos is setting up my phone on a tripod, complete with a ring light.

I quickly switch into my shoes, which look like something my grandma would wear to a funeral, and then nod, signaling Carlos to start the timer. I put my finger to my ear as if I'm getting vital information from an earpiece and then lift the spatula, my pretend microphone, up.

Here goes nothing.

CHAPTER 5: CALLAGHAN

There's nothing like being humiliated on national TV and in front of your college coach to ruin a good mood. At least my parents didn't waste their time making the trip. Thank God for small favors.

A shootout.

The fucking final came down to a fucking shootout. We'd scored within the first five minutes of the first half and then proceeded to do virtually nothing else for the rest of the game.

At least we had shots on goal. The Miami Wave only had two the entire game, both coming in the last seven minutes of play in the second half.

To be honest, I was a little bored standing there, watching my teammates nearly a hundred yards away. It's hard to stay focused when the ball barely crosses midfield. I had a few tap outs and a few throws and one lame corner kick, but other than that, I might as well have been twiddling my fingers. But as fatigue set in toward the end of the second half, the boys got sloppy.

Actually, only one boy did. Brandon Nix. First of all, he had no business being that far back in the penalty box. Then, he should have kept his damn hands to himself. He's lucky he didn't draw a red card for that clothesline. But it did give the Wave a penalty kick.

The thing with PKs is there's no amount of training that will guarantee you can stop every one. Time moves too quickly. In the end, you just have to take your best guess at where the shot will be. Guessing wrong results in a goal.

I knew he was shooting left, mid to upper range. As I launched myself in that direction, the ball whizzed over my gloves. I was inches too low.

Doesn't matter. I missed and we tied. The boys weren't able to do anything with the remaining time or the stoppage time, nor even in the overtime.

Since it was the playoffs, we went to a penalty kick shootout. Normally the game of soccer is played eleven on eleven. When it comes down to a shootout, it becomes a one-to-one match. Everything else about the rest of the game is erased and there is only the kicker and the keeper. Me.

Each team gets five chances. The world record in Global Games play for saves is four. If I were literally the best in the world, I'd only be able to stop eighty percent of shots.

As luck would have it, I'm not the best in the world. I managed one incredible stop. The Wave made the other four. Unfortunately, Pressley Samson whiffed his shot, going right over the top, and Brandon Nix went wide.

And just like that, our season was over.

I had to pray that it wasn't the final for my career as well.

While I wanted to stay on my knees on the field and wallow in my own anguish, I wouldn't have that be the last image the press caught of me before the off-season.

I stood up and shook hands with the opposing team. I hugged some of my teammates. I didn't punch Brandon Nix in the face, so at least that was one good thing.

Coach Dawes is on the sidelines. "Hard break." He's not what anyone would describe as verbose.

I nod, not trusting myself to speak without crying. That would be even worse than losing.

"Are you in town for a bit? Can you come up to campus and talk to the team?"

I nod again, willing to do anything he asked of me. Coach Dawes set me on my path. He was a man of few words, but when he spoke, you knew they were important. I've adopted a similar philosophy.

He got recruiters to come and watch, resulting in my original deal with a farm team for the Nevada Renegades. Whenever possible, he comes to games.

It's more than I can say for my own parents.

Sure, if we'd made it to the final, they would have been there, but they weren't going to waste their time flying out to Indiana—*again*—if it weren't a high-stakes match. In other words, they were only going to come if it were the championship match and there would be TV coverage.

I'm not putting words in their mouths. It's what my mom texted me when I asked if they wanted tickets.

I'll have Justice's assistant, Heaven, get me a rental car and switch my flight back to Boston. Heading down to Bloomington for a day or two might not be the worst idea in the world.

It was a good time in my life. I was supported by solid teammates and a good coaching staff. I'd say I was happy then. It'd be nice to recapture some of that feeling.

Before heading off the field, I make my way to the sidelines where eager fans are waiting. I take several selfies with those who think I'm special. I'll be splashed across social media, these people using me for their fifteen minutes of fame. Story of my life. As I hand the phone back, one girl—probably in her early twenties—says, "You're so serious. Why don't you smile?"

I shrug. "I'll smile when our performance is worthy of it. There wasn't much to smile about tonight."

The mood in the locker room is quiet but not somber. You'd think the team would be more upset than they are. Looking around, I seem to be the only one who is gutted by this loss. We don't get to go to the finals. This is it. Our season is done.

Is my career?

It will be if I don't get selected for the National Team and get to play in the Global Games.

The following morning, driving into campus, I feel my spirits start to lift. The three and a half years I spent here were probably the happiest of my life.

Sad, but true.

Coach Dawes was more of a father figure than my own father. We had a magic and chemistry on that team that I haven't found since. And losing that was hard on me. Looking back now, I know I didn't handle things as I should have.

It wasn't that I burned bridges per se. It's more that I left without looking back. The chapter was closing. It was time to turn the page and not re-read anything. Over the years, it's been perceived as an attitude and snobbery. That I thought I was "too good" to associate with those I deemed "lesser."

It wasn't that at all.

Truth be told, I don't really know how to people.

I know how to play soccer, and that's it.

Ask any of the women I've dated.

Ask my ex-wife.

Katherine often told me I didn't know how to relate to others. I didn't listen to her. I tried to, though. At least I did until I found out how good she was at relating with others, if you know what I mean. I wasn't good at the emotional connection crap when we were dating, and it's not like it improved for the year we were married. Mostly because I was focused on my season, and she was focused on her boyfriends.

Those things generally don't make for a successful relationship.

She was more interested in being a WAG than a wife. I know, WAG means Wives and Girlfriends, but she wanted the title and prestige, not the actual relationship. She wanted me for my name and my status and for something that I wasn't. I wasn't going to be one of those guys all over Instagram and ClikClak, helping to build her business as an influencer.

It's not my jam and never will be.

Hell, the only reason I even have accounts is because Justice made me. His assistant, Heaven, created them and updates them more than I do. It's always weird to visit my profile and see the stuff she uploaded. But I trust her with my logins.

Heaven probably knows more about me than any woman since Katherine. Actually, she probably knows more about me than Katherine ever did. Katherine married a sports star. I'm totally positive she didn't give two shits about who Callaghan was, other than a professional soccer player.

Not many people in my life have cared about that person.

Probably a good thing, because I'm not sure who he is either. Everything in my life revolves around the game, even in the off-season. Let's face it, there's no off-season. Not really. There are no games and no formal practices, but the training doesn't stop. The rehab doesn't stop. The pain doesn't stop.

Driving into Bloomington, it occurs to me that the last time anyone expected anything from me besides soccer was when I was here. That was a long time ago. Teachers expected me to be a student and learn. And outside of the team, I even had a friend who expected me to show up and study. Sure, Hannah and I became friends because she was on the girls' team and we had a class together, but as we trained in the gym, we eventually moved past soccer.

She was one of the casualties when I left school to go to Nevada without looking back.

It was easier for me to cut ties than be pulled in multiple directions. I had—have—one job, and that is blocking shots on goal.

I've never figured out how to have my attention on more than one thing at a time, and soccer's always been the number one priority, so I deleted all my social media and left my old life behind. That way, there was no temptation to relive my glory days in Bloomington.

Now, staring down at what might be the beginning of the end of my career, I have no idea what a life outside of soccer will look like. The mere thought sends waves of panic rippling through my body.

And that mindset, going into practice and talking with the Hoosiers in the gym, might not have been the best for creating a motivational speech. They were ranked second going into the start of this season but finished a disappointing fourteenth. Most people won't understand that being the fourteenth-ranked D1 collegiate team in the nation is disappointing, but seeing as how my team finished in the top four, I get it.

It's number one or nothing at all.

As the team gathers 'round me, I offer these uplifting words of wisdom. "You're a disappointment. You know it. I know it. Don't worry, I am too. We have one job to do, and we failed miserably. No one wants you for anything other than your ability to put a ball into a goal. To outrun, outshoot, and outscore your opponent. To block the shots and make the saves. And when you don't do it, you let everyone down. You need to leave everything behind except the game. Be the game. You are nothing if you can't win."

I try not to see the disappointment on Coach Dawes's face when I leave campus. Avoiding relationships and expectations has worked for me thus far. I just need to keep doing it.

Except, as I fly back to Boston, I can't help but think about what I said to the team. Sure, leaving everything else behind is great when you need to be ready for a game, but what happens when the game is over? What do you have then?

CHAPTER 6: HANNAH

Holy shit, Carlos's strategy is working. Not for getting a job with ESPN, but for getting traction on ClikClak. My videos are starting to get views. Like a few thousand apiece. Especially for the dog park series.

It certainly helps that there's a corgi there named Sir Fluffybottoms—I shit you not—who thinks he runs the show. But today, it's a whole new ball game. A tiny demon chihuahua showed up and literally made a Great Dane cower. I've been studying my dog puns and practicing my sportscaster's voice.

Not to mention, I sort of love having my face all pretty and stuff. Not enough to learn how to do it all myself, but I'll enjoy having Carlos at my disposal before he moves on to be a makeup artist to the stars.

I've never been one to embrace my feminine side, but I could be convinced. I've even started wearing mascara to work.

Today, I have to film my sports gossip features. It's where I talk about the best, juiciest sports news that has little or nothing to do with actual play. It's the stuff even non-sports people like to hear about.

The stories are relatively easy to find on the internet. Someone cheated on their significant other. A random tweet about a hidden relationship.

I have files and notes all over my phone so I'm never without content ideas. Now I know why Carlos wanted me to quit my job. This is pretty much all-consuming. But it's not paying any bills yet, so I still have to work in catering.

To manage, I batch-create whenever I have the time. I take out my list of topics, record several videos, and then edit and publish them later. The juiciest stories get the first videos, with other ones in store for when I don't have time to film. I'm going to make a bunch when I get off work tonight.

If I can keep up this rate of growth, I might be able to parlay this into something to send on come the spring. That's the plan: At least four months of social media presence to show I have some staying power. I need to keep up with consistent posts so I keep gaining more followers. I doubt I can depend on my growth being linear. If that were the case, I'd be in the millions when I plan on sending out resumes and applying for positions.

As long as I make myself finally do it.

The thing with having your dream ripped out of your hands once is that it makes you a little hesitant to try for it again. There's a big part of me that knows I probably was never going to make it as a professional soccer player. While Indiana was a D1 school, we weren't that highly ranked, at least not compared to the men's program. And it's not like I was the best on the team. I wasn't even consistently a starter.

But still, I was supposed to have two more years to improve my physical game, and then who knows what could have happened? I could have been the next Abby Wambach. Instead, courtesy of a crazy medical thing, I nearly died and said goodbye to my soccer career.

It sucked royally.

It's been so much easier not to get my hopes up again. Every time I do, I'm disappointed. It's safer not trying. It might not be fulfilling, but at least I'm not getting crushed. I stay in the moment and don't look toward the future. It's best not to have expectations.

I'm a survivalist.

As I see my views and followers rise, it makes me nervous. If I'm successful here, I'll *have* to do something with it.

I have to try.

I take a deep breath and continue my search, trying to ignore the feelings that are making my chest tight. I can't help but think about everything that went down out in Bloomington that set me on my current path.

Callaghan Entay.

As much as I want to blame him, it's not all his fault. I mean, it most likely wouldn't have happened if not for our night together, but it's nothing either one of us did on purpose.

At least that's what the doctors said.

Rare medical fluke.

What bothers me is that he didn't stick around to even be aware of what I was going through.

Not that I thought one night of amazing sex would turn him into a devoted boyfriend, but we were at least friends before. Or I thought we were. Maybe he would have visited during my long recovery.

Maybe not.

We'll never know.

I close my eyes, willing my feelings to return to their tiny boxes; their dormant status, like some ancient spell in a fantasy novel.

However, like in a fantasy novel, once the box is opened, things are never the same. Apparently, that's where I'm at now because the main gossip story on the sports pages involves none other than my former friend and one-night stand, Callaghan Entay.

What are the freakin' odds?

It's like the universe is deliberately messing with me by putting him in my path.

I watch the video, saving the site. Man, he comes across as a conceited ass.

I mean, he is, but still, this video of him telling a fan that the performance of the Boston Buzzards was nothing worth smiling about is not a great look for him. But then, like the gift that keeps on giving, there's more footage of him, in a facility I recognize well, giving possibly the worst motivational speech in the history of motivational speeches.

Yeah, the optics on this are not going to be in his favor.

I don't envy his agent and publicist on this one. Especially not this year, when he's in contention to not only be named to the National Team for the Global Games but also to get the start as their goalkeeper.

As much as I want to ignore this story, it's a slow news day for salacious sports gossip. I bookmark the pages so I can make a video when I get home.

Throughout my shift, I cannot keep my mind from wandering back to Callaghan. The first day I saw him on campus. Watching him in the weight room. Realizing he was watching me back. Bonding during a European history class that I had no business being in, but it fit into my practice schedule.

Such are the sacrifices of an athlete.

It didn't mean I didn't have to bust my ass to make the grades, though. Until everything went down, I'd been on track to graduate summa cum laude.

All that changed after one stupid night with Callaghan.

One night that left me scarred—literally—and scared. A piece of me was gone that I'd never get back.

A literal piece. One of my kidneys.

I want to hate him.

My emotions mix as my gut churns. What am I even feeling right now? There's definitely some anger. More than I thought I was holding onto. It was so long ago. But as much as I don't want to admit it, there are still those butterflies too. The stupid butterflies I used to get every time I looked at those chestnut-brown eyes. I mooned over him for years. Both before and after it all went down. God, I was pitiful. It's probably a good thing he isn't smiling in the video. There'd be a good chance my panties would melt if he did that.

My undergarments are safe though. He's not smiling, and it's not like we're going to be hanging out again any time soon.

Or ever again.

Even with him here in Boston, the odds of ever running into him casually are virtually non-existent. I *may* have stalked his social media a bit to see what he's up to. I mean, that's totally normal to do with one's ex. Not that he was my ex. All we were was a hookup.

Still, totally normal behavior.

The few glances I had at his social media were enough to know that it's probably an assistant posting on there for him, as intermittent as the posts are. They're too cultivated. Too perfect. And mostly of him, not the environment around him. I bet he doesn't even know his own logins. It's highly unlikely we'll reconnect through social media.

I'm safe.

Not to mention my gossip features don't get as many views on ClikClak as my dog park videos, so odds are he'll never even know if I make a video about him. As long as I don't say anything inappropriate, like how he has a magical tongue, it'll be fine.

I watch the videos of him again. This is for research, obviously. I take the time to write out my script. I even practice it in the mirror. I can't do a half-assed job with this one.

Finally, I'm ready. I sit at the table in my kitchen, a sheet over the door behind me to look like a backdrop. It makes me look professional while hiding an ugly brown door. I smooth my hair down once, twice, before getting up to check my makeup one last time. Then I wipe my damp hands on my thighs.

I wasn't even this nervous when I made my first ClikClak. I've never had a good poker face, and I'm afraid—somehow—people will know that I slept with Callaghan Entay all those years ago.

I don't want people to go digging about my time at IU. I don't want them to know I knew him. I don't want anyone to put two and two together about what happened after.

It's embarrassing, really.

I stand up and shake my head and my shoulders, jogging a little in place. Not that different from what I used to do on the sidelines while I was waiting to sub in. That's a good mindset to be in. I've got to have my best game face on.

After wasting too much time, I'm finally ready. I sit down, turn on my ring light, clear my throat, and use my best deadpan, expressionless voice as I start recording.

Today's hot take comes courtesy of the United States Soccer League's Callaghan Entay.

I play the video of him in the background.

After the Boston Buzzards lost in the semifinals to the Miami Wave, goaltender Callaghan Entay was recorded doing the following: while taking pictures with fans, Callaghan refused to smile, stating that the Buzzards' performance was nothing to smile about. Following this encounter, Callaghan went on to give one of the least motivational speeches in the history of motivational speeches to the men's soccer team at Indiana University, where he is an alumnus. Apparently, he's taking the dark and brooding thing to the next level. So, following the sage advice of Cally—er—Callaghan Entay, I will refuse to smile until my account grows by ten thousand followers. Until then, there's nothing much to smile about.

Before I can overthink, I tag it, write my caption, and hit publish.

Only then do I start to think maybe it wasn't the best of ideas. I definitely fumbled his name. He tolerated very few people in the world calling him Cally, for obvious reasons. There was a girl on campus who used to whine at him. "Oh, Cally, when are you going to take me out?" Naturally, I picked it up, mocking him in the same tone of voice. I remember his mouth lifting into an uncharacteristic smile.

To see a true Callaghan Entay smile was a gift.

I should definitely delete it. My hand hovers over the button, but then I relax. Eh, it's not like anyone's really going to see it. I won't include it in my audition reel because I doubt there's a demand for dry, deadpan sports news delivery. Not to mention they'd just assume I messed up his name.

It does give me the idea to do the gossip videos in the style of the original content though. If someone is drunk, I'll pretend I am too. If someone is avoiding paparazzi in sunglasses and a hoodie, that's how I'll dress too. I'll put some props on my table to reflect the mood of the video I'm featuring.

I'm a genius.

I hope that Callaghan Entay never sees this. Chances are, even if he does, he won't remember me. It was a long time ago. He was popular on campus, and he went on to have a pro career. He even played in the British Football League—the BFL—for a while.

I'm fairly confident I take up no mental space for him. He certainly moved on quickly enough. He wasn't smitten from the get-go. He doesn't carry the baggage I do.

Lucky bastard.

I can only imagine the video I could do about what happened all those years ago. I shake my head and move around the apartment as if I can bob and weave around all the memories that are assaulting me.

I need to focus on my purpose. Callaghan Entay has cost me enough. Time to put him and his brooding good looks back into the past where they belong.

All I have to do is find the next big story, focus on my career, and once again, forget about him.

CHAPTER 7: CALLAGHAN

C: Did you see the story on ESPN.com?

While normally I wouldn't be thrilled for my phone to be dinging with text alerts this early in the morning, getting a text from Chadwick Campbell, the backup goalkeeper, is a rare thing.

Basically, he only texts when the world is ending, like when they canceled the season for COVID.

I have to get up and go train anyway. Plus I need to see the PT about my shoulder, which is still aching after my last diving save attempt two weeks ago. My appointment isn't until ten. I can take a few seconds to look before I get up and eat.

Without responding to CC, I open up my phone. It's easy to find the top story. *Curse of the Birds* by Chassen Donato.

I roll my eyes. Stupid title. I don't want to read this. It's about birds. Why the hell do I care?

I text Chadwick back.

Me: Who gives a flying fuck about birds?
CC: Keep reading.

I follow his directions, my mouth falling open. Oh shit, it's about Xavier Henry, talking about his career in the BFL. Jesus, I hope they never talk about my stint there.

Somehow, Callaghan Entay never lived up to his potential.

That quote will haunt me until the day I die. It's nothing compared to the ghosts chasing Xavier Henry, which are outlined in explicit detail in this article. The exposé continues to talk about his agent, and none of it is favorable. This guy perpetuates the stereotype of the slick wheeler and dealer, which is not at all whom I'd picture Xavier working with.

I sit up a little straighter as I get into the next part of the article though. It's about his wife, Ophelia, who is apparently some sort of ClikClak star.

As well as a sex worker.

And she wrote a smutty porn novel about Xavier.

But that's not the worst part. I don't know how it could get worse, yet somehow it does. The slimy agent is AWOL and suspected of embezzlement, Xavier was linked to the Boston Buzzards, totally violating his contract, and their entire marriage is a fraud. The article ends with Bob Miller, the man who signs my paychecks, saying there are no formal business dealings with Xavier Henry.

Damn, I thought I had it rough. His career is done. He'll never set foot on the pitch again.

It's too bad. We could really use him on the Buzzards. I read the article again. It sits like old food in my stomach. None of it sounds like Xavier. He always struck me as honest and hardworking. He definitely was never one to skate by or dog it.

Even back in England, he didn't seem like the type to get caught up in the party scene, which is why the whole Phaedra Jones thing surprised, well, everyone.

He never spoke up or said anything, which was pretty much admitting to his guilt. I wonder if he'll take the same approach this time around.

Of course, he doesn't have an agent right now to help him out. That's another thing. Xavier Henry is straightlaced. I can't see him being behind the scenes of an embezzlement scheme. I should reach out to Justice and see what he can do.

I don't know why I want to help, other than, deep down in my gut, I like Xavier. And I know how bad the press can be sometimes. I text CC back.

Me: Guess we can't count on him defending us this year. Too bad.

CC: You know what they say … fooling leads to crying. But I never pictured him hiring a sex worker and faking a marriage.

Yeah, me neither.

But this is Henry's issue to deal with. It doesn't directly impact me. I should get up and start my workout. I don't have to be back at the Buzzards' training facility until tomorrow, but at my age, if I have too much downtime, I'll never get moving again.

For a moment, the thought of not having to work out again sounds heavenly. I've been pushing my body so hard for so long. I don't remember having a day without pain. Without bone-crushing fatigue.

I'm not sure I'd know what to do with myself.

But that's the problem. That's why I keep pushing. I don't know what to do or who I'd be without that.

I'm about to get out of bed when my phone dings again. I expect it to be CC, but it's Heaven.

Heaven: Have you been on ClikClak this past week?

I usually only get texts like this from her when there's something non-flattering in the news like another woman claiming I'm her baby daddy or something. After one too many of those stories, I started getting a lot more selective about whom I spent time with. And trust me, there's been no one recently.

Me: No, and I swear I haven't impregnated anyone.

Heaven: I'm not saying you did, but you should go take a look.

She sends me a link to a profile. I click without giving it much thought. What I see makes me bolt upright. I swear my heart glitches.

It's a video of me. Mocking me. A totally expressionless recount of me refusing to smile for that girl after the semifinals game and my terrible showing at Indiana. It was posted four days ago and has over fifty-thousand views.

But that's not what has sent me into possible cardiac arrhythmia.

Holy shit, it's Hannah.

I glance at the profile name. @HannahLaRosa. It really is her. She ... she ... she's totally making fun of me.

Why?

I click on her profile. She's into sportscasting. There are tons of videos with random sports facts. Even more with sports gossip, like the one about me today. And then ... there are a bunch of videos with her wearing suits, standing outside a dog park.

I'm transfixed, watching her speak into a ... is that a spatula?

That's right, Carl, Sir Fluffybottoms will be a free agent at the end of this season. He ran a 10.6 in the combine, which is amazing considering his legs are less than twelve inches long. But he still has competition in the market. Duke and Max bring serious golden retriever energy and are likely to be drafted higher than Sir Fluffybottoms. That being said, he's still a contender for Good Boy status. That's all I have from Rawhide Arena. Back to you, Carl.

I watch every single video.

Some more than once.

Okay, I watch them all multiple times. She's changed, yet I still see the Hannah I once knew. The Hannah who used to challenge me to squat contests, knowing she'd never win. The Hannah who ended up in the wrong history class but worked her ass off and got a better grade than I did. The Hannah who made fun of the way girls pursued me, never realizing the only one I wanted in my bed was her.

Oh, Cally …

The Hannah who was so exquisite, naked, and beautiful in my bed.

The Hannah I sent out my back door, knowing my roommates were watching, and forgot about the minute the call from the Renegades came in.

That's not true. I didn't forget. I simply had to close one chapter and start another. A sacrifice that seemed worth it at the time. Now, I'm not so sure.

I follow her profile.

My phone pings with another text.

Heaven: Did you see it?

Me: Yup

Heaven: I'll have it taken down.

Me: No, don't. It's fine.

Heaven: It's not fine. The original videos are bad enough. You don't need any more publicity.

Me: I'm sure this will all blow over. There's bound to be another scandal any day now. Have you seen the piece on Xavier Henry on ESPN.com?

Heaven: Are you sure? I'll have it pulled.

Me: Leave it alone.

In frustration, I toss my phone to the end of the bed, only to dive for it a moment later. I open Instagram and search for Hannah. The content here is totally different. This appears to be her personal account.

There aren't tons of pictures of her in there, but from the few selfies I do find, she looks good.

There's also nothing about soccer on her Instagram, which is odd because her ClikClak account is all sports. Or sports parodies.

The Dog Park Games is some genius material. I watch them all again. And again.

She smiles at the end of one of the videos and instantly I'm transported back, the feeling punching me in the gut.

"You know what, I don't think you're the hot shit you seem to think you are. In fact, I'd bet money you go home alone tonight." Hannah took a step closer to me, her finger poking my chest.

"You wanna bet?" I licked my lips, looking at hers. They were mere inches from my own. I wanted to taste them. I'd wanted to for a long time. She'd never given any indication the feeling was mutual, so I wasn't going to make things weird by hitting on her.

"Yeah, I do. I don't think you get laid all the time. I think you're too focused on soccer to waste time on women, but you also don't want anyone to know that. You're not going home with anyone tonight, Cally." I didn't realize there was any space left between us until she closed the distance, her body pressing into mine.

I was on fire and instantly hard.

"You want me to put my money where my mouth is?"

She nodded.

"So it's a bet?" I asked, an eyebrow raised.

Hannah nodded again.

Her head had barely stopped moving when I lifted her chin with my hand and captured her mouth with mine. That's all it took.

I drop my phone and cover my eyes, trying to press the images of her out of my memory. No matter how hard I try, they all come rushing back.

I look at the clock. Damn, I'm going to miss my PT appointment if I don't get moving. I'm not the type to run late. I can't afford the hour I just wasted watching Hannah on ClikClak.

This. This is why I don't have relationships. I can't afford to be distracted. Losing in the semifinals means I'm going to have to work that much harder to get named to the National Team. Harder training. Harder diets. Harder ... everything.

But thinking of Hannah and our night together all those years ago, there's another part of me that's hard.

Dammit.

I don't have time for this.

I jump in the shower, blasting the water on cold. It's the last thing my muscles need before what's sure to be a grueling workout and therapy session.

Right. That's what I need to focus on. Getting stronger. Jumping higher. Moving faster.

Block the shot.

Go to the Global Games.

I just need to put Hannah out of my mind, like I did when I left for Nevada. As my phone dings with another text from Heaven, I have a feeling that's going to be easier said than done.

CHAPTER 8: HANNAH

I stare at my phone. My video about Callaghan Entay is hovering in the fifty-thousand views range. A solid turnout for me for a video of this type. My dog park games usually pull in a few hundred thousand views.

But that's not what I'm staring at. It's Ophelia, the girl from the bathroom at The Tower. The bride. Her story is all over the news. Not even just ClikClak, but like the *news*-news. ESPN.com covered it.

And holy hell, is it juicy.

There's no way I can't make a video about it. It's literally the sort of thing I should be salivating over. But here I sit, phone in hand, unable to do anything about it.

It feels wrong.

Granted, I only talked to her for a few minutes, but none of what's in the story seems like the person I met. I would *never* have pegged her for a prostitute or call girl. It doesn't make sense in my head.

I google Ophelia Finnegan.

On about the third or fourth page is her LinkedIn profile. She has an MBA from Boston University. She majored in accounting. She's held positions at a number of places in the accounting departments and as a bookkeeper.

I look at the byline for the article and immediately pass judgment. Chassen Donato is an irresponsible journalist. He should be reporting for Page Six or TMZ rather than ESPN, if he's going to spread gossip like this.

ESPN needs reputable reporters, like me. Ones who know how to use a spatula as a pretend microphone.

I dig into his background a little, including stalking his Instagram profile. The last picture on there is from Thanksgiving. He was in West Hartford, Connecticut. Something about that rings a bell, but I can't put my finger on it. But then I see it. In the background of his picture.

It's Ophelia and Xavier.

I zoom in. Yup, it's them.

I switch to Ophelia's Instagram. Her post from Thanksgiving is a graphic, wishing everyone a good day. However, there is a location stamp. West Hartford, Connecticut.

Two hours later, I've found that Chassen Donato is dating Makayla Nieves, whose mother, Georgia, is sister to Carolina Finnegan, Ophelia's sister-in-law.

What a small world it is. And social media makes it even smaller.

I'd really like to know what happened at that Thanksgiving dinner last week. Chassen Donato's face is all over ClikClak.

I dislike him immensely.

I hope he enjoys his fifteen minutes of fame because he should never work in this business again. I take his irresponsible reporting personally. Here I am, making an ass out of myself so even a local station will notice and give me a chance. This douchecanoe already has a foot in the door at my dream job and breaks the story of the century.

Except it might not be.

Hell, maybe it is, but there are definitely some errors in his reporting, not to mention a personal bias, which he has not disclosed anywhere that I can find.

Not that I mentioned I got hot and heavy with Callaghan Entay, but my story was more satirical than anything else. And I'm not being paid by the largest sports station in the world.

What could Ophelia have done to incur this wrath anyway? If I were in his shoes and found myself at Thanksgiving dinner with Xavier Henry, you can bet I wouldn't be reporting a story full of birds, embezzlement, sex workers, and fraud.

I search Ophelia's profile on ClikClak but there's nothing there. She's taken it down. It's probably for the best. I can only imagine the messages she's been getting.

I switch back to Instagram. Her Thanksgiving post was the last one. I open up Wattpad and search for her story, *Stolen Stars*. It's short and spicy, and really hot, if you like pirate vampires.

I can't see any way in which it resembles Xavier Henry in the least. Another false claim in the Donato article.

I see that I have several messages, mostly asking if I want to be an influencer. But then I come across one from what looks like a spam account, but the message stops me cold.

@BookLuvr3: Hi, Hannah. I don't know if you remember me, but I met you in the bathroom at The Tower a few weeks ago. It was an event for the Boston Buzzards, and you said you knew someone on the team. Well, long story short, I need to get in contact with someone from the team. Things are a mess, and it's all my fault, and I need to fix them. I was hoping you'd be able to make an introduction on my behalf. I know this is weird and creepy, but I promise you I'm not. I'm just super desperate because I really messed things up for my husband, and I might have cost him his career.

@BookLuvr3: By the way, this is Ophelia Finnegan.

@BookLuvr3: I mean Ophelia Henry.

@BookLuvr3: I'm not used to it yet. It's so weird, changing your whole name and everything. But if I can't figure out how to fix this, I'm going to have to go back to Finnegan.

@BookLuvr3: I like being Ophelia Henry.

I start to respond immediately but can't think of what I'm going to write. I mean, obviously, I want to help her. She wouldn't be reaching out if she were guilty of all the things the article accused her of. Not to mention I've already found numerous flaws in the story.

Nothing makes me more irate than crappy journalism.

But in order to help, I'd have to contact Callaghan Entay. The one I just made a video mocking.

Yeah, I don't think that's going to happen.

Another message pops up.

@BookLuvr3: You never said who it was on the team that you had a past with, but Callaghan Entay follows you on ClikClak. If you don't want to reach out to your old hookup, maybe you could DM him for me? I just need someone from the Buzzards to listen. I'm trying to get through to management, but I'm covering all my bases—I know, wrong sport—in case that doesn't work. Failure is not an option.

It cracks me up that Ophelia rambles in her messages, just as she does in person. I'd find it more amusing if I didn't have to digest what she said about Callaghan and ClikClak.

He follows me on ClikClak.

He follows me.

I kick myself for not being aware, but my account is growing so fast that it's hard to keep track.

He has to have seen the video.

I think I'm going to throw up.

Maybe he followed me before. Maybe he's reconnected with all his friends from IU. Yeah, that's got to be it.

I jump to my feet, pacing. If I'd have known he was going to see it, I would never have made that video. I only did it because I was sure his socials were run by an assistant.

Relief floods my body and my legs turn to Jell-O. His assistant. Of course, they're monitoring his social media. Not Callaghan himself. He didn't follow me.

There's no way.

But I realize Ophelia is waiting for a response. What am I going to tell her? No, obviously. I'm not reaching out to Callaghan's account, even if it isn't him.

Especially if it isn't him. I mean, what am I supposed to say? Remember how I basically doubted your manhood and then you spent all night proving to me how much of a man you were and then I snuck out your back door? You look well. Can I have a favor for someone who talked me off a ledge in the bathroom once? And I was on the ledge because you were in the room and I hate you but if I'm honest, you make my girl parts tingle a little still.

Jesus, now I'm rambling like Ophelia. I swear, Callaghan Entay nukes all coherent, rational thoughts I normally have in my head.

There is no way in hell I can reach out to him.

I don't respond and darken my phone, putting it face down on the couch next to me. I try to watch TV, but I can't focus. The phone sits there, taunting me. I know that article on ESPN.com is crap. And Chassen Donato is getting away with putting misinformation out there.

That's not what a responsible journalist does.

Gah!

I flop down, burying my face into a cushion. I should put my personal feelings aside and reach out. Even if it is an assistant, perhaps he or she could help.

I pick up my phone and do the responsible thing.

Me: I need to know the whole story.

About four paragraphs from Ophelia later, I've gleaned that the only thing in that article that's true, aside from the fact that Xavier's family owns a hawkery, is that the agent is as crooked as the day is long and that he steered his client in the wrong direction.

Ophelia also informed me that their marriage is no longer fake, but that it also won't help Xavier get his American citizenship. No duh. A quick google search could have told her that.

But I get the feeling that Ophelia acts on impulse rather than research.

I want to help her if only to shut an irresponsible journalist down. But also because I like her. She's hard not to like.

Though helping her means I have to contact him. I have to. I know I do.

I still don't want to.

The past is bound to come up. The horrible aftermath that took my life and my career and my plans. The fallout from one stupid dare. One stupid night. I can't totally blame him. It was a fluke thing. But it still happened, and I shut down for a long time.

He got to live his dream. He's had it all, and I'm finally trying to start at thirty-two.

No, it's not his fault.

The analytical part of me knows that. The bitter, resentful part of me wants to blame him. Why do women always get stuck with all the shit afterward?

At least I didn't get pregnant.

From what I hear, Callaghan's been named in several paternity claims, though none of them ever proved he was anyone's father.

Crap. I have to do this. If not for Xavier and Ophelia, for responsible journalism everywhere.

Me: Hey—I need a favor.

CHAPTER 9: CALLAGHAN

ey, Cally. Cally Entay. You're so hot." TJ Doyle dissolves into a fit of laughter, thinking he's much funnier than he actually is. I put him in a headlock to discourage him from calling me that.

Ever since that video that Hannah made with that *tiny* little slip, I'm now faced with the nickname I've spent my entire life trying to evade. Really, my parents should have known better. It's not like they call me Callaghan. They call me Cal.

And Cally.

But still, the ribbing from my teammate is not what's crawling under my skin, making me feel like I'm on fire. I look at my texts again.

How dare she?

She makes fun of me, makes me seem like a gigantic asshole for the entire world to see, and then texts me that she needs a favor.

Granted, I haven't talked to Hannah LaRosa in years, but I thought she was different. She's not. She's just like everyone else who wants something from my career to benefit them.

It's the only reason I hold value to anyone, including my parents. They were well off, to begin with, but this adds status and clout. I mean, my mother wishes I played a sport that people "actually cared about," but it still gives her something to brag about at the club.

This text from Hannah, out of the blue, irks me. So I let her know.

Me: No, "Hi Cal, how've you been?" No, "You look good." No, "I'm sorry for making you into a laughingstock on social media." Just diving right in with the favor. Classy.

As soon as I hit send, I wish I could take it back. It's not her fault. It's the way the game is played. Everyone wants something from me. I'm simply surprised that Hannah would hit me up so abruptly and out of the blue like that.

Hannah: I could have led with: "Hi Cal. Thanks for screwing me seven ways from Sunday and then never bothering to call." Would that have been better?

Ouch.

Me: Stuff happened. Life got crazy. I had to focus.

I know it's lame, even as I type it. It's not a shock that I don't have relationships based on my personality instead of what my career can do for someone else.

Hannah: You have no idea. But that's not why I got in contact. Trust me, I wouldn't have reached out if it weren't important.

Before I can reply there's another message.

Hannah: Plus, you're the one who followed me. Stalker.

Damn, she hit the nail right on the head.

Me: After you did a story on me. Who's stalking who?

Hannah: I'm trying to build a social media following so someday I can get a job that doesn't involve me serving drinks and prime rib. Sportscaster. You were in the news. Fair game.

Me: You made me look like a jerk.

Hannah: You did that yourself. Fans want someone nice. You were a dick.

Me: Was not.

Hannah: Was too. And anyway, none of this is relevant.

That makes me sit up straight. If it's not about her video or her career, what could she want from me?

Me: Then maybe you should get to the point. If you want to be a sports reporter, you can't bury the lede. So what is it you want from me?

The phone goes silent.

I'd worry about it, but I've got to get to training. It's off-season, but I'm still working every day with Claude Kenley on my strength and conditioning.

Two hours later when I return to the locker room, sweaty and spent, there's still no reply from Hannah.

Shit.

A wave of guilt and remorse crashes over me. Not dissimilar to the feeling I get when I think about people I've cut off because I didn't know how to balance my career and relationships. I know I do it, but it doesn't stop me from repeating the cycle over and over.

One of these days, I'm going to find myself without soccer and without anything else. I'll be totally alone because I won't have anything to offer people anymore. That thought terrifies me more than anything.

I scroll up and re-read the texts from Hannah. She doesn't seem like a cleat chaser. She doesn't seem like she's trying to use me. Well, maybe, because she wants something, but at least she asked directly. She didn't cozy up to me and try to play me for my fame.

I appreciate her honesty and candor. And she still gives as good as she gets. I can't let this be our last interaction for another dozen years.

Me: Sorry, I guess my humor didn't translate through text. How can I help?

Me: Hannah, I'm sorry. Really. What do you need? I want to help.

My phone stays silent until about midnight when it starts pinging away. The speed with which the texts are coming indicates she's pissed.

Hannah: Never mind. I'll figure out a way to help myself.

Hannah: Forget I contacted you.

Hannah: I don't want anything from you.

Hannah: But to be totally clear, it wasn't for my career. I was trying to help a friend. And actually, I was trying to help you too, but you're too much of a conceited ass to see that.

Hannah: I gave up on my dream for way too long, no thanks to you. I'm not going to stop until I succeed, so someday, our paths may cross in the professional sense. Forget you knew me. I don't want to know you.

I text her back, but they all go unanswered. Okay, I get that I was insensitive, but her reaction is totally out of proportion.

Except that doesn't jibe with the Hannah I used to know. She was levelheaded and pragmatic. Until that night when she totally goaded me into sleeping with her.

Not that she had to try that hard. Or really at all. All I was waiting for was the green light. She wasn't like the girls I usually hooked up with, but that's what made me want her. I know that's a stupid clichéd line, but Hannah was more real. She didn't care about me playing soccer because she did too. If she thought I was special, it was for some other reason.

Like she actually liked me for me.

Not many people ever have. There's not much there to like, besides soccer.

I guess I've blown any chance I had with her.

Hell, I blew that the day I left Bloomington without looking back.

I should move on now as I did back then. But for some reason, I can't stop thinking about her. I spend way more time on her ClikClak profile than I should. Then her Instagram. Then I google her.

She's in Boston.

How the hell did she get from Indiana to Boston?

I try to remember where she's from, but I can't. That's the downside to being so focused on soccer. I lose a lot of details about other things. And people.

Normally it doesn't matter, but right now, it feels important. What have the last twelve years been like for her? Is she still playing soccer? Did she ever go pro? How'd she end up here?

Somehow, it was safer to think of her halfway across the country. Knowing that she's a short drive away … Hell, I go up to Boston all the time. I could drop by and see if she'll tell me what she needs help with.

Maybe I could run into her at the dog park where she films. I mean, I don't have a dog, but I'd be willing to get one if it gave me an excuse.

Wait, why am I thinking about this? Until three days ago, Hannah LaRosa hadn't crossed my mind more than once or twice in the past dozen years. I rarely dwell on things from my past. Now I'm internet stalking her, thinking about ways in which I can casually bump into her.

This ain't right.

Even though I know it, I can't stop my mind from racing with possibilities, which is why I find myself on the treadmill at 11 p.m., trying to work my already tired body until I all but collapse from exhaustion. It's been nearly twenty-four hours since Hannah texted me, and I can think of little else.

But the next day, it's no better. I scroll back through our text messages. What does she mean by "no thanks to you?" What could I possibly have done to her? Why is she blaming me for giving up her dreams?

Normally, I'm patient and even keeled. To be a successful goalkeeper, you have to be.

However, this feels anything but normal. Oh shit, what if she got pregnant that night? She wasn't sleeping around, that I know for sure. So if she did, it would be mine. Not even a gold-digging false accusation this time.

I try to picture it, Hannah, with a small child in tow. Except he wouldn't be small, would he? They. Them. They'd be about eleven or so, right? I don't know if it is a boy or a girl, but in my head, I'm definitely picturing a boy. Does he play soccer? With our combined genes, he would be a standout, for sure. But competitive sports are expensive. How is she affording the travel soccer leagues and all that goes along with it?

It takes a lot of sacrifices to make a D1 athlete, let alone a pro one, which is part of the reason I give my parents a pass for their attitude toward me. They sacrificed a lot. I owe them.

I scour Hannah's social media again. There's not much in there. Definitely no kid, but I know some people try to keep minors out of the public eye. My heart swells a bit. Hannah's a good mom.

If any of my one-night stands had to actually have my kid, she would be the one I'd pick.

But then I realize how incredibly douchey that sounds. Jesus, I am a douchebag of epic standards at this point. She obviously didn't get in contact with me for a reason. I bet she thought I'd be a bad father.

Let's face it, I probably would be. My marriage only lasted about nine months, and Katherine's number one complaint was that I didn't pay enough attention to her. That, and I wouldn't give her unlimited access to my bank account. Considering she always had something going on the side, I thought that was in my best interest.

I look down at my phone again, but there's still no response from Hannah. I'm fairly confident that I won't be hearing from her again. Whatever it is, she must not need it that badly.

Which is fine if it's not about something big, but why else would she reach out to me? And she said it would help me out too.

Damn, it's got to be a kid.

I need to find her. Boston's a big city though, so where would I even start? A quick internet search reveals seventeen off-leash dog parks in Boston and Cambridge alone. Who knows if she's in one of the outskirts?

But then I see it. The Instagram post pops up. It's an artsy, angular view of The Tower, where we had our reception prior to the playoffs. The caption, "I owe, I owe, so off to work I go."

She works there. And—I verify the time stamp—she's working now. As a goalie, my reaction time is stellar. It's what I get paid to be good at. I put those skills to work and within about three minutes, I'm in my car, heading north on I-95. Google Maps said it would take thirty-nine minutes. I'm there in twenty-five.

Parking's normally a bitch, but I luck out and see someone pulling out only a block away from the venue on Arlington Street. I hop out of my Rover and practically run the block.

And … now what?

What am I supposed to say? Hell, I'm in joggers and a hoodie, so it's not like I can even pretend I'm there for an event as a coincidence.

Then it hits me. I was here. Was she? Did she see me? She could have told me about our kid then and she didn't?

That was only like three weeks ago. What could have changed that *now* she needs my help? What if he's sick? What if he needs a kidney? I can't give him mine. I mean, at least not for another few years until my career is done. Maybe she just needs health insurance for him.

I can't let my kid die because I'm sick of being used. No one's ever going to call me father of the year, but I take care of my own. Hannah should know that.

Of course, when she tried to ask for help, I shut her down.

I have to make this right.

She's here, working her ass off to provide for our kid who's probably dying or something. The media would certainly have a field day with this one. No, I've got to fix it. I have money. I have connections. It's time I use my soccer career to help out.

CHAPTER 10: HANNAH

Hannah, can you please come here for a moment?"

It's never a good sign when your manager pulls you aside mid-shift.

"Hang on a minute, Dave. I've got to run these salads out to my section." A five-course meal is a carefully orchestrated event, and if we don't want to be serving dinner at 10 p.m., I need to keep things flowing in my section. I have it down to a science.

Dave shifts uncomfortably, "Brenna will take your section."

My stomach drops to my feet, and I immediately begin sweating. I wish I could pull my mask off, but if I'm only in a little bit of trouble, I don't want to give him an excuse for another demerit—or whatever it is he has against me—though his mask sits firmly underneath his nose.

"Dave, what's wrong?" I ask as I follow him out of the dining room. He heads toward the elevator and hits the down button. The offices are upstairs and the first two floors are empty tonight. There is no reason for us to be going down unless it's something epically bad, like being escorted off the premises.

Shitballs.

I try to subtly inhale through my nose and let it out slowly, willing my deep breathing to calm my nerves that are now bouncing more than a toddler on a trampoline with teenagers. This would be so much easier without this stupid mask on.

"Dave, what's going on?" I ask, pretending my voice didn't crack.

He won't look at me, instead staring at the wall of the elevator like it's the Mona Lisa.

Somebody died. That's got to be it. I pull my cell phone out, but there are no messages, voice or text. If it was one of my parents, my sister Nicole would have called. And vice versa.

Surely if someone had died, there would be a message of some kind, so what else can it be?

I'm being fired. That's the only logical explanation. It would suck, of course, but maybe it's a blessing in disguise. Maybe this would finally force me to try to get a job as an actual sportscaster instead of making my stupid pretend and satire videos for ClikClak.

Though truth be told, even doing that is more than I was doing a month ago.

This is it. I'm being dismissed and escorted off the premises. Another walk of shame.

Hopefully, after this one, no one calls me "Back Door Girl."

"Dave …" Now I'm practically whining. If I'm being fired, I'd at least like to know what for. Everyone

YOU BELONG WITH ME

sneaks a lamb chop now and again. I'm not the only one.

"There's someone here to see you. He says it's an emergency and was quite … insistent. He said it was life or death. Please don't be too long, and this will be your break for tonight."

Well, if I have a break, then that implies I still have a job, so that's one win. But who could be here? Carlos knows better, but you never can tell what constitutes an emergency in his book.

The last person I expect to see standing in the lobby is Callaghan Entay.

I stop in my tracks, leaving a good twenty feet between us.

The audacity.

I pull my mask down, not wanting to look any more foolish than my black-on-black uniform and high bun makes me look. We won't mention the black orthopedic non-slip sneakers I'm forced to wear. They're practical and comfortable as hell, but not what I want to be wearing when I run into the hottest man on the planet.

"Why are you here? I'm working." I can't help the words from flying out of my mouth. I'm being rude, but seriously, what the hell?

"I know, but you said you needed help. And you said it wasn't for you, and it would help me out. But you also said I was the reason you weren't a sportscaster, but you wouldn't tell me why."

I fold my arms and roll my eyes. I never pictured Callaghan as being a man who couldn't accept no for an answer, but on the other hand, I'm not sure he ever heard it that much.

"You were being an ass. I don't need your help that much. I'll figure out another way." I'm not sure how, but I won't let him know that. I haven't heard from Ophelia in two days, so I don't know if she was able to get through to the main office of the Boston Buzzards. I keep sending her all the information I can find to refute the article by Chassen Donato, hoping she can make sense of it all.

I start to head back upstairs.

"I thought about it all night. I can't stop thinking about what you said, and I finally figured it out."

That stops me in my tracks. How? Other than following each other on social media, there's nothing to link me with Ophelia or Xavier Henry. It would be a super stretch to put us together.

Then it hits me. He has no idea. There's no possible way he could. Yet there he is, Callaghan Entay, looking fine as ever in fitted joggers and a hoodie, confident as all get-out.

He has no clue. As a goalkeeper, he has excellent jumping skills. It'll be interesting to see how he's used them jumping to conclusions. This could be fun.

"You did, did you?" Slowly I turn back around, raising my eyebrows.

He nods.

"I bet you didn't."

"I bet I did." He takes a few long steps, closing the gap between us.

I smirk and shake my head. "No way. You'll never figure it out."

"But I did, and I'm here. That's got to count for something. Would I have raced up here if I wasn't confident I knew what was going on?"

I roll my eyes again as he steps closer. Is it getting hot in here?

"Okay, if you're so smart, tell me then. Tell me why, after all this time, I texted you for help. And tell me how you figured it out." This should be good. I know I'm wasting my precious break time, but it's nice to see Mr. Cool, Calm, and Collected a little agitated for once.

Callaghan sucks in a deep breath. "Well, you said it wasn't for your career, even though that's what makes the most sense. You also said you had to put your career on hold because of me."

I nod. It's really hot in here.

Cal looks at my face before dropping his gaze to my hands. Before I know what he's doing, he grabs mine in his, squeezing them a little more tightly than is comfortable.

Also, my hands are sweating. A lot. Gross.

I don't want Cal to think it's because of him. It was mostly from the elevator ride in which I convinced myself that I was being fired or someone had died.

Okay, it's a little from him.

Or a lot.

My body is betraying me right now, remembering all the ways he touched me.

"Hannah, I'm not mad. I understand. You did what you thought was best. I don't blame you."

"Blame me?" Now I'm dying to know what he thinks is going on. I so desperately want to tell him he's probably not anywhere near the truth, but I need to hold my hand. Not the literal ones he's still grasping tightly. The figurative ones that give me an advantage, at least for the next few minutes.

If I do this right, there's a chance I can still get his help with the Ophelia situation.

"You made the choice you thought was best at the time. I left. I wasn't dependable or reliable. Hell, I didn't even keep in touch on social media, which was the least I should have done. It's okay."

I'm totally lost. What the hell is he talking about?

"Cal, I think you're—"

"Han, it's okay. I'm not mad about the baby. Child. Kid. Whatever. I understand why you didn't reach out before, but you can now. My kid is not going to want or need for anything."

Kid?

I don't mean to laugh in his face literally, but that's what sort of happens.

Okay, there's no sort of about it. I let out a large, unattractive noise that can only be described as a guffaw.

Now, Cal pulls me into a hug, crushing me to his chest. "I can't imagine how much of a struggle it's been all these years for you. I'll take care of you and the baby. We can figure something out."

This is the most ridiculous thing. If I didn't know better, I'd think I was being pranked. Laughter wells up, putting incredible pressure on my chest. My whole body shakes against him, trying not to let my true emotions show while he auditions for Father of the Year.

Cal must mistake my laughter for tears, because now he's patting the back of my head, pressing my face down into his shoulder. If didn't know better, I'd think he's trying to soothe me. Mostly because he's going, "Sssh, Han. I've got you. I'll take care of you both."

Now I really am crying, but only from laughter. Even in the depths of my imagination, I could not imagine a more ridiculous scenario than the one I'm in the middle of right this minute.

"I don't know why you waited this long to reach out to me. Is he sick? Does he need a kidney? We can get my family tested to see if someone's a match."

With the mention of that word, my laughter stops abruptly, real tears threatening now. My posture shifts to ramrod straight and if he doesn't let me go this second, I'm going to go wild.

Callaghan must feel the change because he loosens his hold and steps back. "Han, what is it? Is it bad? Let me know how I can help."

I smooth down the front of my pants. There's something spilled on them, probably salad dressing that'll leave a stain.

I hope Cal got it on him and his clothes are ruined.

The loss of a pair of pants would be minor compared to the losses I've had.

CHAPTER 11: CALLAGHAN

This is worse than I thought. At first, she was crying, but if I didn't know better, I'd say she's mad now. Not just mad but like seething, raging angry. I take a step back, hoping the distance will help her calm down.

If I'd known about the kid, I would have been here sooner. She's got to know that. This is partly her fault, for not getting in contact.

Her voice is low and even, in stark contrast with the fire brewing in her eyes. She crosses her arms over her chest. "So, if your child needed a kidney, you'd ask family members to get tested? You wouldn't get tested?"

I want to avoid her gaze, but I hold it. It's the least I can do. It's the bare minimum of what I owe her. But I can't take it and look at my feet as I admit, "They haven't made final selections for the National Team yet, but I've got a good shot. And then the Global Games are this summer in Paris." I don't need to explain. She knows what I mean.

It's one of the things I always enjoyed about spending time with her in college. I didn't have to explain about early morning workouts or diets that I couldn't stray from because I was trying to protein load. It wasn't that I didn't want to have fun; I simply had priorities. Hannah understood. She didn't pressure me to change. She knew what I was doing and why.

Her eyebrows pinch together before she hisses, "Callaghan Entay, you could not be more wrong about everything. I've got to get back to work."

"So no one needs a kidney?" That would be a huge relief. I sort of feel like a douche for not giving my kid a kidney, but it's more the timing of everything. After the Global Games, they can have anything they want.

Tears well up in her big brown eyes. I see her lip quiver. Oh shit, she's on the verge of crying.

I don't think I can handle tears. Not from her.

Before I stop to think about what I'm doing, I grab her hands again. "Han, I'm sorry. I don't want to make you cry."

She lets out a bitter laugh. "You have no idea."

"Then tell me. Tell me what's going on and how I can help you. Anything. I'll do anything."

In this moment, I mean it. I never want to see this look on her face again. If I can do anything to make it go away forever, I will.

Even give her a kidney.

She pulls her hands away as if I'm on fire. "Really?"

"Anything." I nod. "Whatever you want, it's yours." I have never felt compelled to make this type of offer before. I can't for the life of me figure out why now, of all occasions, these words are leaving my mouth.

"I will never ask you for anything for me. Trust me on that. I don't need anything from you. But if I text you someone's name, will you contact her? She's trying to clear Xavier Henry's name and see if she can salvage his career with the Buzzards."

This—this is about Xavier Henry?

"Why?" I ask, absolutely dumbfounded. I'm so lost.

"Because some douchebag wrote a terrible article that is mostly untrue, and it's going to cost him his career if someone doesn't step in. Text her and she'll give you the proof that you need. Ophelia needs a way to talk to management. Bjorn Janssen would be great, but Bob Miller would be even better."

I am impressed that Hannah knows the names of both the head coach and the owner of the Boston Buzzards. I shouldn't be surprised though, after watching her ClikClaks.

She's a sports trivia aficionado. Of course, she would know this.

My ex-wife didn't, but Hannah does.

"Okay, I'll talk to Coach tomorrow. But what else do you need from me?"

Hannah stalks away. Just before she reaches the elevators, she turns and spits, "Never mind. I don't want anything from you. I never did and I never will."

I probably deserve that.

Or do I? Is there a dying kid or not? She never said there wasn't. She never said there was.

She did say the favor was about Xavier Henry.

So that's how this could benefit me. He'd be a huge asset to the Buzzards for sure. Not that I don't like Adam Lazarus as a person. As a defender, it's a different story. He's a weak link on our team and we all know it. Adam is one of the last few leftovers from pre-COVID when the Buzzards were dead last in the league.

He was one of their better players then, but Miller used the shutdown to rebuild his team. Considering we made it to the semifinals this year, I'd say the strategy was working. I'd say we'd look even better with Xavier Henry on our defensive line.

On the other hand, the article on ESPN.com said that Miller denied being in talks with Henry. With publicity that bad, he would have to say that though. I think about what Hannah said. Someone was trying to clear Henry because that article was crap. It didn't sound like him, the guy I knew when I was in the BFL.

The press can be brutal, especially when they have a salacious story to run with. I've no proof of whether the story is true or not. Nothing tangible, that is. Hannah contacting me, especially with her reaction to me tonight, should be evidence enough.

On the other hand, Henry did show up at our reception with his new bride in tow. Literally. They were on their way home from the courthouse if his Instagram feed is any indication.

But I did see them together. The way they danced, never tearing their gaze off each other. The gentle hand he put on her back. The death glare he gave me when I was checking her out. Those are not things a man does if he doesn't have some semblance of feeling toward his partner. Those weren't things he was doing because someone was watching.

Those are things a man in love does.

Or at least what I imagine a man in love would do. I've never felt that strongly about anything, other than soccer. But people give you funny looks when you give your cleats or shin guards loving caresses.

On my way home, I text Coach Janssen. It's hovering on too late to get in contact, but I reach out nonetheless. I'm not sure what I'm even going to say that's not going to sound completely ridiculous, so I simply ask to meet with him before I come in for my workout.

Because of the hour, I'm not expecting him to reply so quickly.

Coach: Actually, I was hoping to catch you tomorrow for a sit-down. 9 a.m.?

Shit. Sit-downs are never good. This is it. The end of my career. The fact that I failed to stop those PKs which cost us a shot at the finals. He's going to start CC. I'm out.

And then there goes my chance at the Global Games.

The one last thing I need to do.

Those thoughts haunt me during the drive back down I-95. It felt like I made the trip up in minutes, but it feels like it's taking hours to get back home.

Home.

My cold townhouse that's new construction and nice enough but feels as empty as my life. It's too big for me at almost 2700 square feet. There are rooms I virtually never go in. I'm not home enough to. But at just under a million, the price was right. It was high-end enough to be fitting for someone in my career.

At least that's what my mother said when she picked it out for me. She's a real estate agent to the wealthy of New Jersey. She's even appeared on an episode or two of *Real Housewives*.

We have very different priorities in life.

It was fine when Mom found it for me. It made Katherine spitting mad since I was still renting an apartment when we were married. She'd been bugging me to buy a "nice little house." I'm not going to lie, part of the reason I bought this place—in addition to not wanting to let my mom down—was to piss off Katherine.

Not super mature, but no one's ever accused me of that.

As I pull into my garage, I start to wonder if my stupid ego didn't bite off more than it can chew with this place. If I lose my spot, then the endorsements are sure to dry up fast. Soccer's not big enough in America to carry me for long with the few deals I currently have.

I was banking on the publicity surrounding the Global Games to get me one or two more big deals so I'd be set for a while until I can figure out what life is like after soccer.

I'd better get started on that.

After a terrible night's sleep, it's finally time to head to the training facility. In my head, I rehearse all the reasons why Coach shouldn't bench me. I'm about a thousand times more nervous than I am on a game day.

But when I'm staring down the kicker taking a penalty shot, I know it's all about the fake out. Trying to psych out your opponent so he second-guesses his plan and falls right into your trap. I'll do the same thing now.

I take a deep breath, trying to center myself.

Without giving Coach the opportunity to sit me down and begin awkwardly demoting me, I open his door and stride in, sitting down before being invited.

"Thanks for meeting with me, Coach. I have some information that may be useful to you and the front office in terms of our roster for next year." I continue on, without giving him a chance to stop me. "The Boston Buzzards as an organization has had quite the growing year. From the bottom of the league prior to the COVID shutdown to making the semifinals is a growth not before seen. Miller has a great vision for this team, and I'm proud to be a part of it. I think with a few more lineup changes, we could go all the way next year."

Coach Janssen sits back, folding his arms over. He lifts an eyebrow. "Really? Do tell."

"No one expected us to go from the bottom to the very top in one year, so I think we outperformed expectations. However, our defensive line still needs some shoring up, and—if the rumors are true—you've been talking with Xavier Henry. Now I know he's got some bad press right now, but I've also heard from a very reliable source that most of that article is false.

He's not like that at all. You should know that since you coached him in Baltimore."

Coach nods. "I agree that the article sounds a bit out of character for him."

"I knew him when I was in the BFL and the whole Phaedra Jones mess happened. That didn't sound much like him either, but he kept his nose out of the news and left without making a stink. To me, that says a lot about his character, not to mention his playing skills. Our defense needs him."

"I agree, but getting Miller to overlook the publicity right now is going to be tricky."

"What if he could refute the article? Would that help?"

"If he could refute it, then why hasn't he already done it?"

This is what's been bothering me. Why doesn't Xavier just come out and say it's all bullshit?

I shrug. "Not sure, but a friend of a friend is gathering proof, I guess. If they have it, will you take a look at it? Do you think Miller will?"

Coach tilts his head, considering my words. "Can't hurt to take a look, I guess. Who is this friend of a friend?"

Shit. How am I supposed to say a girl I hooked up with a long time ago knows someone—

"Ophelia." The name pops into my head. Hannah said it. Even as it leaves my mouth, I put two and two together. "I'm pretty sure that's the woman in the article, but my friend is reliable and says they have proof the article is bullshit."

"I met Ophelia. Interesting woman. But I agree. The article is totally out of character for the Xavier Henry I know. I coached him for four years and knew him before that. Is that what you wanted to discuss? Because I have something to talk about as well."

Dammit. I think I'm gonna puke.

"Callaghan, even this conversation shows me that you're interested in the welfare of this team, and you're a solid judge of character. As such, we'd like to name you co-captain with Pressley this year."

You could knock me over with a feather. "Co-captain?" I manage to sputter out. While it's not uncommon for the goalie to be the captain, I'm not sure I've ever been thought of as leadership material.

Mostly because I take this game too seriously and hold my teammates accountable when they fuck up. I mean, it's not unreasonable, but it also doesn't win me any popularity contests.

But being named co-captain means I'm keeping my starting position and that I possibly still have a chance at the National Team.

Score.

CHAPTER 12: HANNAH

Never have I ever been so livid. Not in all my life. Three days later, I'm still seething.

I also try not to think about the fact that he's been at the forefront of my thoughts for the past three days. I thought I was past that. Past him. My trauma boxes are all opened up, and my shit is everywhere.

I funnel those emotions into anger.

Who the hell does he think he is?

But that's not even what makes me so mad. He wouldn't give up a kidney for his kid because it would mean the end of his career. He didn't say it in so many words, but it was there. We both knew what he meant.

And that intention slashed deeper than he will ever know.

Of all the body parts he has to mention are the ones of mine that were impacted the most. You know, the one I might actually need someday because one has already died.

On one level, I get it—it was a random fluke. One of those things where everything in the universe has to line up just perfectly for it to happen.

Unfortunately, it happened to me. While the rational part of me knows that I most likely wouldn't have had a professional soccer career like Cal has, it wasn't totally off the table until I got sick.

I was supposed to have internships though, as part of my major. Those were supposed to funnel right into the workforce and eventually the career of my dreams. Since I had to defer schooling and finish it piecemeal, I lost the chance to intern, thereby getting my foot in the door.

My career still hasn't rebounded.

And while it was extremely bad luck to end up how I did, if I hadn't spent the night getting freaky with Cal and then snuck out of his house the next morning without even going to the bathroom, I can say I definitely would not have ended up with a urinary tract infection at that precise moment in time.

It wasn't just any UTI. Oh no. When I go big, I go really big. Like two weeks in the ICU and another four in the hospital big. Then there were the three weeks in rehab, gaining back the strength to simply stand up and walk. I didn't know that's how it was going to end up.

At first, when the tell-tale symptoms started, I tried to ignore them.

Then I drank cranberry juice.

And went to the bathroom every ten minutes, feeling like I had a bladder full of razor blades.

Apparently, I was one of those stereotypical college girls who got a UTI from a drunken one-night stand. At the time, I was just thankful it wasn't an STD.

But it didn't go away like it should have, and over the course of the week, I kept feeling worse and worse. Sure, I tried to tell myself that it was because the men's soccer team had a brand-new nickname for me.

Or that I was upset that Callaghan left without saying goodbye after the most amazing night.

I mean, I get that our night together didn't mean anything to him. Not like it meant to me. But I thought our friendship would have meant something. At least enough to stay connected on social media. It was as if he ghosted his entire past, me included.

Eventually, I stopped peeing constantly, so I thought the UTI was better, even though I felt like shit. I was tired and nauseous, but the pregnancy tests were all negative.

Thank God.

And then I pretty much stopped peeing altogether.

For the record, that's what happens when your kidneys shut down. My little UTI turned into a kidney infection and then I was septic. I legit almost died. I ended up in rehab because it turns out that lying in bed for over a month can really sap your strength away. I had to learn to walk again. I felt like a newborn deer on ice skates.

At least I kept all my limbs as well as my life.

I was truly lucky.

Almost half of all sepsis infections end in death.

My left kidney never rebounded, failing completely, and my right is not 100 percent. There's a decent chance I will end up needing a transplant one day if Righty decides to take an early retirement.

At least I'm not still on dialysis. That could have been a real lifelong possibility. Hell, it still is.

In addition to working at less than half of my kidney capacity, I've had to deal with other awesome long-term sequelae of sepsis, including things like insomnia, random rashes, periodic hair loss, anxiety, and bouts of PTSD. It's the gift that keeps on giving.

My illness was an abrupt end to my soccer career as well as life as I knew it. I lost my scholarship to IU and had to finish school while living back home in Ohio. When I finally did graduate, I had one interview with a small independent TV station out of Derry, New Hampshire. I didn't get it, but I stayed in Boston to try and figure my life out. Staying in New England made sense, as there were a lot more options for jobs. Not to mention, it's a hell of a lot closer to the ESPN headquarters in Bristol, Connecticut, than Ohio is.

And a mere decade and one pandemic later, here I am. Making an ass out of myself on ClikClak, hoping to get one more shot at what I lost all those years ago.

No, what I have here is an opportunity.

It's been a long time coming. I pull out my phone.

Me: I don't think my connection with the Buzzards is going to work.

Ophelia: That's ok. It was a long shot. Thanks for trying.

I feel as if I've let her down.

Me: This isn't the end. Let me put my journalism skills to work. Between my sports knowledge and your writing, we can probably get enough proof to exonerate Xavier.

Ophelia: <heart eyes emoji> Really? You still want to help? Why?

Me: Of course, I want to help. Just because the one guy I know on the team wasn't the way in the door, it doesn't mean we can't bust the thing down ourselves.

We are women, hear us roar.

Me: In the interest of full disclosure, I am trying to launch a career as a sportscaster. I want to be reporting from the sidelines someday, maybe even for ESPN. So if nothing else, I'm mad that someone who actually works there would publish such garbage, and that it got through in the first place.

Ophelia: Right? He was a douche at Thanksgiving, and then even douchier to write that article. Xavier won't talk to me, not that I blame him. I shouldn't have published the book when I did.

Me: Um, I read it, and unless Xavier is undead, I don't see how it's actually related to him at all.

I giggle and blush at the same time. Her book, *Stolen Stars*, is about a vampire, living as a pirate sometime in the 1800s. It's about as far from Xavier Henry as you can get.

Ophelia: YES! It's like that douchecanoe didn't even read the book but just assumed I was writing about X.

Ophelia: Still, the timing was pretty bad.

Ophelia: I have a gift for that. I need to start thinking before I act. I can be a little impulsive.

From her ClikClaks, I'd say she can be a lot impulsive. I wonder if she has ADHD or something. Not that it matters. We need a plan.

Me: We need a plan.

Ophelia: Agreed, but I'm bad at plans.

Me: Give me a few, and then I'll get back to you.

About two hours later, I've got a plan.

I don't know if it's a good one, but it's a start. We are systematically taking apart the article and proving it wrong. I'm putting together a slideshow presentation about why Xavier Henry would benefit the Buzzards' defense.

This is where Cal would have been useful. Bastard.

I don't need him. Like I said, being with Callaghan Entay was the start of my villain origin story. I channel my inner Thanos. *Fine, I'll do it myself.*

I email Ophelia my detailed plan of action. She's got a lot of people to get in contact with, including Phaedra Jones and Bob Miller. I wrote up bulleted notes for her for each talking point.

There's a lot riding on this, and I'm not sure it's going to work. It'll be a great story someday. Hopefully, Ophelia and Xavier will let me tell it.

Even if they don't, I'm doing the right thing.

One week. That's all it takes for Ophelia to put her plan into action. I'm not sure how she got all the pieces lined up so quickly, but apparently, everything's in place and ready to go.

Except for Ophelia's confidence.

Ophelia: You have to come with me.

Me: And do what?

Ophelia: Be my moral support. I wouldn't have half this info if it weren't for you.

She wants me to go to the Boston Buzzards' headquarters and meet with not only Bob Miller and Coach Janssen, but Vinny Camacho and the Commissioner of the USSL, Tanner Suarez, as well.

Being on the inside would be a massive advantage for the story I'm working on. Ophelia told me I could, of course, but I still need the green light from Xavier.

Since he's in the dark about the whole thing, that approval will have to wait.

But if he sees me there, helping, he'll be more inclined to return the favor, right?

The only thing holding me back from jumping at this opportunity is the slim chance I'll run into Callaghan. Who knows if he'll be there, but the mere thought of it is making the butterflies in my stomach dance.

I still can't believe he tracked me down at work.

I can only imagine what I looked like to him. I shudder. I'm not the girl he used to know, that's for sure.

I didn't think he could get better looking than he was in college, but he's aged like a fine wine. He's in peak form, not that I know that from spending hours watching footage of him online. I definitely wouldn't have done that.

And if I did, it would only be for research.

Researching his thigh muscles maybe.

Goalies do a lot of plyometric training. Explosive jumps require strong quads and glutes.

I glance down at my own legs, thick and curvy. It's been a long time since I worked out. Hard to think that something that was such a part of my daily life and my identity could be gone so quickly.

I'm fairly confident that most of my ClikClak followers would have a hard time believing I was once a D1 athlete. I don't have to prove it to them. I don't have to prove anything to anyone, with the exception of the fact that Xavier Henry is a good guy.

But as I stand in front of my closet, I suddenly feel more self-conscious about my body than I have in years. I'll be with Ophelia, who's a good seven inches shorter than me. I'm going to look like a giant— or an ogre—next to her.

I don't have a lot of appropriate wardrobe options. I wear my server clothes and sweatpants. There's not a huge need for much else. I have some of the suits that Carlos has thrifted for me, but I can't see myself walking into the Boston Buzzards' administrative offices dressed like that.

It's one thing for someone to laugh at my ClikClaks. It's another thing entirely for them to laugh in my face. Plus, this is serious business, and I don't want my retro suits to detract from that.

Finally, I settle on a pair of slim-fit black pants. I'd bought them for work, but they're not comfortable enough to move around in. I pair them with the black pumps I wear in the ClikClaks.

Okay, the bottom doesn't look bad. Now for the top, because I'm pretty sure wearing only my bra is not going to get us the attention we're looking for.

Though one benefit of gaining weight is that my girls are a lot more impressive than they were at the height of my soccer days. If all else fails, I'll use them as our backup plan.

I find a white shirt and a blazer that doesn't quite button all the way. It'll be fine for our purposes. I look professional enough. Hell, no one's going to be looking at me anyway. I'm just the moral support.

And to help guide Ophelia back on track if she goes off the rails. There's a good chance of that happening.

Ophelia picks me up at two. The meeting is set for three. Apparently, Xavier's been staying with the strength and conditioning coach, and he's been letting Xavier work out at the facility each day after the team finishes their workouts. We haven't received a full confirmation from the Buzzards that they'll still consider Xavier, but that's a really good sign.

Now, if I just manage to avoid Callaghan Entay while I'm there, I'll call this day a success.

CHAPTER 13: CALLAGHAN

Being named co-captain has its perks.

In addition to the snazzy "C" on my jersey, I'm privy to some insider information. Like the fact that Claude Kenley's been working out with Xavier Henry every day.

Unfortunately for Xavier, it was a slow news week in the sports world when his story broke, so it lingered on for longer than it should have. Sucks for him.

If I'm not mistaken, something's going down today. Coach asked me to stay late and talk to Xavier. There's a big meeting, and it's on me to get Henry from the gym to the conference room.

I've showered and returned to the training field, where Kenley has Henry finishing our circuit. The Buzzards have a "friendly" competition for time and reps. It's supposed to motivate us to do our best. In reality, there's a lot of wagering that goes on. I'm currently number three. Not bad for the one position player who doesn't actually have to run.

Henry is in amazing shape. He moves with power and grace, agile but controlled. We need him on this team if we want to go all the way. I hope whatever is going on in the main building today is going to get him here.

I know there are issues because he's a British citizen and all, but certainly, they can figure all that out. The USSL is focused on developing American talent, especially after the men's team failed to qualify for the last two sets of the Global Games.

I don't really care. The US Men are going this year, and I'll be damned if I'm not named to the team. I'm so close I can taste it. If the leadership role gets me there, so be it.

I'll do anything for this.

I wait for an opportunity to get Henry's attention. He finishes his circuit, all but collapsing on the turf. He presses his fists to his face, and I can feel the agony he's in. Claude Kenley, our strength and conditioning coach, claps from the sidelines. "Holy shit, Bird Man, you're a beast. You hit the highest reps of the team."

Damn. The current prize for that is a grand and a bottle of Macallan Rare.

"Too bad I'm not on the team," Xavier growls in response. You can feel the tension rolling off him in waves. I start walking in, hoping to get to Xavier before he explodes. I've never known him to be an angry guy, but he's got a lot to be upset about right now.

Kenley's voice is cheerful and also trying to calm him down. "Yeah, I wish I could put your name on the leaderboard. It might spark a fire under these lightweights to know they've got serious competition."

He winks at me, knowing Henry still has no idea I'm here. "How do you feel about Scotch?"

I'm on. "Who you callin' a lightweight?"

Henry pops up, horror on his face. His eyes dart toward the door. He looks as if he wants to make a break for it. "Fuck, Kenley, I don't want you to get in trouble."

"Actually, I came to talk to you." I sit down next to him, glancing to see if anyone is around to hear. I've got to make this convincing and inspirational and shit. That's what a co-captain does, right? "I've got to make this quick though. Word on the street is that you're totally screwed right now."

Okay, no one's ever going to be quoting me as a motivational speaker. Just as long as it doesn't end up on ClikClak again.

Hannah darts through my brain. She'd have a field day with this.

"Good word travels fast." He lies down on the turf.

"I got it from an inside source." I glance up at Kenley. I wonder how much info he's privy to. Probably more than me. Frankly, I only know as much as I do because of my conversation with Hannah. "Listen, those of us on this track know what it can be like. We get targeted for things all the time. Do you know how many paternity tests we've taken as a team?"

Kenley laughs. "Just you personally."

Bastard.

"The majority are unfounded. Kenley's working with you, helping you out. That leads me to believe that there's a chance you might not be as diabolical as the press is making you out to be. But you need to start speaking up for yourself."

He really does. If he's innocent, we need to hear it from him.

"I'd like to hear this for myself." I startle a little bit when the voice behind me says this. It's Coach.

Is he here because he didn't trust me to not mess this up? Shit.

Henry gets up, running his fingers through his hair but follows Coach Janssen and Kenley. After a curt nod from Coach, I follow the trio, providing support.

And to make sure Henry doesn't run away.

The conference room might as well be a firing squad. Bob Miller is there, plus a handful of Boston Buzzards' legal staff. Tanner Suarez, the Commissioner of the USSL, is in the room as well.

I'm not even in the hot seat, and my mouth goes dry.

When Vinny Camacho, owner of the Baltimore Terrors, walks in, I feel for Xavier. He's still technically on the Terrors yet was working out on Buzzards' property.

That's a big no.

It's grounds for immediate termination.

Which is what happens within the next few minutes. I'm standing in the back of the room, watching this unfold. It's a player's worst nightmare. I feel sick for him.

His career is done.

He's too good for that.

I slyly pull out my phone and text Justice what's going down. I'm not sure there will be anything left to salvage for Henry, but maybe Justice can do something.

From what I've gleaned, practically the only salacious thing in that article that's true is that Henry's agent is missing, along with a bunch of money. He's going to need new representation.

I don't call in many favors with Justice. Hell, I don't call in many favors with anyone. I'm usually on the receiving end of being asked for things. As such, my agent recognizes the importance of this, so he's happy to talk to Xavier if needed.

Xavier signs the papers that officially terminate him from the Terrors. Damn. He may not need Justice's help after all. He might be beyond help. Vinny Camacho stands to leave amid a trail of sarcastic comments when Bob Miller tells him to sit back down.

You could hear a pin drop in the room.

Camacho, an asshole of epic proportions if I've ever met one, throws out insult after insult about Xavier. "He's as shady and ruthless as they come. Need I remind you that he almost killed poor Phaedra Jones? Tanner, think about it. What if it was your daughter? Edmund Jones was right to ban him from the BFL."

This is where I want Henry to jump up and defend himself, but what happens next is even better. Coach Janssen gives the cue and on the large screen at the front of the room, a Zoom link opens showing an attractive blonde with a British accent.

Holy shit, it's Phaedra Jones.

I'm not sure how all of this fell into place, but, I repeat, holy shit.

I wish I had some popcorn, watching all this unfold. Phaedra goes on to explain that she was driving and that she begged Xavier to cover for her, which he did, at the cost of his career.

But that's not the most incredible thing.

Phaedra is on this video, making her addict's amends, because of Ophelia.

Xavier also can't believe what his bride has been up to. That girl's got some moxie.

Coach Janssen stands up. "She's been quite busy, and quite persuasive too." He pulls out a stack of papers and drops them on the table in front of Henry.

"What are these?" I'm glad Henry asks because I'm dying to know too.

"The emails and documentation to refute nearly every single point in the ESPN article. I've had several phone conversations with her, and at my request, she sent these over to me with alarming volume and speed. She can be charming, yet with dogged determination, as you well know. One would never expect that level of tenacity from her."

My phone buzzes silently in my pocket. I don't want to tear my eyes away from what's going on in the room, but I need to see.

Justice: Whatever he needs. If you say he's good, I trust you. Tell him to call me.

As I'm reading the text, I hear Miller say, "One-point-two for three years plus the standard bonuses."

Damn.

Justice will be happy with that commission. It's a win-win for everyone.

Especially for the Buzzards when Camacho's face turns bright red, practically exploding at the offer to the player he just terminated. Bob Miller remains calm. "I understand if you want to have your representative look at these, but I also understand you are currently without representation."

This is my moment.

I step forward. "Can I offer a solution? My agent, Justice Williams, would be more than happy to look at it and represent you. He's expecting your call."

Henry looks around the room, bewildered at what's going on. Then the door opens, and Ophelia walks in with ... Hannah? What's she doing here?

Ophelia explains, knotting her hands nervously in front of her. "Don't be mad at me for sticking my nose in. I ... I had to fix this. And you know me. Before I could stop and think, I was messaging Phaedra and Hannah and emailing Bjorn when Mr. Miller wouldn't take my calls."

Hannah looks anywhere in the room but at me. Until Henry crosses the floor in four steps, picking his wife up. As her legs wrap around his waist and they embrace like something out of a cheesy movie, I finally feel Hannah's gaze shift to me.

What would she do if I crossed the room like that to her?

I shake my head. Where the hell did that thought come from?

Miller clears his throat. "Ahem, are you two finished?" Then he mutters, "So much for the marriage being just for show."

Seriously, it wouldn't surprise me if he laid her down and started screwing her right on the conference table with everyone still in the room. They really are in love.

Of course, I could see that the night at The Tower.

I grab a piece of paper and write down Justice's contact information, sliding it on top of the contract.

It's time for me to leave.

Hannah also senses she's no longer needed. I wonder why she was there in the first place.

"Why are you here?" It comes off way more gruff and abrupt than I mean it to. I try to backpedal. "I mean—"

"Ophelia needed moral support. Plus, I did a lot of the research for her, and she thought if they had sports-specific questions, I might be better off answering them. She can be a bit … scattered."

I laugh. I can see that. Ophelia could be a poster child for Adderall.

What she said hits me. "You … you did a lot of the research for this?"

Hannah crosses her arms over her chest. Her very full chest. It's magnificent. I work extra hard to be polite and keep my gaze on her eyes as she speaks. "Um, yeah. It's not a secret that I want to be a sportscaster or sports reporter. Researching this stuff is my jam."

I smile at her. I can't help it. "Well, I think you must be good at it, sarcastic videos aside. It looks as if we've got a new player for our defense."

I start to walk down the hall, thinking Hannah will follow me to the exit. But she doesn't. She stands there, nervously glancing back at the conference room.

"What?" I ask. "You coming?"

Hannah's gaze drops down. "Um, Ophelia drove me here. I have to wait for her."

I think about the passionate PDA in the conference room. I doubt Ophelia's going to want Hannah for a third wheel when they're finally done in there.

"I'll give you a ride home. They might be a while."

Hannah doesn't move.

I raise my eyebrows at her, waiting for her to say something. Do something. Anything, really. "Han?" I say softly.

"I live up in Boston. Charlestown."

Makes sense, with her working there and all. "Okay."

"It's a long drive."

"It's not that long, and what else are you going to do? Do you know how much an Uber would cost?"

We stand there, staring at each other for a long moment. What is she thinking about? I try to read her face, but her expression is smooth. Her tobacco-colored eyes stare back at me, unblinking.

Even though I've watched her videos over and over on ClikClak, it's a bit surreal that she's standing here in front of me. She's composed and calm, not at all like she was when I saw her at her work.

This is the Hannah I remember from college. Put together and unflappable. Controlled on the field and in the gym. Until the night before I left, I didn't know she could lose control like that.

And boy, did she ever.

"Let me do this for you." The words surprise me. I'm not known for being magnanimous and giving. Probably because people are usually trying to take from me. I don't usually get the chance to offer before they ask.

From the small breath Hannah takes in, my words must surprise her too. "Okay, fine, but I'm not going to talk to you in the car." Then she's back to silence. I stand there, not sure what to make of her until she tilts her head to the side and widens her eyes as if to say, "Are we going?"

I walk to my car, Hannah following behind me. I know this was the right thing to do, especially since Hannah helped get Xavier signed with us and all, but I'm totally regretting my decision.

There is no way I am not going to mess this up with Hannah.

Again.

CHAPTER 14: HANNAH

tay cool. Stay cool. Stay cool.

I chant that inside my head, trying not to let any emotion show. I'm wearing my interview face, which I've spent hours practicing. It's neutral, not betraying the absolute turmoil that is running speed drills in my stomach.

I have to spend almost an hour in a car with Callaghan Entay. My brain cannot even begin to process the thoughts moving through it faster than Usain Bolt.

Tell him you almost died.

Ask him to help you get a job.

Does he still like maple walnut ice cream?

I bet he's still a great kisser.

He left you and never looked back.

How many women has he slept with since you?

Is he going to be named to the National Team?

Maybe he'll do an interview with me.

Can I lick him again?

The ideas whirring through my mind make me dizzy. I close my eyes and clench my teeth, willing them to stop.

"Are you okay over there?"

Slowly I lift my lids and give him a side-eye.

Callaghan holds up his hand in defense. "Just asking. I don't want you booting all over my car if you're carsick or something. You look a little pale. Like, paler than you usually are."

It's a good thing he's pretty because he's definitely not wooing women with his prose. "I'm not going to throw up," I say through gritted teeth. Though, on second thought, it might not be out of the realm of possibilities.

I'm thinking too much. Too hard. This is a simple car ride, and then I never have to see Callaghan Entay again. I don't need him to achieve my dream. I've got a plan that might even be working, and I'm going to stick with it. I can sit here for the next forty-five minutes or so and then move on. We don't even have to talk.

It would be better that way.

"Okay, so what's with the ClikClak? I've seen the videos."

"Oh? Which one did you see?" I cross my fingers that it's not the one where I'm totally making fun of him.

"I've watched them all."

Just when I didn't think the pit in my stomach could grow any bigger, it becomes a quicksand sinkhole. Actually, that would be great if it really was, because then I could let it swallow me whole.

He knows about the video. Of course, he does. I knew that. But I still don't want to think about him watching me in that video. Mocking him. Maybe he won't bring it up.

"All?" I squeak out. I don't know why I need his confirmation. I know he saw *it*.

His gaze darts toward me for the briefest of seconds, an eyebrow cocking. "Yes, all."

His words hang in the car. I try to swallow, but it's not going so well. Finally, I manage to croak out, "Well, you need to get some hobbies then."

"Like making ClikClaks?"

I shrug, not that he can really see it. "It's a living." I quickly rephrase. "I mean, it's not. Not yet. But hopefully someday."

The disdain is evident in his voice. "You mean, all you want to do with your life is make stupid videos about dogs and make fun of athletes?"

From the bitterness in his voice, I wonder how many times he's watched my video about him. I struck a nerve.

"That's not—"

Callaghan cuts me off. "You know, some of us are out here, giving our hearts and souls for the game. We sacrifice everything. Our lives, our relationships, our bodies. And then someone asks a stupid question when you're feeling your lowest of low, and *that's* what lives forever on the internet because of people like you."

His knuckles are white on the steering wheel. Yeah, well, he's not the only one in this car who's riled up.

"People like me? Oh, come on, Callaghan. ClikClak didn't cause your PR issues. It just documented them. You're a fantastic goalie, no doubt about it, but you seriously lack people skills. You always have. It's a good thing you're super-hot because otherwise, you'd never land a woman."

Oh shit. Please tell me those words did not leave my mouth. Those are brain-only words and have no business being spoken aloud. But from the look he gives me, I know without a doubt those words were very audible.

I should apologize.

"So, you think I'm hot?"

That's what he got out of that?

"Look in the mirror. Everyone with eyes thinks you're hot. That's not a big revelation, so don't let it go to your already overinflated ego. But you know what I mean. You don't really have a way with words."

He's quiet for a minute before saying, "That doesn't give you a right to make fun of me." He's hurt. He'll never say it, but I can hear it. I'm going to apologize and pull the video.

Then he keeps talking. "I didn't say anything wrong. The team blew it. Brandon Nix and his shit-ass temper blew it. If he hadn't drawn that penalty, we'd have won. There are eleven men on the field, but they left it all to me. And do you know what percentage of PKs are saved? It's ridiculous to put it all on one player and then not expect him to be upset that the rest of the fuckwits on the team may have cost him his shot at the Global Games."

"Eleven." My answer is automatic.

Callaghan shakes his head, his rant interrupted, and looks at me. "Eleven?"

I nod. "At the topflight level of soccer, eighty-five percent of penalty kicks are scored. Eleven percent are saved, and the other four percent are totally shanked by the kicker, as evidenced by Pressley's and Brandon's kicks. So, not including the PK that tied the score, you saved one out of five. That's a 20 percent save rate. No one would fault that performance. You pouting like a baby at the end, well, that's another story. You have to control that for the press. You should know by now you don't say that kind of stuff in public. Ever. The game face needs to stay on."

Callaghan swerves over three lanes of traffic on I-93 to pull off to the side of the road. He puts the car in park and turns to stare at me. I stare back.

"What?" I finally ask. I can't hold his intense gaze anymore, so I look down at my hands, tightly knotted in my lap.

He's got one elbow resting on the steering wheel and the other leaning on the center console. Suddenly, the interior of this Range Rover seems very small.

"How do you know that?"

I don't even bother to hide rolling my eyes. "Just because I don't have a penis doesn't mean I don't know about sports."

Callaghan's eyes narrow. "Are you stalking me?"

This makes me laugh. You know, one of my loud awkward bleats. "Get over yourself. Been there, done that, have the scars to prove it."

Oh shit. I can't believe I said that. I quickly cover. "I doubt you remember conversations we had

YOU BELONG WITH ME

in college, but my career aspirations remain the same. I want to be a field sportscaster for ESPN. I'd settle for Fox Sports. I want you to turn on any big game, and I'll be the one on the sidelines calling it. The next Erin Andrews or Pam Oliver or Lesley Visser. I know sports."

His head tilts slightly, his gaze drifting up and to the left. "Well, yeah. So, is that why you follow soccer?"

I sigh, letting my head flop back to the leather headrest. Closing my eyes, I say, "I follow all sports. I don't know what I'll be able to get a job covering, so I want to be prepared."

"Then what are you doing making ClikClaks?"

I open my eyes and look at him. "I got a little off track with my career, and since I wasn't able to go through the normal pathways, I've got to do something to make myself marketable. Apparently, nowadays, a big social media presence can open more doors than personal letters of reference or internships."

I still can't believe it's true, but I'm trusting multiple sources who say that companies look at this stuff now. Carlos was totally right.

"So ClikClak fame is not the end goal? No pun intended. Speaking of which, do you still play soccer?"

I look at him and then glance down at my frame, ample and lush. "Do I look like I do?"

Of course, this causes his gaze to drop too. If I'm not mistaken, it spends a disproportionate amount of time on my breasts.

"Yoo-hoo! Eyes up here." I wave my hands, pointing to my face. When he's finally looking at my eyes I say, "No, I gave it up."

"Why? Don't you miss it?"

The lump in my throat threatens to choke off all my air. It certainly prevents any words from coming out. Part of me wants to tell him what happened to me after he left, but I know, deep down—way deep down—it really has nothing to do with him.

It's not his fault, but he was an easy scapegoat for a terrible situation. It feels good to be mad at him rather than at myself for being so stupid.

Another part of me is trying not to have a panic attack reliving that time in my life. I do okay if I think about what happened. When someone else brings me back, it's hard to be right back in that time of fear and pain.

I take a deep breath and count to ten before responding. I don't think I want to get into all of it with Callaghan. At least not now. "I miss the team. You know what it's like when you have one that clicks. I certainly don't miss burpees."

I really hated burpees.

"I've never been away from the sport long enough to miss it." His voice is quiet. I can't tell if he wishes to be away or if he's scared to be away from it.

"I didn't have—this is just how things ended up for me. Certainly not what I'd planned, but I'll figure something out someday." I wish he'd start driving again, so I can get out from under his intense gaze.

Not to mention, I kind of have to go to the bathroom.

Not kind of. That large coffee this morning is doing me no favors. And being this close to Callaghan makes me nervous. Really nervous. My nerves certainly aren't helping the situation.

Since my remaining kidney is already working on borrowed time, I don't like to stress her out. I need him to start driving again. Now.

"Can we please get going? I need to get home."

Callaghan looks at the steering wheel and then back at me. He looks lost and confused. I don't want to have to spell it out for him, but he's not moving. And the more I think about it, the more the urgency grows.

"Listen, if you don't start driving right now, you're going to need to get your car detailed. I'm warning you. Mother Nature is calling, and I'm going to have to answer."

Awareness finally dawns in his eyes, and he shifts back into his seat, putting the car in drive. As soon as there's an opening, he pulls out. I look at passing signs to see how far we are from my place.

Dammit, we're not even to Quincy yet. I'm not sure how far the next exit is. It might be only three or four miles, but that might as well be forty to my bladder.

There's a very good chance I will wet myself in this car. I've gone through a lot of embarrassment in my life, but I'm not sure I'd ever be able to live that one down.

"I implore you, please get off at the next exit."

Cal gives me a side-eye, but I feel the Range Rover accelerate. He weaves through traffic. I clench every muscle in my body, trying not to rock back and forth. Finally, he gets off at exit 11, flies down Granite Street, and then hangs a sharp right to pull up in front of a Dunks.

You couldn't get more New England if you tried.

I make it in and to the bathroom in the nick of time. Once I'm done, I sheepishly get back in the car. Cal just looks at me.

"That happen often?"

I shrug. It does. I won't feel like I have to go, and once I do, it's an emergency. It's not great, but it's better than the alternative. The infection that raged through my urinary tract left a lot of damage. "Yeah, it's a thing. We don't ever need to mention it again." I look down at my hands. "That won't be hard, because we don't ever need to talk again."

He doesn't start the car.

I lift my eyebrows. He continues to stare at me. "What?"

"Why won't we talk again?"

I lift my shoulders, letting them drop. I'm not sure how to articulate this without sounding pitiful.

"Hannah …"

He almost sounds like he's pleading.

How do I say that being around him reminds me of the most terrible chapter of my life? I had a lot of therapy after I almost died. I still only have one functioning kidney. He's a trigger. Even though it wasn't his fault, he's still the catalyst that started the ball in motion.

Also, because I was totally in love with him and he ghosted me. It took me years to stop fantasizing about him walking back into my life. That started when I was in the hospital. I hoped every day that he'd show up. That was not super helpful in my recovery.

"Cal, you're a famous athlete. You're at the top of your game. You're about to be named to the National Team. I'm a waitress."

"You want more."

"Yeah, but the odds of that happening are not in my favor. We're just not in the same circles. And even if we were, why? Why do you care if we talk again? I wasn't interesting enough for you to keep in touch the first time around," I say quietly.

He looks at his hands, gripping the steering wheel, even though he's made no move to take the car out of park. "I thought we were friends once," he says finally.

I stare straight ahead, trying to think of a response.

He puts the Rover in drive and heads back toward 93. We sit in silence for a bit before I offer, "We were friends. Or at least as good of friends as you can be. You're rather single-focused, and I'm guessing that focus is never on anything but soccer."

I'm not trying to insult him. It's simply the truth.

Callaghan nods. "Can I tell you a secret?"

It's my turn to nod.

He continues. "I'm not the best out there."

"Um, your stats would say otherwise." His statistics are seriously impressive.

"I'm not inherently the best. I'm only that good because I work so hard at it. I put everything I have into this game. If I didn't, I probably wouldn't still be playing."

"I doubt that. I don't think you give yourself enough credit."

He shakes his head. "You don't understand. I have to do more. More training. More supplements. More analysis. More than everyone, just to keep up. I don't have time for anything else. Trust me, I've tried, and it nearly cost me my career. But I wouldn't expect you to understand."

I was all on board to be sympathetic to the woes of his personal life—until that last part. Immediately I'm bitter. My emotions take over.

"Yeah, well, I'm the last person you should complain to about stupid shit costing your career. After all, you cost me mine."

Oh shit. I did not just say that.

CHAPTER 15: CALLAGHAN

I whip my head so fast to look at Hannah that I almost swerve into the pickup next to me.

I knew it!

We do have a kid together. I think back to our last conversation about the issue. She didn't deny it. She didn't say no. In the media, that's as good as saying yes.

And speaking of media, she probably knows about all those paternity cases I was named in. I bet she doesn't want to be another girl like that.

I have to know.

I'm tempted to pull the car over again, but since we're in the midst of downtown Boston traffic, I instead follow the GPS, sitting in silence.

It's fine. I can be patient. I can wait.

I'm bringing her to her house. It'll be apparent soon enough if there's an eleven-year-old in residence.

Of course, I'll have to get inside. I can't just storm in, as much as I want to. I could ask her, but with the attitude swirling around her now, she's likely to say no.

That's fine. I'll take a page from her book.

I pull into an on-street parking spot just past her place. "Do you mind if I use the bathroom? I've got a long drive home."

She rolls her eyes but exits the car without saying anything. I take that as a good sign. I hop out and hurry after her to the door. Her building is a three-story brick with peeling black-painted trim. I look up and try to imagine a small child in this building.

I can't.

Never have I wanted to be wrong so much in my life.

Hannah doesn't speak to me as she walks up to the second floor. She opens the door and walks into a small living room. The whole place is light and bright and there's color everywhere. Bright rugs and couches and artwork.

Not a toy in sight.

Do prepubescent kids play with toys? I glance at the TV. There's no gaming system. I'm pretty sure preteens play with those.

"Bathroom's down the hall."

I walk down the narrow hallway, trying to look in the bedrooms on my way. One is pale grays and aquas, while the other looks like a unicorn threw up in it.

I never pictured Hannah as a rainbow-sequin-unicorn person.

Which is what I say to her as soon as I'm done in the bathroom.

"That's because I'm not. That's my roommate's room."

I look around. "Oh, is she here?"

Hannah smiles. "*She* is not. Carlos should be home soon though."

Right.

I look down at my feet. There's definitely no kid stuff around.

"Okay then, thanks for the ride. You should probably get back on the road. You don't want to get off schedule with your training regime."

I meet her gaze. "Hannah, I'm not going anywhere until you tell me how I ruined your career. Did you get pregnant or not?"

She laughs a bitter laugh, shaking her head in denial. "I only wish."

The startled expression on my face has her immediately recanting that statement. "That's not what I mean. I didn't want a baby, and I certainly wasn't trying to get pregnant from you. It would have been horribly inconvenient, especially considering how you never looked back."

"Then what could I possibly have done to you? I mean other than never calling you after we slept together. I know that was a dick move, but there were extenuating circumstances. If there's no kid, then why are you bitter?"

"There's definitely no kid. But do you really think you're the only guy ever to blow me off after a hookup? They're called one-night stands for a reason."

I look at this attractive, brazen woman before me, trying to picture what kind of fool—other than me—would blow her off. Hannah's like the physical embodiment of a Renaissance painting. Soft skin, a great rack, and hips that I just want to grab. Why would guys not call after sleeping with a goddess like her? Idiots.

That includes me.

Also, I'm totally relieved that there's no baby. Child. And for the first time, it's not relief that I'm not saddled with a woman and a kid. I'm happy that I didn't leave this all for Hannah to do by herself.

I take a step toward her. This is killing me. I don't know why, either. Maybe because she's made it clear that she doesn't want anything from me. I'm not used to that.

It's actually quite attractive that she doesn't treat me like I'm special. She gives me shit and doesn't let me off the hook.

Plus, she knows sports.

Maybe it's because she knew me back when. Before I was famous. She's familiar and comfortable like going home should be. Not that my own home has ever felt like that, but what I imagine it to be.

I clasp her hands. "Hannah, tell me what I did."

She pulls her hands out of mine, turning away. She sits down on the couch and motions for me to take a seat. I look at her expectantly.

"I … I got sick. Really sick after … you know. I ended up in the hospital. The ICU. It was really bad. I almost died."

That's shocking. "Oh my God, Han. I'm so sorry. That sucks." I pause for a minute. "But what did I do? How did I make you sick? How is it on me?"

She takes another breath before starting again. "That morning ... after. I needed to get out. All your roommates were there—"

"I remember." I remember her hair, a mess. I remember her searching around my room for her clothes. I don't know if she ever found her underwear. She was wearing one of my jerseys with her bare legs and ass hanging out. God, the sight of my name on her back made me want to claim her again. I wanted to ask her to stay and go to breakfast with me, but she was totally panicking. I knew she was embarrassed and ashamed. It's like she knew I wasn't good enough for her and didn't want anyone to find out.

"So I left without even going to the bathroom."

"You practically ran out the door. To be honest, I'd never had anyone want to leave like that before. I thought you must have regretted it."

Regretted me.

Hannah blinks rapidly. "Um, what?"

"You know, like you had beer goggles on and that's the only reason you came home with me, and you were ashamed of being with me."

"Have you seen you? And when you forget about trying to act like a jock, you're actually a decent human being. I thought your friends would give you a hard time about bringing me home, and I didn't want to hear the comments about being your pity fuck."

There is no way that's what she actually thought. I need to set that record straight. "Dude, lots of guys on the team wanted to nail you. They were too afraid you'd kick their asses if they ever made a pass."

She used to do this thing where she'd roll her shorts up so they were super short and then wipe her sweat with the hem of her shirt. I don't think she had any idea what that did to me. Good thing I was usually wearing a cup.

She tilts her head. "Me?"

It's my turn. "Have you seen you? You are gorgeous without being all made up and fake. You were fierce on the field, and you didn't take shit from anyone, least of all me. You weren't into all that girly shit and drama. You were like one of the guys, if we wanted to screw each other."

I don't think that came out right.

"I think there might be a compliment in there, but I'm not sure."

"You know how good my motivational speeches are."

Hannah laughs. "Legendary."

I return her smile. "So you thought you were sparing me? It's not because you were ashamed?"

She shakes her head. "If I thought people would have believed me—that you were after me—I would have taken out a billboard. But contrary to popular belief, female athletes don't always do well with dating. Men, that is. They seem to be intimidated by us. Or maybe it's just me. That was my experience anyway."

"So you don't regret sleeping with me then?"

Her face falls as she looks away.

"I wish I could say I didn't regret it, but I do."

It feels like she's kicked me in the gut.

She stands up, so I do too. There's not a lot of space between us. I step forward, making it even less. I can't take my eyes off her mouth. "Hannah, I don't want you to hate me. I don't want you to regret me."

Her full lips part slightly. I want to claim them, as I did that night so long ago. Will she taste the same? Will she feel the same? I want to find out.

"Hannah," I whisper, just as our mouths are about to touch.

"Han, I've got twenty to do your makeup because we're going out tonight!" The door flies open and Hannah's roommate—I'm guessing—comes in like a storm of energy and chaos.

Hannah jumps back, putting way too much space between us.

It's probably a good thing too. I'm thinking things about Hannah that I've no business thinking about. Especially since she already regrets me once.

The roommate—Carlos—comes to a dead stop. "Am I interrupting something?"

"No!" Hannah exclaims loudly. "Not at all. Cally was just leaving."

The way she slips so effortlessly into my nickname does things to me. Things it shouldn't, especially since every other vibe I'm picking up from her is nothing but prickly.

Carlos gives me a slow up and down. "Why? He should come out with us tonight."

I look down at my hoodie and joggers. Not exactly dressed for the club. "I … uh …"

"No, that's quite alright. You have to get home. I'm sure you have training early in the morning or something."

"I do get a day off every now and then." Not that I take them, but she doesn't need to know this. I should rest. Kenley keeps telling me I'm pushing too hard.

I don't know how to stop.

"I'm not going out anyway. I've got work to do tonight." Hannah crosses her arms over her chest. Actually, it's slightly under her chest, making her breasts strain at the buttons of her white button-down.

It's glorious.

"I thought you were off tonight. I made plans." Carlos puts his hands on his hips.

Hannah turns to face him, like I'm not still standing right there. "I don't have to go to work, but I need to work. You know, ClikClak. I'm trying to write some more material. I want to start sending inquiries to stations after the holidays. I need to have a great portfolio."

Carlos lets out a dramatic sigh. "You're right. You do need to get your house in order. I'm happy to see you've finally stopped moping and are taking the bull by the horns."

Hannah's face grows red. Her eyes shoot daggers at her roommate. "Got it. I'm lazy and unmotivated. Nothing I haven't heard before." Then, it's as if she remembers I'm here. Finally facing me, she says, "Thanks for the ride. And thank you for the agent thing. It was a good sign for Xavier and Ophelia."

I am summarily being dismissed. On the other hand, Hannah's not usually forthcoming with praise. She's not wrong in her assessment of Henry joining the team. "Yeah, well, he'll be good for the Buzzards."

"I know. You need him." Her tone is aggressive like I'm not listening to her.

"I know. I'm agreeing with you." My tone is matching her aggression, like we're arguing instead of seeing eye to eye.

"Don't you have to go?"

I try to read her expression. I'm used to staring opponents down, watching their body language, looking for their tells so I can determine which way they're going to shoot. But with Hannah, there's nothing giving it away.

It's too bad she's not still playing soccer. She'd make one hell of a penalty kicker.

"Okay, then. I ..." I don't know how to finish that thought. I see myself out and to my car.

It's only when I'm almost home do I realize Hannah never exactly told me how sleeping with me ruined her life.

CHAPTER 16: HANNAH

O*phelia: <heart eyes emoji> I can't thank you enough. <heart eyes emoji>*
Ophelia really does love that emoji. She adds it to everything, along with her trademark "XOXO" signature. I guess if I were as happy as she is, I'd probably add stupid emojis too.

In spite of myself, I smile. Her life is the thing of dreams. Her fake marriage turned out to be anything but. Xavier is head over heels for her. The feeling's definitely mutual. Thanks to ClikClak, her book is doing amazingly well. Even Ophelia admits it's cheesy smut, but that doesn't stop people from devouring it. The next one will be out in a few weeks.

Instead of feeling jealous of her perfect life, I take it as a sign to work on my own.

Okay, I wallow for about ten minutes first before I bite the bullet and initiate a search on the internet. No matter how successful my ClikClak videos are, I doubt ESPN is going to come knocking on my door. I'm going to have to work my way up.

It'll be fine.

Kurt Warner was undrafted and stocking shelves in a grocery store for $5.50 an hour when his big break came with St. Louis. Okay, he was still playing in the Arena Football League during this time, so he wasn't totally out of the game.

I glance at my phone. I'm not either. Comparing ClikClak to the Arena Football League is a stretch, but what the hell? It's a metaphor, and that's bread and butter to sports reporters and athletes alike.

I wade through listings for newspaper reporters covering high school athletics. That would be starting at the bottom. Like way down. Sports editors.

Too bad Ophelia is the writer, not me.

There's a weekend sportscasting job in Binghamton, New York. I drove through there once. There's not much there. I bookmark it, but it would be a last resort for me.

Then, I see it.

It's not ESPN, but it's perfect. Sports reporter. Online. A hybrid job, with some work in New York. Seems doable. It's an English company, looking to expand into the US. Cool. They want someone with knowledge of the law. Probably so they don't get sued, like Xavier is about to do to Chassen Donato. I can fact-check. I'm really good at that. I look at the other requirements. Encyclopedic sports knowledge. Check. Social media experience. Check. And remind me to hug Carlos. Live blogging. Check. Audience analytics. Check.

I'm so golden.

Sure, I gloss over the fact that I don't actually have a year of journalism experience, other than college. I'm sure I can impress them with the stories I've done thus far.

The pay is awful. It's actually on the high side for this field, but it will not get me far in Boston, especially not if I'm commuting to the Big Apple. I'd better plan on keeping my job in catering. People think that just because you're on TV, you must be rich. It's so not the case. Realistically, I'm not sure I can afford to follow my dream.

But I have to try.

All I need is to do some fantastic reporting—of real sports, not the dog park variety—and send those videos in with my resume. Maybe Xavier will let me do a story on him. Telling his side.

Ophelia did say they owed me.

I can feel my excitement growing. For the first time since I was admitted to the hospital all those years ago, my dream seems like it's within my reach. I can practically touch it.

Before I stop to think, I'm enthusiastically filling out the application and writing the cover letter. I promise an exclusive story from a current professional athlete if I'm granted an interview.

And then I hit submit.

The minute the green check comes up, I want to vomit. What did I just do? Ophelia and Xavier never agreed to help me. While I'm sure they will, what if they don't?

"What if" is not responsible journalism. I'm no better than the reporter who almost ruined Xavier's career.

My stomach churns.

I haven't even started, and I've made an unforgivable mistake.

Maybe they won't respond. That would probably be for the best. The pay is terrible. I'd have to move.

Maybe I'm just not meant for this.

I go back to the job listing for the weekend job in Binghamton. Oh God, it's to cover one D1 college sports events, a golf tournament that I've never heard of, and then cover high school athletics.

At least I meet all the job requirements. They stress social media too.

I submit my application to them.

It's bottom of the ladder, weekends and three days a week, but I wouldn't have to make promises that I can't keep.

And submitting that application doesn't make me want to yak, so there's that.

Okay, I'm still in literally the same place I was six weeks ago when I helped Ophelia and Xavier out, but I feel maybe one step closer to success today.

Ophelia: And guess what? We're getting married. For real. We booked it at The Tower because, well, you know.

Me: OMG, perfect. Let me know, and I'll make sure I'm on the schedule.

Ophelia: That would be great, but no climbing out the window this time.

I bury my face in my hands. I cannot believe that was my reaction to seeing Callaghan Entay again. Though it makes sense. I learned one time that the body's sympathetic nervous system takes over in moments of survival. Most people are familiar with the fight-or-flight response. There are actually four Fs associated with the response. Fight, flight, freeze, or the other F-word.

Callaghan triggers every single one of them in me.

I'd better hope that I never have to spontaneously interview him. Lord only knows what will come out, but I'd bet a year's salary that it would be fodder for the blooper reel.

Me: If I know ahead of time that he's going to be there, I can mentally prepare myself.

With some Xanax maybe.

Ophelia: Chances are good he'll be there. The ceremony's going to be small. Family and a few close friends, but I'm sure Xavier'll invite him. If only for the help with the agent stuff.

I have to admit, both Callaghan and I did play a role in Xavier getting signed to the Buzzards. I wonder what the public would think of that. Cal doesn't have the best public image, no thanks to his interview prowess, so it might make people like him a little more.

Especially since he was just named to the National Team.

His dream is coming true.

The odds are in his favor, so he probably doesn't need me doing a story on him to help. Frankly, it would help me a lot more than it would help him.

And Red Sox Nation will root for the Yankees before I ask Callaghan Entay for help with my career.

For those of you non-sports fans out there, that means never.

I need to stop thinking about him. He's been on my mind—a lot more than I'd like to admit—since that fateful night when I met Ophelia. But it's hard.

Especially when I get a message from him every few days.

Usually, it's nothing important. A ClikClak video or some meme. A reminiscence about college, like *whatever happened to …*

I should take comfort in the fact that he didn't keep in touch with anyone else either. It wasn't personal that he blew me off. He was focused.

And it's paid off.

He's not only on the National Team but their starting goalkeeper. It was announced this morning. I search out and watch the video footage from the announcement at the Buzzards' training facility. Callaghan is showing off, blocking shots and diving. On the last dive, he hits particularly hard, bouncing off his shoulder. He seems a little slow to stand, and there's an unmistakable look of pain on his face. The video cuts away.

Maybe it was a stinger.

He's probably fine.

His adrenaline is so high, he probably didn't feel a thing. He's got to be elated. I should make a ClikClak about this announcement. Or at least send him a message. We never exchanged numbers so we're in each other's DMs on ClikClak.

Me: Congrats!

I shouldn't expect a reply right away, but I'm sort of surprised when the message goes unread. Unanswered.

Okay then. The minute he gets a better offer, he forgets about everyone from his past.

Apparently, nothing's changed with Callaghan Entay.

And I doubt it ever will.

CHAPTER 17: CALLAGHAN

*F*uck.

The pain lances through my shoulder and arm. I've done this before, so I know exactly what it is. But this time, it's worse. Not just because of the timing, but the injury itself.

I knew the second I landed that I didn't roll my shoulder under enough. Rookie mistake, but I'm no rookie.

I should have reported it immediately to the trainer and physician, but I didn't. The shoulder was touchy to begin with. The announcement that I made the National Team is still a top news story and garnering me all the attention I've been looking for. Being diagnosed with an AC joint separation right now would be disastrous.

I have to play through it.

I'm sure it'll be fine in a few days.

I ignore that it's already been a few days, and each day keeps getting worse.

Maybe I can get the athletic trainer, Johnson, to tape it or something. I've been taking anti-inflammatories, which I don't normally like to do, and trying to manage it conservatively. I'm doing lots of lower body drills to keep my legs in shape, but eventually, someone's going to notice that I can't lift my arm up.

Fuck.

While it's still technically the off-season, we only have about four weeks to go until the official training season starts. While I *could* take a day off or two, it's probably not advised.

I don't have much of a choice.

Three days after I'm named to the National Team, I text Kenley to let him know I won't be in to work out.

Kenley: Fame going to your head already?

Me: You know it.

The next day, the shoulder is no better. In fact, I think it's worse. This isn't the first time I've separated my collarbone from my shoulder blade. I'm sure those ligaments have given up their last ghost. How many ghosts are there to give up? Are shoulder ligaments like cats and have nine lives? How many times have I sprained this joint? At least eight.

If that's the case, then my career is over.

I'd need surgery and would miss most of the season, which is yet to even start.

That's the worst-case scenario.

The best case is that I'm just getting old and I don't bounce back as well as I used to.

I mope around in my place, not even bothering to turn the lights on. I'm going to become a hermit and sit here in my bathrobe until the end of time. It seems like a solid plan.

I manage to sit for about seven minutes before I have to get up and move around. I'm not sure being a hermit is a good career plan for me.

But speaking of careers, I need a backup plan if my career is ending. I pick up my phone, wincing as I forget that I can't reach with my right arm.

Me: I can't go into details, but I could really use a huge endorsement deal right about now.

Justice: Another paternity suit?

Me: No. And I'm being serious.

Justice: As was I. Keep your pants on. I was actually just going to call you.

I don't have a chance to respond before my phone rings. I prefer to deal with people through text messages only, which my agent knows. He only calls when it's big.

"Is it big?"

"I think so. It's what we've been working on, but there's a catch."

Isn't that always the way?

"What?" I don't mean my tone to be so clipped, but my patience is at an all-time low. Mostly because I'm frustrated with myself, but I like to take it out on everyone around me.

It makes me super lovable.

"I need you to hear me out before you answer. Listen to it all before you say no."

"You're not selling it well so far."

There's a silence on the line. Then Justice takes in a deep breath before explaining. "You need to go to New York for about four days, so you'll have to skip training."

In the past, when endorsement deals have been on the table but they required me missing training, I passed on them. What good was cashing in on my soccer career if I didn't have a career? And the only way to keep the career was to train and practice and play. I wasn't pissing that away to stand around in a suit trying to convince people to buy a watch.

I don't even wear a watch, for Christ's sake.

"When?"

I swear, even through the line, I can feel Justice's shoulders sink in relief that I didn't automatically say no. His career depends on my success and the more deals I have, the more money he makes.

"Friday."

"This Friday? Like tomorrow?" Shit. That's not much notice. On the other hand, I doubt my shoulder will magically have healed by then, so really, the timing couldn't be better. I can't practice anyway.

"Yeah. It's a whole weekend convention. There's a cocktail reception on Friday and then trade shows throughout the weekend. They want to casually talk to you on Friday, have a formal sit-down on Saturday, and then, if you manage not to blow it, do a photo shoot and formal announcement on Sunday."

Justice has left out one important detail.

"Who's it for?"

The name makes me suck in a breath.

It's one of the biggest names in athletic gear. Even without paid endorsements, my closet is full of items bearing that brand logo. They don't usually have soccer players in their campaigns. Not enough name and face recognition.

This is huge.

"I'm in."

We go over the details, including travel and wardrobe expectations. Of course, my casual wear is almost always joggers, so it's easy, as long as I make sure to include those with the right logo on them. Heaven emails me my itinerary of flights from Logan to LaGuardia and reservations at the hotel approximately one block away from the Javits Center.

What a week. Named to the National Team. A campaign with one of the biggest brands out there. But as I reach out to lift my travel bag up, I'm painfully reminded that it might be gone already.

I wish I had someone to call. To share the news with. To talk about my fear of never playing again. But as I sit, phone in my hand, I realize there's no one.

I suppose I could call someone on the team. That could get a little messy though because we're all basically competing for the same endorsement deals. On the team, personal victories still go toward the greater good. This is entirely for personal gain, so it could breed feelings of resentment. That's not what I want. I just want someone to talk this through with me.

I think about calling my mom, but she won't be interested until the endorsement deal brings her swag, and even then, it's not her style. If I could land a deal with lululemon, she might be more excited. And she definitely won't be thrilled that there are more games for her to go to with my addition to the National Team roster.

Dad, undoubtedly, will criticize me for injuring myself, if he takes the call at all.

As my thoughts swirl down, I consider calling Hannah. She might not like me all that much—for reasons she has still yet to explain—but she'd at least appreciate the situation. She'd know what it meant. She'd understand my vacillating between extreme euphoria at landing this deal and massive panic that my career is done. She would understand the implications and the nuances. I just want to hear her voice.

Huh.

She's not in my contacts. I could have sworn during all of our communication that I added her there. I could send her a DM on ClikClak, but knowing Heaven could be reading them too pulls me up. This is personal, and I have no one to share it with.

I guess I'm truly on my own.

CHAPTER 18: HANNAH

It all happened so fast. I guess that's how it usually goes down. I'd sent out resumes and filled out applications. I attached my ClikClak handle so they could see me in action.

I didn't expect to hear anything. Let alone within a week. And certainly not for anything that'd have me sitting on a bus in South Station, heading to New York City to cover an event.

They're calling it an "opportunity."

The "they" is *The Looking Glass*. You know, Britain's largest entertainment news. They've covered sports in England—football especially—and now want to expand their American market. They like my portfolio, and I'm onto the next round for consideration.

All I have to do is make more ClikClaks for a specific assignment. I'm to go in, blend in, and find the news plus human-interest stories. I will be there for two days, and I have to make at least ten videos. I'll post drafts to *The Looking Glass* account, and if the videos pass muster (their words, not mine), they will get officially published to *The Looking Glass*'s account.

Without showing my face or other identifying information, I'm to report on behind-the-scenes happenings.

Basically the gossip.

But sports gossip.

It doesn't matter. I'm practically as good as in.

All I have to do is be amazing.

Which is easier said than done, because Gunther, with whom I corresponded, didn't actually give me details about the event. That's test number one.

Like any good journalist, I immediately started researching based on the information provided, which is practically nothing besides the location. Also, while I can navigate Boston with my eyes closed, I'm pretty lost when it comes to New York City. Sure, the city's on a grid, so that should make it much easier than Beantown, but when have I ever preferred the easy way out?

It appears to be a product launch for the premier sports footwear manufacturing company. It's their annual showcase to talk about their products, campaigns, charitable causes, and to announce which athletes will be the face of the brand for the year. Basically, it's three days of patting themselves on the back and creating publicity by inviting all sorts of high-profile people to walk around in their merch.

Any pro-athlete's wet dream.

Hell, most kids dream of this sort of thing from the first time their parents drop them off at the ball field.

I know I dreamt about being the face of this brand and having my name on a sneaker.

Uncovering the details of the event was a small first victory, immediately met with my first obstacle. I don't have a pass for this. I have to find all this information without actually being on the inside. But in reality, that's the second obstacle. The first: what the hell am I supposed to wear for something like this?

Also, I'm supposed to blend in. No one can know that I'm there for *The Looking Glass*. It's all very cloak and dagger. I feel like I'm a spy or undercover agent.

All that time recuperating in bed watching the entirety of *Alias* now doesn't seem to be a waste of my time. I wonder if Bradley Cooper will be there ...

But I didn't have time to get lost in a daydream because I had to pack. What I was packing was the problem. Carlos hadn't been available to consult, so I had to put my big girl panties on and figure this one out for myself. Tonight is a cocktail hour. I have one dress—a red body-con dress with an almost dangerous slit—that makes me feel like a million dollars. I roll that up and put it in my suitcase, along with a full-body slimming undergarment that is guaranteed to cut off all my oxygen. I don't have too many other options, so I throw in the outfit I wore to the Buzzards' Headquarters with Ophelia, and then a selection of athleisure, all bearing the name brand of the conference host.

I hope no one will notice that they're several seasons old.

I'll be on my own for hair and makeup, but I've been paying attention when Carlos works his magic.

Plus, it's not like I need anything fancy. I need to blend in and fly under the radar.

So here I am, on the 12:30 bus that will drop me off at Port Authority with about two hours to get ready for cocktails. But first, I need to find a place to stay. I type "hotels near Javits Convention Center NYC" into TripAdvisor and am rewarded with numerous choices. Unfortunately, all the close ones are out of my budget, which is only marginally higher than the cost of a youth hostel.

I'm going to need to pick up extra shifts at The Tower to cover the cost of getting a new job. And considering I had to beg co-workers to take my shifts for the entire weekend, I'm starting this whole venture in the red. The bus ticket alone was fifty bucks. I navigate to several travel websites, price shopping. I find something in Times Square, which is still less than a mile from where I need to be. Walking a mile is nothing. The reviews aren't terrible, so that's one more thing done.

However, by the time my bus pulls into Port Authority, I'm starting to get nervous. I've been studying the map of Manhattan, and the hotel I booked is in the opposite direction from the convention. Do I take the chance and go to my hotel first and then head down? Do I go right to the convention center and change in the bathroom?

Screw it. I'm going to my hotel first. I have plenty of time. There's no need to stress.

Except when I get there, it's raining. Inside the building. Apparently, the massive water cistern on the roof failed and there are ten thousand gallons of water seeping down into the hotel.

Plan B.

I hustle over to the Javits and then head for the bathroom. This is probably a better plan anyway because between my winter coat and hat and carrying not only an oversized purse but a suitcase, I'm sweating and my hair is plastered to my head.

Thank goodness for dry shampoo.

On the other hand, this is one of those plans that's definitely better on paper than in reality. I'm pretty sure Jennifer Garner never fell over nearly landing her face in the toilet while trying to get into her fancy dress. In fairness, the dress isn't the main problem.

It's the shapewear.

A favorite saying of my dad's floats through my head as I jump up and down, willing this spandex to allow my body to slide through it. I know my body looks good once I'm in it, but I always forget the work it takes to get there.

It's like shoveling ten pounds of shit into a five-pound bag.

There used to be a time in my life when I didn't have to wear shapewear. When I was an athlete, I never thought about it at all. But being sick meant I couldn't work out. The muscle mass I lost simply by being in bed was amazing, and not in a good way.

Needless to say, it's all been replaced by softer tissue.

And that soft tissue does not want to be stuffed into this shaper. After ten minutes of wrangling, almost going headfirst into a public toilet, bashing my hip—and elbow—on the toilet paper dispenser, and accidentally stepping on a public bathroom floor with my bare feet, I emerge from the stall.

It's definitely more Chris Farley in *Tommy Boy* than Angelina Jolie in *Salt*.

No matter. I head to the sink and work on my makeup. Understated but adequate. That's all I'm going for. After shaking out my hair and liberally dosing it with dry shampoo, I pull it back, twisting it a few times before using a small claw clip to hold it in place. Silver hoops and a few thin silver chains complete the look.

The last thing I put on is my leopard-print wedges. They fit the vibe of the red dress without actually being heels. First, I'm tall to begin with. Second, I'd rather wear sneakers or cleats than heels. Third, and the biggest reason, I can't walk in stiletto heels.

I do have to say, I polish up real nice.

I shove all my traveling clothes and toiletries back into my suitcase and head to the coat check. I put on my most convincing pity look, make up some semi plausible excuse about my room not being ready, and ask the young man working the desk to secure my bag. Maybe I lean forward slightly so my cleavage is on display.

It works.

On to the next part of the plan.

Also, if this plan to infiltrate fails, I could always try to pass myself off as one of the waitstaff.

As I follow the crowd up to the fifth floor and into the pre-function area, I realize there's one detail I overlooked. How to actually get in. Everyone, it seems, has their bright orange lanyards around their necks. Even the fit women in their microscopic dresses don't seem to mind the additional fashion accessory.

I look down at my chest, sort of hoping one has appeared. Unfortunately for me, it hasn't.

If I could go in and get a drink, I could hang out just beyond the doors and make it look like I belonged there.

Holy shit, I think Serena Williams just walked by.

Be cool. Be calm. She'd probably fall over too trying to put on a girdle in a bathroom stall.

When I see LeBron enter, I know I'm in over my head. Security is tight. This is a who's who of the sporting world. There are bodyguards milling about, and there are probably more than I can even recognize.

If I try to sneak in, I'm going to get ejected faster than Brandon Nix when his mouth starts going.

Seriously, he holds the USSL record for most red cards in a season.

Think. Think. Think.

There's got to be something I can do. Some way to find out news to report. Hell, I just need to make a fifteen-second ClikClak. Then, I hear the name. My ears tune in, only able to decipher a few things. But it's enough.

"Michael Jordan, new line."

With security so tight, I can't even get into the bathrooms on this level. I take the escalator down to the fourth level where I rush to the bathroom and pull out my phone and quickly log in to *The Looking Glass* account. I position the camera so it only gets the side of my jaw, my ear, and my shoulder.

Christmas may be over and done with, but there's one more thing you will want to add to your list for the upcoming year. Word on the street is that His Airness himself will be announcing a new line for the upcoming season. What will it look like? Place your guesses in the comments. As soon as I get more information, I'll be sure to let you know!

With the vague positioning and the use of a voice filter, I'm sure no one will recognize me, which is part of the assignment. I wonder how long it will take for anyone at *The Looking Glass* to even see that I uploaded a video.

A text alert on my phone indicates I won't be wondering for long.

Gunther: Brilliant tidbit. Keep 'em coming.

Me: I can't actually get into the event. I need a pass. Any chance there's one waiting for me at the desk?

Even as I type it, I know the answer.

Gunther: <laughing crying emoji> Oh, you Americans and your sense of humor.

Great.

Gunther: But, we do have other staff members—and prospective staff members—there. You don't want to let them scoop you.

No pressure whatsoever.

All I need to do is find a way into that room. I glance in the mirror, hoping I've magically transformed into a sex kitten or puck bunny or some other siren that some stud would find irresistible.

Nope, still me.

I mean, I look okay for me. Not as good as when Carlos paints my face on but better than when I'm at work. But probably not enough to fake seduce someone into adding me as their plus one.

Letting out a resigned sigh, I leave the security of the bathroom to mill about, hoping to hear more gossip. If I can't successfully eavesdrop, this whole thing will stop my career before it even starts.

CHAPTER 19: CALLAGHAN

This is easy. The endorsement deal of my dreams is within my grasp. No one on the Buzzards even knows I'm hurt because I'm doing this. It's the perfect cover. But it has me on edge. It's too easy.

My hotel is a short walk, only a block or so away from the Javits Center. Once I'm checked in, I shower, shave, and get ready for the cocktail reception. At least no one is here to see me grimace as I slide my right arm gingerly into the sleeve of my favorite suit coat.

I head over and check in, receiving my pair of passes. Heaven didn't tell me I could bring a date. Not that it would have mattered—it's not like I have anyone to bring. I shove the extra one in my pocket and head for the main door to the event.

But then I see her.

Shit.

Why the hell is my ex-wife here?

While our divorce wasn't the stuff of legend, it was far from amicable. I doubt she has a positive word to say about me.

The feeling is mutual.

I feel sorry for the latest poor bastard she's managed to ensnare. He's got to be a big name. There's no other reason for her to be here tonight.

I quickly turn around and look for an escape.

What am I doing? This is my night. I shouldn't be running from her. I'm the one who belongs here. And it's not like I'm sorry our marriage ended. I'm much better off without her.

It sort of makes me feel like I'm living out one of my nightmares. One where I'm on the field defenseless, about ten players are charging me, preparing to take their shots, and suddenly my legs are stuck in the ground and I can't lift my arms.

And hell, one of those things is true right now.

Katherine and I didn't part on good terms, and my success following the end of our marriage has got to be a thorn in her side. She's going to be nasty.

If only …

"Callaghan! Is that you?"

Dammit. Katherine's spotted me. I whirl around, looking for any possible way to escape this encounter. My eyes land on the escalator. I have to shake my head because I'm sure I'm having a hallucination.

Except even when I open my eyes, she's still there. Hannah LaRosa, looking fine and fierce in a fitted red dress.

Holy shit. I practically start to salivate at the curvy vision in red.

"Callaghan!" I can hear Katherine's voice getting closer. She'll be at my side any moment. Before I can make a plan, my body is in motion.

Reacting. Doing what it does. Moving without thinking.

Blocking the shot.

I take four large strides which puts me directly in front of Hannah. "There you are! You finally made it." My voice sounds way too chipper for me, but I can feel Katherine's eyes on me. I encircle Hannah's waist with my left arm and pull her body flush with mine. Her eyes grow wide with shock.

I don't blame her. It's not like we parted with good feelings when I left her place that day two months ago. I give her a quick wink and then dart my gaze to the right, where Katherine is nearly upon us. I lean in and whisper into her ear, "Please."

I'm sure that to the outside observer—my ex-wife in particular—it looks like I was leaning in to give Hannah a kiss on her cheek. So, for good measure, I do just that. Her skin is warm beneath my lips, and it takes all the strength I have not to linger.

Hannah's voice seems a little out of breath. It makes her sound sexy. I don't mind at all. "Sorry to keep you waiting, Cally." Her gaze meets mine, and for a brief second, I forget that there's another world around us.

"Who's this?"

My arm is still around Hannah, keeping her glued to my side as we face Katherine. I try not to notice how her curves melt perfectly into my body. "This is Hannah LaRosa. Hannah, this is my ex-wife, Katherine."

Though the movement is probably imperceptible to anyone else, I notice how Hannah's body immediately tenses up. I tighten my grasp.

"It's a pleasure," Hannah says without extending her hand. Most likely because it's trapped behind me. I feel her finger poke into the small of my back.

Katherine is staring at Hannah, her mouth slightly agape. I glance over. Hannah's skin is flushed. The last time I saw it this shade, she was under me wearing nothing but this lovely hue. I feel the heat rise in my own skin at that memory. The dress hugs her curves in all the right places. From this angle, I have a view of her cleavage, which is spectacular.

She might be going along with things for now, but I doubt she'd take kindly to me burying my face in it. But hell, if she were on board, the things I could—

"Callaghan!" Katherine's voice is sharp, pulling me out of my daydream. "Is it true? Are you being signed?"

I have to laugh. Neither Katherine nor Hannah know what to do with that response. "Oh, Katherine. It's nice to see things never change. Were you hoping to reconcile once I sign and am suddenly worth a lot more?"

Katherine glowers at me. "Do you really think *she's* here for anything else? It's not like you bring a whole lot to the relationship other than your fame and money, Callaghan. I mean, what could you possibly have in common? Why else would she be with you?"

My ex-wife has never pulled any punches before, so it doesn't surprise me that she hits below the belt. Also, because these are the thoughts I think to myself on a daily basis anyway.

"Actually, Cally and I have known each other for years. *Years.* He was a fantastic lay before he ever signed with Nevada, and he's only gotten better with age." Hannah reaches over and gingerly brushes my hair back off my forehead. "Not to mention, I very much appreciate a man who can not only give me multiple orgasms but can also discuss how the Battle of Kosovo in 1389 was directly responsible for the start of World War I."

I'm not sure if I'm more stunned by her orgasm content or the fact that she still remembers random trivia from that history class all those years ago. However, if given the opportunity, I know which subject I'd like to revisit later.

And it has nothing to do with Archduke Franz Ferdinand.

Katherine is momentarily rendered speechless. I'm going to owe Hannah so big. I look at her, smiling brightly. "Are you ready to go in?"

Her own smile tightens a little at the edges as she starts to pull away. "You know, I still can't find that damn pass. I must have set it down somewhere, but I can't for the life of me remember where."

I reach inside my coat pocket and produce my spare. "You mean this one here?" I finally let Hannah go for as long as it takes to put the lanyard over her head, my knuckles brushing along her collarbones and the neckline of her dress for a brief instant.

Jesus, this small touch has me growing hard.

Hannah's smile relaxes. "I should have known you'd have it." She dips her chin before gazing up. "Thanks," she says so quietly I can barely hear it.

"Ready?"

Hannah nods, and once again, I slide my arm around her waist, this time escorting her into the large event space. The room is dark and loud. It's opulent and modern and the background din will make it hard to have a conversation. A waiter passes by with a tray of champagne. I grab two flutes, handing one to Hannah.

"Thanks," I say. "Katherine's ... a lot. I didn't want to have to deal with her tonight of all nights."

Hannah downs about half the contents of her glass before saying, "Is she right? Are you signing with ..." She nods to the large corporate display at the front of the room.

I shrug, ignoring the stab that shoots through the front of my right shoulder. "If all goes well, I could even get a billboard in Times Square."

Hannah finishes her glass and immediately grabs another one. "Well, then, here's to you, Cally Entay. You're finally as hot as your name implies. You finally have it all."

I laugh at her humor and meet her toast.

Even though I should be satisfied with the direction my life is going, as I look at Hannah, I can't help but think there's one more thing I want that I might not be able to have.

CHAPTER 20: HANNAH

Holy shitballs.

I'm in.

Callaghan Entay is about to sign a lucrative endorsement deal, and I know about it before anyone else. This is what I should be focusing on. Instead, all I can see is that he's looking at me as if I'm a plate of pastries that he wants to devour.

And you don't get to my physique without a sweet tooth, so the feeling is definitely mutual.

Which is so weird, because I want to hate him. He left a wave of destruction behind that took my body—and heart—years to recover from. He's cocky and arrogant. His drive is so powerful that it causes him to ignore everyone around him.

That has not changed.

I wouldn't exactly call him a giver, except maybe in the bedroom.

But from the pinched look on his ex-wife's face, maybe he's not even generous there anymore.

That's a shame.

I should be focusing on the real reason I'm here, but all I can see is that pleading look in his eyes as he said, "Please." My insides turned to a gelatinous mush. I would have done anything he asked.

A swell of power rises within me as I get the impression that Callaghan Entay doesn't ask for help often.

Cal won't let me leave his side. Which, for my purposes, is the best place to be. I don't even have to eavesdrop. It's the best of the best of the athletic and sporting world, and Cal, as the starting goalkeeper for Team USA, is a hot commodity.

I take my phone out and grab some video, scanning the crowd. I'm not sure what I'm going to do with it, but it'll be useful for something. I grab a selfie or two, managing to perhaps get some major sports names in the background. I'd love to get a picture of Callaghan, but I certainly don't want to be obvious about it. Maybe I'll walk around the room and get one from a distance.

But when I try to wander off, his arm snakes around my waist and pulls me back to him. After about the third or fourth time he does it, I finally call him on it.

Raising my eyebrows, I say, "I'm not your property or prisoner." I really wish I could raise one at a time. It'd make my statement so much more powerful.

He glances down at where our bodies meet. "Can I consider you my security blanket?"

"Really?"

He leans in, his breath hot against my cheek. "Especially if you'd consider draping yourself all over me tonight."

I ignore the clench deep in my abdomen. Instead, I burst out laughing. "Oh, my God. Callaghan Entay, that is terrible. Is that the crap you're spewing to get someone into your bed? Do these lines really work for you?"

His face is still close to mine, and I can feel his cheeks widen into a smile. I pull back to look at him. He's laughing too. "Dammit, Hannah. Still a ballbuster, I see."

"No, but seriously, do those lines work?"

He lifts up one shoulder and lets it drop in nonchalance. "I don't even have to talk."

"With pick-up attempts like that, it might be better that way. But, if you're not talking, what are you doing?"

His eyes sparkle. "I just smolder in their general direction."

My laugh is loud and unattractive. I don't care. His response calls for a full-on head-tipped back, belly-holding, open-mouth cachinnation.

"Sshh," Cal hisses. "You're drawing attention." But he's still smiling too. A real one that goes all the way to his eyes.

I now have tears threatening to spill down my cheeks. "What are you going to do? Silence me with a smolder?"

"I could use my best line from our days at Indiana."

"If you try the Hoosier-daddy questions, I'm so out of here." I admit, it is a clever play on the IU mascot, but it doesn't mean it's not painful.

Now his eyes darken with a devilish glint, his smile even wider. Some might find a Callaghan Entay smolder seductive, but his smile is what makes me weak in the knees. As in right now. I press my thighs together, which doesn't actually help the situation. In fact, the tension makes it much—much—worse.

This is the kind of playful banter that ended us up in bed all those years ago.

I shake my head, trying to clear it from all these errant—*and naughty*—thoughts running through it. I'm here for a reason, and I need to keep my focus on that.

Sleeping with Callaghan Entay derailed my life once. I'm not going to let it happen again.

I grab another flute of champagne, this time to keep my hands occupied, and put some space between our bodies. *Focus. Focus. Focus.*

"Let's mingle. I'm sure there are people you need to schmooze with, right?"

Cal gives me a wry smile, letting out a little sigh. "It's why I'm here. The deal's not final yet. It's like a last round tryout." He looks down at his feet. His shoulders appear to slump a fraction.

"Hey—" I put my hand under his chin to level his gaze with mine. "What is it?"

"Kick a ball in my direction, and I know to stop it. This"—he gestures to the room of suits and dresses—"is outside my element. I don't know what they want from me. What else do I have to offer, other than my athletic ability?" There's worry in his eyes. "That's all I have to offer anyone."

I let go of his chin and take his hand. "You offer the promise of greatness. That drive and hard work are what it takes to be the best. The hallmarks of the brand. You show up and you just do it. No questions asked. But, there's one thing you could do." I don't wait for him to reply before launching into my advice. "Lighten up a little. Smile more often. I know you think you have to be balls-to-the-wall serious all the time or else you'll lose your momentum, but it makes it hard to relate to you. Most people don't have your inhuman drive. You're hard on your teammates and everyone around you. I'd bet most people don't realize you hold them to that standard because you hold yourself to an even higher one. But sometimes, you have to let it go for a minute. Don't glower. Don't smolder. Smile."

He tilts his head as if questioning everything I'm saying.

"Even David Beckham smiles in his ads from time to time. Go look him up on Pinterest. I guarantee more than half of what pops up immediately—the most popular pins—are of him smiling, at least a little."

He pulls the top lip back in a grimace, baring his teeth.

"You look like a deranged animal." I laugh.

Callaghan laughs too. "That's the market I'm trying to corner. It's an underserved niche." Then Callaghan's gaze goes from mine to something—or someone—behind me, and he straightens up. His posture is tight, and he clearly has his game face on.

"Mr. Conners." Callaghan nods and extends his hand. I step back so I'm out of the way. Bryce Conners is one of the higher-up execs. He definitely has decision-making power. God, I hope Cal doesn't blow it.

"Thank you for the invitation this weekend. I appreciate your consideration."

Good. He's off to a good start. He's stiff, in the zone. I drift into the background, letting him do his thing. Or at least that's what I intend to do. One thing Callaghan Entay is known for in the goal is his wingspan, and he takes advantage of that to reach out toward me to take my hand.

I see it coming and manage to evade his grasp, his fingers lightly brushing my hand as I step away. This is Cal's chance to seal this deal, and I don't want to mess it up for him by saying something stupid. Just as I think I'm in the clear, his arm extends another few inches and his massive hand wraps around my wrist.

Heat floods through me, thinking about that hand and what it can do, on and off the field. You know what they say about men with big hands.

With a small yet firm tug, I'm back at Callaghan's side. His nearness, his scent, the enormity of this occasion is going to my head, making me the smallest bit dizzy.

Or maybe it's the champagne.

Either way, it's an effort to stay on my feet and not colossally embarrass myself in front of the executive from one of the largest athletic brands in the world. Maybe Callaghan senses it, as his hand returns to my waist, steadying me. There are too many emotions swirling around in my head to be able to focus.

Dammit, why does this man have this effect on me? I swear, no one else does.

And at this moment, when I could be getting some sort of insider information to report for *The Looking Glass*, all I can think about is climbing Callaghan Entay like a tree.

That thought pulls me up quickly. I straighten up a bit, trying to put some distance between our bodies. I can't be melting into him, thinking about peeling his clothes off. I'm here, and I have a job to do.

Tonight, nothing's going to stop me from getting a story.

But even as I'm paying attention, frankly it's hard to hear over the din in the room. Before I can compose a coherent thought, Bryce Conners is moving on. Callaghan's body seems to collapse into mine as the tension relaxes.

"Where did you think you were going? I needed you." Cal smiles at me. He grabs another flute of champagne and hands it to me. He takes one for himself and holds it up in a toast.

I clink my glass against his. "Eh, I didn't want to accidentally say something to mess this up for you. Let's face it, I don't belong here." I gesture with the flute to the room.

"Why would you think you'd say something to mess it up? You're very good on your feet. Don't forget, I've seen your videos." He leans in, saying this into my ear. His hot breath sends shivers down my spine. "And you've always been my good luck charm."

I close my eyes at his words. He did always call me his good luck charm. Usually, it referred to him landing a chick, but considering he got called up the day after he slept with me, it may be more accurate than not. "For some reason, I can't seem to think clearly around you." My voice comes out in a breathy exhale.

He pulls back enough so I can look into his deep dark eyes. "The feeling's mutual."

A dozen years have passed, but I feel exactly as I did that night. *The night*.

This is not good.

I take a step back, downing the rest of my champagne in a large gulp. "I, uh, should probably get going." I'm stepping backward, nodding like a bobblehead doll.

I wonder if Cal will get his own bobblehead one of these days. I'd most certainly have to get one.

Before I lose the strength to tear myself away from him, I turn on my heel—thank God I'm wearing wedges—and hightail it to the door. With a pace I don't think this body-con dress was meant to handle, I rush toward the escalator, heading down the four flights until I reach the coat check on the first floor.

My pace is abruptly halted when I realize I've got nowhere to go. I have no hotel room.

Shit.

I trade my ticket for my coat and suitcase and pull out my phone—which is nearly dead now—and start a new search for a place to stay that won't require me to sell my only remaining kidney to afford it.

But at least I got away from Callaghan before I did something stupid. I know if I spent one more minute with him—if he touched me one more time—it would be over for me. Maybe it's because I've had several glasses of champagne. Maybe it's because I haven't had sex in a while. Or maybe it's because that man makes me weak in the knees and hot in my nether regions. All I know is that if I don't get away now, I'll be the one begging him.

"Hannah—wait!"

CHAPTER 21: CALLAGHAN

I can't tell you the last time I chased after a woman.

Frankly, I haven't found that many worth the chase.

"Hannah—wait!" I yell. I'm drawing attention, but I don't care. Let someone take a video and make it viral. This is nothing to be ashamed of.

I'm not even winded when I catch up to her.

"Why'd you take off? Where are you going? Why do you have your suitcase?"

"I've got to go. And I ... um ... got in late so I didn't have time to check in before. So, you know, I've got to go. Check in."

I glance at my watch. It's close to midnight. "Did you tell them you were checking in late? Most places won't hold the room this long without prior notice."

She looks at her phone and then her gaze darts to the left. "Um, yeah. It's fine. I'll be fine."

It couldn't be any more obvious that she's lying than if a giant nose started growing in the middle of her face.

"Then I'm taking you there. Let me get an Uber. What's the address?" I'm used to staring down challenges. I don't know why Hannah is running or being evasive, but I'm not letting her go anywhere.

Not again.

"Hannah," I put my fingers on her jaw, turning her face toward mine, much as she did to me earlier. "Where are you going?"

She rolls her eyes one last time before her resolve melts away. "Okay, fine. I don't have a place to go. When I tried to check into my hotel earlier, there had been a flood of some kind. Did you know those big water tanks on the roof can leak into the building, and it's like thousands of gallons of water? Like I need something else to worry about when I'm staying in a hotel. That I'm going to wake up and my room is going to be like a scene from *Titanic*. But anyway, now I have to find a place to stay that I can afford, which is pretty laughable. Are you happy? Is that what you wanted me to admit?"

I drop my hand. "Why didn't you say something? And no, I'm not happy. This is a shitty situation, and I don't want you to have to deal with it. I can help you out."

Hannah shakes her head. The lights in this lobby are too bright for the dark January night. There's not much activity here on the first floor, and it feels like we're the only ones left in a club when they turn the lights back on. She looks tired. "It's not your problem. I'll figure it out. I'm not gonna ask you to help me."

For some reason, the song *Ain't Too Proud to Beg* pops into my head. She's the one who needs the help, but all I know is I can't let her walk out of here and out of my life.

"You're not asking, I'm offering. Those are two very different things. And the way I see it, there are two possible solutions. The first is you let me get you a hotel room. My hotel is only a block away, and I'll get you a room there."

"I'm not taking your money." She juts her chin out slightly. "What's option two?"

I can't keep my mouth from stretching into a sly grin. "You can stay with me."

"And let me guess, you have a room with a king bed."

"It's a room in downtown Manhattan. The bed takes up most of the floor space, but it does have a view of the Empire State Building." Every fiber of my being is begging her to pick option two. Touching her tonight has brought back a torrent of memories of the way she tastes and feels, and I'm practically crawling out of my skin, desperate to be with her again.

"Oh, Callaghan, there you are. I thought I'd missed you!"

Fuck. I was so enraptured with Hannah, I didn't even notice Katherine approaching.

I want to physically take hold of Hannah so she doesn't use this distraction to escape, but, despite what the public may think of me, I'm not a dick. This is her choice to make freely.

"I couldn't be so lucky. What do you want, Katherine?" In the bright fluorescent lights, Katherine's makeup is glaring. I'm not sure what I ever saw in her.

"I was hoping we could go for a drink." She puts her hand on my arm. "You know, for old times' sake." I shake her off. The audacity of that woman.

"Actually, we need to get going. I'm pretty tired. Cally, do you mind taking my suitcase?" Hannah rolls it toward me before squaring herself toward Katherine. "I got hung up and didn't have time to check into our room before. I didn't want to be late for Cally on his big night, but I can't wait to see that view of the Empire State Building. I bet it'll be an amazing backdrop for the rest of the night."

Damn. Hannah is so quick on her feet. She'll be a fantastic sideline reporter.

I take her suitcase handle with my left hand and casually throw my right arm over her shoulder. Or at least I try to make it seem casual and not like someone is driving a thousand knives into me. With her shoes on, Hannah's not that much shorter than I am, and lifting my arm that high makes me wince. Hannah sees my expression and knits her brow slightly in concern.

I give my head a gentle shake, trying to communicate it's no big deal. Our backs are to Katherine now, but Hannah's keeping up the act. She leans in and whispers, "Are you okay?"

Her breath, so near and warm, sends all the blood rushing south. I'm fairly confident she's putting on a show for Katherine. If that's the case, and we'll be parting ways in the lobby of the Marriott Courtyard, I'd better take this last chance to shoot my shot.

I turn my head so our lips are just inches apart. "I'll be better after I do this." I close the distance between us, my mouth on hers. It's a brief moment, but it's enough to make me hard.

Damn, I want this woman.

Her body melts into mine, driving me absolutely crazy. She exhales slightly, and with a willpower I didn't know I possessed, I pull back. "You ready?" I ask.

Hannah nods, and without looking back at my ex-wife, we walk out into the cold January night. Our teeth chatter and our bodies shake in the sub-zero temperature. If it were any more than a block walk, I'd be hailing a cab or calling an Uber to prevent Hannah from dying of frostbite.

Hypothermia is a good motivator for walking quickly, and we reach the hotel in record time. The cold was a good distraction too. I'm pretty sure the only reason I'm able to say what I say next is because of the drop in my core body temperature as we walk into the lobby.

"Let me see about getting you that room now."

Instead of heading toward the front desk, Hannah walks toward the elevator bank. I stop dead in my tracks, a little stunned at her brazen strut. I wish she didn't have her coat on, as I'd give anything to see her voluptuous ass sashaying away in that sexy red dress.

Hannah gives me a quick glance over her shoulder. "You coming?"

I sprint after her. The elevator door opens and once we're inside I say, "You keep asking like that, and the answer will be an immediate yes."

Hannah laughs. That big, throaty, open-mouth laugh of hers. "Again with the lines." She shakes her head.

"Well, considering you're here in the elevator with me, they seem to be working, no?"

"Only you, Cally. Only you."

I turn to look at her. "Only me what?"

Before she can answer, the doors open. We make our way to my room, and I unlock the door, stepping aside so she can enter first. It only takes about five steps until we're both staring at the bed.

My throat is dry. I shove my hands in my pockets to prevent them from reaching out and grabbing Hannah. The ball is in her court. I'm not going to pressure her into anything, no matter how badly I may want it. "I can get you your own room. It's no problem."

Hannah tucks a lock of hair behind her ear. "Do you want me to go?"

"Do you want to go?" I need to hear it from her directly.

"I asked first. What do you want?" Her voice seems to drop an octave or two.

I lick my lips, thinking about all the places on her body I want to put them. I need to be subtle and smooth. Hannah isn't one for lines, and she certainly doesn't want a player. I go for brutal, naked honesty.

No pun intended.

"I want to strip you down naked and lick every inch of your body. And after that, I want to bury myself in you until the sun comes up."

Real fucking smooth.

"You don't mince words, do you?"

"You're driving me crazy, Han. I can't stop touching you, and I don't want to. I keep remembering what you feel like. What you taste like. I feel like I'm starving, and you're the only thing I have an appetite for." The words shock me as they tumble out of my mouth. I'm not used to having to work this hard.

I'm not usually the chaser.

But this woman has always challenged me, and I've always found it incredibly hot.

She drops her gaze to the floor. Crap. I knew I was coming on too strong. But in her presence, I can't keep my chill.

"I'm sorry, Han. I didn't mean to make you uncomfortable. You can stay here, and I promise I won't touch you. If you don't believe me, we'll get a second room. Can we just forget what I said?"

She looks up, her eyes a little glassy. "You want me. Like this?" She gestures to her body.

"Um, yeah."

She tilts her head. "You do know I'm not wearing sexy lingerie under here. There's no red lace thong or Victoria's Secret bra. It's shapewear meant to smooth out my lumps and bumps so I don't look like I have more rolls than a bakery. It's about structure and support, not being sexy."

I know what she's getting at, and I could not care less. I'm not even going to acknowledge such a baseless concern. I take a step toward her. "I don't care. If I have my way, in about thirty seconds, it's all going to end up in a pile on the floor anyway, and you're going to be naked and beautiful stretched out on that bed, with me between your legs."

Apparently, sweet Hannah LaRosa likes a little dirty talk, because that's all it takes. Her mouth is on mine, her tongue eagerly moving. We're a tangle of hands and tongues, mouths and bodies. There's an absolute frenzy as clothes go flying.

Okay, that shapewear thingy is a little harder to remove than I'd anticipated, and I wrench my right shoulder trying to yank it down. I can ignore the pain slicing through my arm though, because once it's down, I'm blessed with a view of the most incredible full breasts.

My God, Hannah is stunning.

"You still good?" I ask before going any further. Her breathless "yes" is like scoring a game-winning goal.

Though I may have the endurance of an elite athlete, I have no ability to last long with Hannah. It's all force and frenzy, motion and moaning. My body on hers. Her body on mine. Sliding inside her, feeling like I'm home.

It's perfect.

She's perfect.

CHAPTER 22: HANNAH

W ell, that was unexpected." It's true. Never in a million years did I think I'd end up back in bed with Callaghan Entay.

Like, never.

I'm not saying I didn't want it, because I can barely remember a time in my life when I *didn't* want him. I simply didn't think it would ever happen again.

And I know I should have taken the offer for a separate hotel room because we all know no good can come from this. There is no reality in which Callaghan and I can ever be anything more than a fling. However, I let the champagne do the decision-making, and it wanted to get laid.

Not that the champagne had to try that hard to plead its case. I was a goner from the minute he whispered "please" into my ear. And then when he kissed me, it was all over. I had to be with him, at least one more time.

No matter how stupid a decision it was.

I, however, will not be admitting that to Callaghan. His ego doesn't need the help. And he doesn't need to know that I'd like this to be more than a fling; that what I feel for him is more than a casual hookup.

I can keep it light and breezy.

"Um, you literally came willingly to my hotel room with me. What did you think was going to happen? And I asked you. You totally verbalized consent." Cal pushes up on his elbow. If I'm not mistaken, he winces slightly. His left hand cups his right shoulder and he lies back down.

Something's wrong.

"Slow your roll, sport. I meant, when I was on the bus down here, and changing in the bathroom at the Javits Center, I did not picture the night ending like this. And what's up with your shoulder?"

If I didn't know better, I'd say he was injured. Callaghan doesn't respond as he rolls onto his back, his face contracting in pain.

Oh my God, what if I hurt him? His career is at its zenith, and our sex was no less athletic than it was a dozen years ago. But this time, there's a lot more of me to go around. I mean, it's for certain that I'm going to be sore for days after this.

But what if I broke him?

"Did I hurt you? What's up with the shoulder?" I repeat. Then I say what I'm really thinking. "Did I break you?"

"It's nothing."

He didn't answer the question. Oh shit. "Cally, tell me. Did I hurt you? You don't have to spare my feelings. I'm realistic about my situation here." I gesture down my body, which is exposed from the waist up. "I know I'm a lot bigger than I used to be."

In reality, he is too, except he's pure muscle.

Cal's eyes fly open. "Are you shitting me, Hannah? Did you just imply that you injured me because of your size?"

I shrug. "It's a legit fair question."

Cal sits up. I notice he doesn't use his right arm to help. He slides back to rest against the headrest, his bare chest glorious on display. I wonder if he'd mind if I licked it.

Again.

His voice is low and dangerous. "I'm going to say this once, and once only. You are beautiful. You were gorgeous in college, and you're even more so now." He trails a finger from the corner of my jaw down my neck and then curves around my breast. "All of you."

While I appreciate his sentiment—and I really do—his words make me uncomfortable. Like he's being serious instead of just having fun.

Because if he's serious, then I don't need to deny that I think of him as a lot more than a casual hookup, and I always have. And I can't deny that his words make me feel tingly and squishy inside.

That they make me feel special.

I can't let myself feel those things for him again.

This can't be more than what it is right now, no matter how much I might want it to be. He's never promised me more, and he never will. He's not in a place to.

I don't know what to think though. It's not like he's using me for status. That's laughable. Callaghan's reputation with the ladies may be legendary, but knowing what I do of him, I have a feeling it's more publicity than reality, just as it was in college. Behind closed doors, he's not at all the man the media portrays him to be. He's so much more. He's brutally honest—to a fault—but it's because he feels so passionately about the things that matter to him. "Okay, well, still, I didn't have this in the cards for this weekend. Or ever again, to be honest."

"It wasn't on your secret agenda?" He smiles, waggling his eyebrows. He totally has the sexy smolder down, but I wish he knew what a freakin' turn-on his smile is. On the other hand, I like that he reserves it for me.

"Um, no. I'm not a stalker." A moment of panic races through my veins and lands squarely in the pit of my stomach. What if he asks why I'm there in the first place? My assignment is top secret. No one's supposed to know who is supplying *The Looking Glass* with their information this weekend.

"Yeah, your name's not Katherine." He shakes his head slightly. "What the hell, man? We've been divorced for years. So, um, thanks for covering for me."

It's my turn to laugh. "Obviously, it was a stretch, pretending to be there with you. I find you revolting, honestly. I just thought I should make it look realistic."

"Well, it sounded realistic when you were screaming my name."

I feel heat flood my face. He does have a point. "There isn't an apartment full of your teammates on the other side of the door to make fun of me this time.

Do you know they called me 'Back Door Girl' after that night?"

Cal scrunches up his nose. "Ouch. That's brutal. They're a bunch of dicks."

"Yeah, well, boys are stupid." I need to change the subject from that night. I don't want to get into what happened after he left. Even briefly thinking about it makes me start to sweat a little. "But what about Katherine? I take it you didn't know she'd be there?"

"No, but it doesn't surprise me. She was always more about being a WAG than a wife. I'm still not sure she knows what sport I play, let alone anything about soccer. I'd bet she was there 'networking.'" He holds up two fingers to make air quotes. "Trying to find her next ex. She never cared about me. Only what my name and prestige could do for her. So I really owe you big time for getting me away from her. I should, like, pay you to always be my girlfriend when she's around."

"Yeah, you may want to ask Xavier Henry if he'd recommend the fake relationship thing." I laugh.

"Considering I just got an invitation for their wedding, I think it worked out alright for them."

The pit in my stomach deepens. I asked to work the event and told Ophelia I'd be there, coordinating all the behind-the-scenes stuff to give her the perfect night. It's not a stretch to think that Cal would be invited, but I certainly wasn't thinking about that last night. That I'll have to see him again, outside this room.

What will it look like?

Will I still be able to pretend that he doesn't affect me?

I get up and go to the bathroom. The jury's still out on whether falling back into bed with Callaghan Entay was a mistake, but at least I learned one lesson from the first time.

A quick glance in the mirror confirms I look like a raccoon since taking off my mascara last night certainly wasn't a priority. I dab at my eyes with a tissue, but it's only making matters worse. I need makeup wipes. Damn, when did I get to be so high maintenance?

When I come out of the bathroom, I squat by the edge of the bed, digging through my bag for some clothes to throw on. As much as I'd like to lounge around in the complimentary robe and slippers, I should probably get dressed. Callaghan's up with a pair of shorts on and nothing else.

Holy hell. He looks even better in the daylight.

He's rubbing his shoulder again.

"Okay, so fess up. What's up with the shoulder?" I ask. I'm pulling out my toiletry bag and finding my makeup wipes. "It hurts. Pretty sure I separated my AC joint. You got any ibuprofen in there?" He nods toward my bag.

"No." I haven't taken any since my kidneys decided to go rogue. Thanks to my categorization as having chronic kidney disease, there are a whole bunch of medications I can't take anymore.

"Seriously? How can you not travel with any?"

"Why don't you have any?"

"I took the last that I had last night before I went to the reception." He looks down. "I, uh, didn't realize I'd gone through the rest of the bottle."

That makes me stand up. "How much are you taking? Are you in that much pain? What does the doctor say? That's super bad for your kidneys." High doses of NSAIDs can reduce blood flow, causing damage. Not to mention they're processed in the kidneys, therefore making them work overtime while reducing their nutrients.

"The doctor hasn't said anything because I haven't been to him. I know what I did. And I don't care about my kidneys. I just need the pain to stop."

His words are like a slap across the face. I inhale sharply and try to remind myself that he doesn't know. He's not saying them on purpose.

It doesn't matter. My mind begins to whirl, the intrusive thoughts that signal a panic attack forming. This cannot be happening right now. I have to get out of here.

"What?" Callaghan asks, registering that something has abruptly shifted in the room.

I shake my head. "It's nothing. If you want, I can run to the store to get you some." I pull on a sweatshirt and leggings. "In fact, let me go do that. It'll be better. I need some air."

Without stopping to hear his protest, I shove my feet into my Uggs, grab my phone and coat, and all but sprint out the door. Yes, some cold air will do me good.

And space.

This is too much. Too much too fast. There's too much history. Too much baggage. At least on my end.

Whether I want to admit it or not, I've always felt that if Callaghan hadn't left—and I hadn't almost died—we could have been something. I'm not sure what he's thinking now, but he's not treating me like a one-night stand.

On the other hand, he once walked away from me and never looked back. He freely admits that he did it and justifies his actions as necessary. Which means he's more than likely to do it again.

And it will hurt so much more this time.

Not only that, but how could I possibly get involved with him when I'm hoping that it'll be my job to report about him? On the other hand, he could probably give me a lot of inside info that could catapult me to the front of the line.

Even thinking about that makes me feel gross. I'd never use him for his status. I'm not like his ex-wife. Plus, the stubborn side of me doesn't want his help. I want to do this on my own.

My phone is in my hand, directing me to the Duane Reade three blocks uptown when it buzzes with a text message from Gunther.

Gunther: You still alive? You started off with a brilliant bit but fell radio silent. The Looking Glass *needs more than a one-and-done.*

Shit.

Gunther: You owe us nine more.

I got distracted.

No, I let Callaghan Entay distract me. And now what am I supposed to do? I've got some video footage, but I doubt anything is scoopable. I need to find out something no one else knows.

The panic that had just started to ebb comes back with a vengeance. It's too much, all at once. My PTSD. My feelings for Cal. The real possibility that I could lose this chance at a job.

I cannot fail again.

I cannot let this slip through my fingers.

I cannot let Callaghan Entay distract me from what I am supposed to have.

My phone buzzes again, but this time it's Cal.

Callaghan: I hate to ask this, but if you really are getting me ibuprofen, would you mind picking up some KT tape? I can't tape my own shoulder, but now that you know, maybe you could help me out?

Gunther: We're anxiously awaiting your next submission.

Before I know it, I'm checking out of Duane Reade with not only extra strength painkillers but a portable TENS unit and a roll of KT tape. I look at the bottle in my hand. I haven't purchased this stuff in twelve years. Sometimes I forget what I went through, and sometimes the whole experience comes rushing back, causing me to relive the trauma and fear as if it were happening again.

Guess which this moment is?

The boxes have spilled wide open, flooding my brain with images I'd rather forget.

Waking up with a breathing tube and on dialysis, strapped to a bed with more tubes coming out of me than I ever imagined possible was an absolute nightmare. And this stupid bottle of ibuprofen brings it all rushing back to me, hitting me with full force.

Gunther texts again.

I've got to send him something. What? I don't know. All I can think about is the pain I used to have. The bouts of insomnia that still plague me from time to time. Not to mention the constant fear that my remaining kidney will fail.

I have to focus so I don't lie down and curl into a fetal position here on the streets of Manhattan. I have to do *something* to get this job. I need to make all my struggles worthwhile. I need something to show for my life.

Think, Hannah, think.

My brain is empty. I could not name a sports statistic if you paid me a million dollars. Tears form in my eyes, and I swipe them away, the bag in my hand hitting my cheek. The corner of the ibuprofen box stabs me. A bottle of pills I can never take.

Panic is replaced by red rage.

I open up my camera and start a video.

"Word on the street"—I pan around so you can tell I'm walking—"is that Boston Buzzards goalkeeper Callaghan Entay is injured. This is not public knowledge, but once it gets out, will it affect his standing on the US Men's National Team?"

I jump when my phone rings with a FaceTime from Cal. I close the video and answer, immediately filled with guilt and remorse that I even thought about reporting that story.

What the hell was I thinking?

I could never send that to Gunther. I can't believe I even let it cross my mind.

As soon as we finish our call, I'll delete it and think of something else. There has to be another way.

CHAPTER 23: CALLAGHAN

I'm relieved to see her face on the phone screen, and even more so when she holds up the bag. "I'll be back in about five minutes unless you want me to pick up something for breakfast."

"I thought we'd order room service if that's okay with you. Just come back."

I sound like I'm begging again. What is it about this woman that has me chasing after her like a lovesick teen?

A minute later she's back, and I'm stripping off my shirt so she can tape my shoulder. Her hands are cold on my skin, but I know it's her mere touch that is setting my blood on fire.

Once she's done with that, she opens up the bottle of ibuprofen and hands me two.

"Two? I need three."

"You need to not kill your kidneys by cutting off all their blood flow."

I swallow the two down with a large gulp of water. "What's it with you and my kidneys anyway? And what do you want for breakfast?"

She takes the menu, flopping down across the bed on her stomach. "I'll take the pancakes. What are you getting?"

"Egg white omelet."

Hannah rolls onto her back and looks at me, still sitting on the floor next to the bed. "I should have guessed. Have to keep that physique somehow."

"I bet your pancakes will taste better. Maybe I can have a taste of you instead."

Hannah shimmies closer so I can kiss her. "Mmm, just like this, but you're going to be maple-flavored," I murmur. "Maybe we should ask for extra syrup." I can feel her smile into my mouth, but before we can take it any further, my phone starts to chime.

Aggressively.

A quick glance reveals both Heaven and Justice are blowing up my phone. "Shit." I scramble to my feet. "I forgot about …" I read the texts. Holy crap. The entire timeline's been moved up. They're ready to bring me on board, complete with a photo shoot today.

No more interviews. No auditioning. No schmoozing. They want me.

I show her my phone and then Hannah's on her feet too. She throws my shirt at me and starts rushing around the tiny hotel room. "You've got a deal to sign!"

We both pause at the absurdity of it. "How could you forget this was in the works?" Hannah pants.

I close the distance between us and bring my mouth to hers. I feel her body melt into mine. When we touch, it's like nothing else exists. "Because you make it hard for me to think straight." It's the truth. I don't even know the last time I let anything—let alone a woman—distract me from my career.

Maybe we should slow things down.

But then I look at her beautiful brown eyes and her body that feels so good around mine … and that mouth that never ceases to stop challenging me, and I don't want to slow anything down.

I want to see how much further this can go.

"Come with me. To the expo. I want to share this with you."

Hannah raises her eyebrows. "Are you sure you want me tagging along?"

I slide my hand into hers. "Most definitely. And just think about all the inside stories you can get for your ClikClak channel. I can definitely get you the behind-the-scenes scoop that no one else will have."

Hannah stiffens slightly. "I don't want your help. I want to do this on my own. I don't want anything from you."

I don't know why she's being so stubborn. I kiss the tip of her nose. "You're the first not to jump at the offer, but whatever. But also, hurry because I think Justice might have an aneurism if I don't get over there to mingle and sign papers."

In just under fifteen minutes, we're exiting the Marriott and heading back toward the Javits Center. I take Hannah's hand in mine as we walk, marveling at how natural this seems.

I have an ease around Hannah that I haven't felt within myself in possibly—forever. When I'm with her, I don't feel like a caged animal, trapped behind the bars of my career but unable to survive without their protection. I may not have the answers, but I don't feel like I need them when I'm with her.

Maybe it's because Hannah sees me.

She doesn't see an athlete. She's not riding my coattails. She's not expecting me to foot the bill. It wouldn't shock me at all if she haggled with me about splitting the room cost.

The answer will be a resounding no.

The minute we get through the door, Justice and Heaven descend upon me. I feel Hannah's grip slip from mine, but before I can grab it again, she's gone, standing in the distance, like Mad Max in the final scene of *Fury Road*. I don't even get to introduce her to them. And now there are execs and higher-ups and meetings.

And paperwork.

And more paperwork.

It feels like hours before I can finally steal a glance at my phone without being rude.

Hannah: Don't forget to smile. You'll make more friends that way.

Me: I don't need any more friends.

Hannah: I'll believe that when I see it.

Me: I've got you.

There's a pause. A definite pause. Then the dots wave. And wave. And wave. I see Justice and Heaven approaching, and I'm going to have to put my phone away in a second.

Dammit, I came on too strong.

This is why I shouldn't feel things and should only focus on the game.

Right as I'm about to put my phone back in my pocket, it buzzes.

Hannah: As long as you don't ghost me this time because your career is taking off again.

I pop onto Hannah's ClikClak to see if she's posted anything from the convention, but she hasn't. That's weird. You'd think she'd want to take advantage of this opportunity.

Perhaps she's as distracted by me as I am by her.

And I'm definitely distracted because I have no idea who this person is standing before me and why she's handing me a bag full of clothes. I look at her and then at Heaven, who's typing away on her phone.

"Heav, what's going on?"

"That's what they want you wearing. Today and tomorrow. And they pushed the photo shoot up. They'll bring you back and do a facial and haircut, and then you'll do the shoot while all the ambassadors are here. Group stuff. C'mon. You've got to get changed."

I'm being herded out of the room we're in and to somewhere more secluded. I don't know if I'm in the bowels of this convention center or what. I text Hannah again.

Me: I apparently have to put on new clothes and do a photo shoot, all GQ style. Except in sneakers and shorts.

Hannah: Now this, I want to see. You probably only have one expression, like Zoolander.

Hannah makes me laugh.

Me: I'll have you know, I can do both Blue Steel AND Magnum.

Me: I'll text you when I know where I'm going to be so you can meet up with me.

Hannah: What if I don't want to? What if I'm busy following around some other star? You assume an awful lot.

Me: So are you going to run away on me again?

Hannah: I won't run if you don't.

She's got me there.

But no matter what happens with my career, I can't see myself ever moving on from Hannah.

Not again.

CHAPTER 24: HANNAH

Time away from Callaghan is good. It's what I need to clear my head and do my job. He's a distraction I didn't count on. And can't afford.

I made up for lost time, cranking out about six videos for *The Looking Glass.* I think Gunther had given up on me.

I'll show him.

I'll show them all.

And I've uncovered some good stuff too. I'm happy with my delivery and the quality of the videos. My color commentary on the aesthetics of the new tracksuits and sneakers, done as if I were calling a game, is brilliant, if I do say so myself.

All I'm saying is I'd better get this job. I'm putting a lot of work into this free content for them, all in the name of my audition.

A quick perusal of *The Looking Glass's* ClikClak channel reveals some of the other stories that have been submitted. I think my stuff is better, but you never know exactly what they're looking for. I need something to elevate myself to the next level.

But as I try to think of what I can make a video about next, my mind wanders back to last night.

I should text Callaghan and see what he's up to.

No, I shake that thought from my head. I don't know what's even going on between us. I try to convince myself there's nothing going on. That it's purely physical.

I'm such a liar.

No matter what, though, I'm not going to be one of those people who use him for his status. It's been something he's dealt with his entire life. I'll figure out how to make my career without pulling him into it.

My phone buzzes with a text, and I anxiously swipe it open, hoping it's him, even though I know he's busy.

Ophelia: Okay, I've got a crazy request for my wedding, but I'm afraid to ask. Will you tell me if I can do it?

I can only imagine what it is if Ophelia thinks it's out there.

Me: Shoot.

Ophelia: So, you know how Xavier likes birds and all? I want to release doves at our wedding. Can I do that at The Tower?

I try to picture how this would work. The wedding is going to be on the fourth floor in the library room. It's got high gilded gold ceilings and, as we've already established, none of the windows open.

Me: Um, well, it's indoors, so I imagine they'd only fly up to the ceiling. They're like 23 feet high, so it would be a pain to capture them again. And they might poop on your guests.

Ophelia: Right. Good point.

Me: Plus, do you think they could survive in Boston if we let them out? I mean, I know doves are basically pigeons, but are they going to be white? That's like the kiss of death in nature.

Ophelia: It's the middle of winter. Maybe they'd blend in with the snow. Instant camouflage.

Me: Or get hypothermia. Don't birds fly south for the winter?

There's no response for a while. I didn't mean to burst her bubble, but it's not practical to release doves. But she could probably have one in a cage.

Me: What if you had one in a cage and didn't let it go?

Ophelia: Will they let me do that?

She's got a point, and I'm sure there's some code against it. On the other hand, I probably won't be working there much longer, so what do I care?

Me: Better to beg forgiveness than ask permission.

Ophelia: OMG, YES. I OWE YOU ONE. BIG TIME. <heart eye emoji>

I stare at her words, wondering if she really means it. But then a text from Gunther pops up.

Gunther: One of our other applicants just upped the ante. Time to pay up or fold.

Shit.

My gaze darts back to Ophelia's last text. She owes me one. She really does.

Me: So I'm applying for a sports reporting job, and I need stories for my social media that relate to sports. *Any chance you would be ok with me mentioning that you're having a wedding?*

Ophelia: Will it continue to make that douchewaffle reporter from ESPN look bad?

Me: 100% yes

Ophelia: 100% yes

Perfect.

It's going to be a fine line that I walk, being in the media while having personal connections, but I'll be able to handle it. I'm honest and ethical. All I have to do is reach out ahead of time, and things should be fine.

It's not like I'd be the first sideline reporter to have personal relationships with players.

Well, one player.

I quickly record the video, filming only the side of my jaw again, talking about the upcoming wedding reception for Ophelia and Xavier, thereby doubling down on the fact that the original article that blew up was totally false. It's a win-win. I get an exclusive story, and I get to exonerate Xavier and Ophelia again.

Gunther: This is brilliant. Henry always gives such good press. How did you get this? This bumps you up in the queue.

Gunther's latest text should make me happy. Instead, I feel a pit form in my stomach. I re-read it. Yup, definitely a pit. Reporting sports news shouldn't make me feel like this.

Before I have time to figure out why I'm uneasy, my phone dings with a text from Callaghan, asking me to meet him in a specific location. I hustle up to the next floor and down a corridor. I'm glad I changed into sneakers, as I'm getting tons of steps in today.

I'm only slightly out of breath when I reach his location. It doesn't matter because what I see before me takes my breath away. Callaghan's changed into sleek black joggers and a fitted t-shirt that leaves little to the imagination.

I mean, I'd seen him naked just this morning, but damn, that man is all sorts of delicious.

Once Callaghan sees me, he does a little spin so I can check out the whole branded ensemble. Through the fitted material, I can see the outlines of the taping I did for his shoulder. I don't know much about photography or photoshopping, but those lines might show up in the pictures.

"Hey!" I wave him over. "I need a private moment with you."

Callaghan grins, and it takes everything in my power not to melt into a puddle. "I've got to do a shoot. I'll take care of you later." He waggles his eyebrows.

I grin back. "It's not that, and I know you will." I glance around the room, looking for somewhere private. "Where did you get changed?"

Cally jerks his head toward a trifold partition set up in a corner. It looks like a medium breeze will blow it over, and not at all private.

It'll have to do.

I take his hand and pull him behind the screen. Cally's hands go to my waist, pulling my pelvis flush with his. I try to ignore the surge of heat that zips through me, landing squarely between my legs. "You can't get me all hot and bothered like this. I have to do a photo shoot in, like, five minutes," he whispers in my ear.

I thread my hands up his back, underneath his shirt. I trace his firm muscles, leaning in as close as I can to get the best grip. "I'm sorry, but this has to be done."

He asks, "What are you apologizing for?" as I find the base of the tape and pull up. I press my mouth to his, stifling his yelp as the tape breaks free from his scapula.

"Sorry," I say. "You could see the outlines of it through the shirt, and I didn't want it to show in the pictures." I change my grip and remove the rest of it, pretending I didn't cause him pain. I add on one more "I'm sorry" for good measure as I stuff the tape in my pocket.

Cally steps back, rubbing his shoulder. "No, good call. I'd be exposed if they want me to take off my shirt."

I shrug. "I mean, it's not unheard of for a professional athlete to be taped or have cupping marks. I think being a little hurt is literally in the job description."

He shakes his head. "The US Men's National Team doesn't want someone who's a little hurt. It could ruin everything for me."

"Isn't someone going to notice you can't lift your right arm well?"

He shrugs. "It's feeling better already. I'll be fine."

From the other side of the room, someone calls, "Callaghan Entay! You're up."

I start to leave the secluded little area, but Callaghan grabs my hand. He's always doing this like he thinks I belong to him. "Stay and watch. Feel free to get some pictures or whatever. You can use me on your ClikClak."

I smile, appreciating his offer. I mean, I'm one hundred percent going to take pictures, especially if his shirt is coming off. "I don't want to use you."

Cally pulls me back toward him one last time, whispering in my ear. "The right thirst trap could blow up your account. And trust me, you're the only one who's going to have this sort of footage."

With that, he walks away. I watch him approach the photographer and listen to instructions. Then I watch him—as well as all the other newly named brand ambassadors—congregate in front of the backdrop.

My first gut instinct is I don't want to use Callaghan as a thirst trap to attract people to my page. I don't want them looking at what's mine.

On the other hand, it could make a difference. I look at the pictures I've taken. There are enough of Cal—with his shirt on—and the group shots to put into a collage video. I assemble it while I wait and send it off to Gunther.

It's video number nine. I only need one more to complete the assignment. I should be able to pull something together.

After what feels like five hours, Callaghan's finally done. I'm trying not to fall asleep in my chair.

He walks over with two people, introducing them to me as his agent and his agent's assistant. They're both beaming like proud parents.

Even Callaghan looks happy. Seeing him happy makes me happy.

The assistant is looking at her phone. "Up next is the meet and greet. Signing autographs, taking pictures with fans, that sort of thing. You're scheduled to be there for ninety minutes. Then we have a dinner with some execs."

Callaghan glances at me. "This is going to get supremely boring."

I smile at him. "For me or for you?"

He cocks his head, matching my grin. "Both."

My phone alerts me to a new text.

Gunther: Bloody hell. This just put you first in the queue. We need you to come in ASAP for a meeting.

This can only be good, right? They know I'm in New York. This was all part of the test. And I passed.

I had to have. He sends me the address.

"Hey, listen. I got invited to meet up with someone about a possible collaboration. I might go do that while you do your thing."

Callaghan nods. "Like from ClikClak?"

It's not untrue. "Yeah, and it could be big for me, so I'm going to go check it out."

"Meet me back at the hotel when you're done?" His eyes are hopeful. "We're going to have a lot to celebrate tonight."

We've reached the meet-and-greet station, and there are loads of people lined up. Maybe they're here to see the other ambassadors, but someone screams Callaghan's name. "You've got at least one fan. Don't forget about me before tonight."

He leans in and whispers in my ear, "I'll never forget you as long as I live. You'll always be mine."

I can't find the words to reply.

Callaghan Entay has taken my breath and speech away.

CHAPTER 25: CALLAGHAN

The meet and greet wasn't nearly as bad as I thought it would be. Sure, I'd rather be on the soccer field, but talking about my sport with adoring fans isn't bad either.

I'm not sure how word spread so quickly that I was here. Granted, I'm not usually one for public appearances, but the fans were clamoring to see me. I think I would have enjoyed it more if Hannah had stayed with me.

I think I'd enjoy everything more with her by my side.

It would have been boring for her. Justice and Heaven, hanging out in the back of the room, looked like they wanted to go to sleep at one point. But they stayed through the event and then dinner.

The whole atmosphere of the meal was an odd juxtaposition, with the finest food and liquor flowing freely, while the guests of honor were dressed head to toe in athletic gear. The finest, naturally, but still, we're all in t-shirts and sneakers. It didn't stop the VIP treatment though.

I ended up seated next to hockey player Bastian St. Ames. His rookie season last year put him in some record books, naming him a phenom. I'm not sure if he's even old enough to drink. Partway through the dinner he leans over. "Can you pinch me? I think I'm dreaming."

Normally I'm not one to make small talk, but something about his blatant honesty prompts me to respond. "Right? Three days ago, I was contemplating if my shoulder had ended my career."

I blame the whiskey for that admission.

"You hurt?"

Reflexively, I rub my shoulder. I can't quite feel it.

I've had a lot of whiskey.

"Yeah, separated my AC. But I haven't told anyone. Just got named to the National Team and don't want to jeopardize my spot, ya know?"

"Totally. That could be the end for you. At least you have this now, though. Frankly, if they're going to pay us to be pretty, it might be worth it to retire. You ever think about that?"

Even in my inebriated state, I know the answer. "No, man. I can't picture a life without soccer."

"But you can't play forever. What then?"

There's a fog in my brain. The room is dim, almost hazy. Or maybe I've had way too much to drink. Images are swirling around and for the first time, I don't see myself in goal. I'm on the sidelines, clipboard in hand.

Whoa. I must be drunk because I'd be the worst coach ever. There's no way that would ever be a reality.

I shrug. "Not sure. No plans to quit. What about you?"

"Imma buy a house by the beach and get myself a boat. That's why I took this endorsement. Consider it a down payment."

"You're going tropical? Aren't you Canadian? And didn't you just get started?"

"Listen, my feet have been cold my whole life. I want to stick them in hot sand and bake away with my woman by my side. I've worked hard, and one day, it'll be time to sit back and relax. This is a finite period of time in my life, and I have a plan for after. Life will go on if I'm not at the rink. I actually think it'll be when my life will finally start."

Bastian's words roll through my head for the rest of the dinner.

The dinner is finally over, and Justice walks me outside. We're on the Upper East Side. I suppose I could walk back to the hotel, but I order an Uber instead.

When my life will finally start.

Soccer is my life. There's nothing else.

Except ... maybe there is, and maybe I'm heading toward it now.

Hannah.

I wonder how she made out at her meeting. I pull out my phone and check for messages, but there aren't any from her.

Me: Blowing me off for bigger and better things? Don't go home with LeBron. He's married.

There's no response.

That's odd, but maybe she's tied up.

Me: I'm on my way back to the hotel. If I'm asleep when you get in, wake me up.

I check her ClikClak but there haven't been any new posts since this morning. Weird, because I could have sworn I saw her making videos multiple times today.

She still hasn't answered my text. Maybe she's already back in the room, fast asleep. Today's been a long day, and it's not like we got tons of sleep last night. I tell myself I'm not going to worry until I confirm whether she's in the room.

Telling myself does very little to stop my mind from whirring with the worst-case scenarios and the absolute panic they induce.

My phone beeps, and I nearly drop it because I'm so anxious to see her reply.

CC: Yo, man. Where you at? You haven't worked out all week.

I'm disappointed it's not her.

Me: In NYC, signing a deal. Be back in a few days.

CC: Don't let 'em wine and dine you too much. You might get soft and lazy, and I'll be in the goal instead.

I know he's fucking with me, but it's enough to send a sobering wave down my spine. He could take my spot. It's a very real possibility.

I exit the Uber and practically run to the room. Hannah's walking out of the bathroom, towel around her body, when I open the door. I grab her to me, lifting her off her feet, her wet hair pressing against my face.

"Oh my God, you're okay. You didn't answer my texts."

"I was in the shower. Plus, my phone's on the charger. It's pretty much dead."

"Where did you go? Who did you meet up with?"

Hannah adjusts the towel around her chest as she sits down on the edge of the bed. There's a faint scar on the left side of her chest, just under her collarbone. I don't know how I missed it last night. I was sure I'd explored every inch of her body. "I was meeting with a media conglomerate. They're possibly interested in my work."

"Like for sportscasting? That's fantastic! It's what you're trying to get, right?" I sit down next to her. "Is it TV? Local or national?"

"It's online and print, not TV. Large social media aspect. But I've got to start somewhere, right? It wasn't even a full interview. I mean, you saw what I was wearing. It was just a quick meeting. It's why I'm in town."

Until this moment, it hadn't occurred to me to wonder why she was in town. It was as if she appeared out of my dreams at the moment I needed her most. "Oh, right. Yeah. I was wondering," I lie.

I stand up, uncomfortable with my lack of awareness. I should be more alert. I've been totally blindsided by her. "Well, I should hop in the shower myself."

Hannah stands up too, placing a hand on my arm. "Cally, what is it? You've got this weird look on your face."

I don't look at her as I pull my shaving kit and clean clothes out of my suitcase. What am I supposed to say? How do I tell her that something isn't sitting right in my gut?

I mean, it could be that dinner and all that booze, but it's more than that. CC's innocent comment, Hannah showing up, my shoulder. I should be on the trainer's table or at physical therapy, not in New York City being wined and dined. I haven't worked out in two days. Maybe that's it. Maybe that's why I don't feel right.

I get out of the shower and swipe the steam away from the mirror. The hairstylist trimmed my hair before the photo shoot, and it's shorter than I'd like.

Another thing out of my control.

Hannah's definitely outside of my control. Frankly, she has me in a tailspin. She's knocked me off my game for sure. All I can think about is her. Why?

The next thought intrudes, slipping by me like a penalty kick to the opposite corner.

I wonder what she wants from me.

She has to want something. Everyone does. Hell, it's not like I'm attracting anyone with my sparkling personality. Maybe my skills in the sack, but she was tolerating me even before that.

And it's not like she was the one hitting on me. Quite the opposite.

No, I came on strong. She didn't even have to try to seduce me.

What if it's all an act? What if she doesn't actually like me? There's not a lot to like.

God, I'm so stupid, walking into another trap, just like I did with Katherine.

But Hannah's not like Katherine. I *know* Hannah. She was a good friend to me in college. But that was a long time ago, and things change. People change.

Something she said pops to the forefront of my brain.

And it's all your fault.

She never did tell me what I could have possibly done that cost her her career. What if she's playing some long game in order to exact revenge on me?

There's only one way to find out.

CHAPTER 26: HANNAH

The meeting with *The Looking Glass* went well. Very well. I have a contract in my bag to review and sign.

It's amazing. This is happening. My career is finally going to start.

Cally walks out of the bathroom, towel wrapped low around his waist. Yowzers.

This is also really happening.

Never in a million years did I see my life moving in this direction. Never did I think that social media would get me the job of my dreams. Well, more like a job adjacent to my dreams. It's not ESPN or Fox Sports or even a network, but it's a foot in the door. And while *The Looking Glass* does appear to be a bit more of a gossip publication than true sports reporting, perhaps I can pull them to the real story of the game.

And then there's Cally. That was totally unexpected.

I look up at him and smile. I mean, how can I not smile when such a fine specimen is standing in front of me with only a towel between me and ecstasy?

My smile falls as soon as I see the clouded look on his face. "What's wrong? Is it your shoulder?"

Reflexively he rolls it back and doesn't even grimace. "I think it's starting to mend. Good thing, too, because I'm heading back tomorrow, and I've got to get back to my workouts."

Tomorrow. This all ends tomorrow. Or does it? But he's talking about getting back to training, which will take up all of his time. As it should. This is his job, and he's at the apex of his career. But what if he pushes too hard and hurts himself more? He was definitely in pain last night.

I lift my eyebrows. "Will you at least talk to the trainer or the PT? They can help. It's not a sign of weakness, admitting something's not right. You don't want to wait until it's too late and then it all blows up catastrophically."

I speak from experience.

"I guess." He sits down on the edge of the bed next to me and takes a long pull from the bottle of water I set out for him.

The last twenty-four hours have been such a whirlwind that I haven't had time to think about what comes after … tonight. "So, we should probably talk at some point."

"What's there to talk about?" His back is still to me.

His words land like a punch to the solar plexus, and I find myself recoiling to the other side of the bed.

I should have known. I should have known that Callaghan Entay will never want more. He's not capable of more. He's only capable of focusing on one thing at a time, and that's his career.

Not everyone gets as easily sidelined and distracted as me.

What is it about this man that can make me forget what all my hopes and dreams are, simply to spend time with him? How could I have been so stupid? Again.

"I just thought ... I mean I know you're busy but ..."

"Yeah, you know what my schedule is like."

I nod, though his back is still to me. "I do. Soccer is your job. It's your life. It's who you are, right down to your molecular core."

He finally turns, stretching out in the bed, his left hand behind his head while his right folds across his bare stomach. "At least you understand me."

I roll away, my back to Callaghan, willing the tears not to start. The sad thing is, I do understand. Sure, I was hurt that he left Bloomington without looking back, but I understood. His career—built on talent and hard work—is something so few ever get to achieve. It's a gift, and he can't waste it.

On the other hand, I don't know if I can walk away this time either. At least the last time, I had the whole almost-dying thing to distract me from my heartbreak. I'm hoping not to repeat that mistake.

I roll back to face him. I have to let him know I don't want this to end tonight. We've only started our second chance. "I'm sure your schedule is packed, but you always know where to find me."

He turns his head to look at me. "Are you sure you want that? Didn't I ruin your life?"

Heat floods my face as my own words ricochet through my brain. Of course, I said that to him. Being in a mere ten-foot radius of Callaghan Entay causes my senses to fly out of my brain. "I mean ... kind of, but not on purpose."

He slides his right arm gingerly up under the pillow. This is more than he was doing with it yesterday, so that's a good sign, right?

"You have to explain. You can't keep saying things like that."

He's right. It's time to fess up. Here goes nothing. I inhale. "So, you know how I left your apartment without even going to the bathroom that morning?"

"I remember you said that and then my roommates started calling you 'Back Door Girl.'" He shakes his head. "That was a douche move on their part, but it shouldn't have ruined your life. How did that keep you from having a career?"

I put my finger over his mouth to shush him so I can continue before I lose my nerve. "No, it wasn't that. It was ... well, I developed a urinary tract infection. Not uncommon after sex. It's why women should always empty their bladders after intercourse. I suppose I thought it was an old wives' tale or something. Unfortunately, it is a real thing."

I lower my hand. "But I was upset at your roommates, and I was upset that you left town without even saying goodbye, so I tried to ignore it. I didn't want to go to Student Health and be another statistic about the ramifications of casual sex, and there was no way I was talking to the team doctor. Especially when everyone knew we slept together. So, I tried to manage it and thought it would go away eventually."

I told him the rest, about how it traveled to my kidneys and the resultant sepsis. The prolonged hospital stay, the dialysis. How my left kidney never recovered and is considered non-functional. They left it in me, mainly because they were worried about my body undergoing the trauma of surgery while still recovering from sepsis.

"You almost died?" he asks.

I nod. "I was considered moderate sepsis. I kept my fingers and toes, so that was good. I do have a chance of getting further infections. It made the pandemic pretty scary for me. And then there's the kidney issue."

"So that's why you quit soccer."

"Um, yeah. At that point, I was trying not to quit life."

He reaches out, touching the scar on my chest. "Is that what this is from?"

"My catheter for dialysis. I was on it for about six months. School took a back seat for a while. I eventually finished, but not at IU. I graduated, but I missed out on all the internship opportunities you normally have that get your foot in the door for broadcasting."

Finally telling him this is a weight off my shoulders. But it's also scary to let him in on my secrets, to show him how vulnerable it made me.

Callaghan looks at me thoughtfully for a moment, his finger still lightly tracing my scar. Then his eyes narrow. "So, how is this my fault?"

"If you hadn't been so cocky and charming, I wouldn't have had to make that bet with you."

"I'm sorry that happened. And I'm sorry I didn't know." He leans in until his mouth is mere inches from mine. "By the way, you lost."

I smile. "I don't remember what the terms of the bet were in the first place."

His lips touch mine before he says, "I don't either, but I'm sure I can think of some form of payment that's acceptable to both parties."

⚽ ⚽ ⚽ ⚽ ⚽

Callaghan won't let me take the bus back to Boston. He insists on flying me up with him. It's quite an uncomfortable moment when he asks why I'm refusing and I have to tell him it's because I can't afford it. This is probably something I'm going to have to get used to if I'm dating a pro athlete.

Dating. Is that what this is? The mere thought of it makes my heart flutter.

"Well, I can, and that's the last we're having of this conversation," he insists.

I have to clench my jaw to stop myself from blurting out something stupid like, "Are we dating?" I still cannot for the life of me figure out why I have no chill around this man. He makes me nervous and giddy and completely saps away all my self-control.

Dating. With Callaghan Entay.

I try to picture what a relationship with Callaghan would look like. He doesn't even live in Boston. Sure, he's only a forty-five-minute drive away, but I don't have a car. I can't picture myself taking the commuter rail to Foxborough to stay overnight.

Not to mention, he's going to be busy. Super busy. Not only will the season be ramping up for the Buzzards, but he'll have games for the National Team too. The Global Games are in July in Paris.

And now he has commercial and endorsement responsibilities on top of it.

This is probably the worst time ever to pursue a relationship. Even if he wanted to be all in—which I don't even know if he does—there's no way he has the time for anything past this flight landing.

I should have thought about that before I jumped into bed with him. Again.

Because I'd be lying to myself if I said this was just sex. At least not to me. Callaghan Entay cast a spell on me years ago, and I've never been able to break it.

But he doesn't know that.

He didn't promise anything.

He doesn't know that I'm falling for him with each cocky grin and that each time he grabs my hand, my heart melts a little more.

The flight is just over an hour long, so it takes us longer to go to and from the airport than it does to actually fly. I steel myself, knowing the fairytale is ending, and I'll probably be a distant memory for Callaghan.

I can't let him know. He's not at fault here. I am, for falling too hard and too fast. Again.

Once we hit land in Logan, I try to distract myself from this downward spiral by turning on my phone. Lucky for me, Ophelia has blown it up with text messages.

That's not unusual for her.

Good. It'll keep me from having to talk to Callaghan and from saying something totally stupid.

Like I love you.

Once we're in Callaghan's car, driving to my place in Charlestown, I start reading them.

Ophelia: Hannah, I'm so sorry. I don't know how this happened.

Ophelia: Xavier's livid.

Ophelia: Do you think it was someone from The Tower who leaked it?

Ophelia: I'm sorry because the story would have helped you. I want to help you.

Ophelia: We owe you, big time.

Ophelia: Maybe you can put your own spin on it? I'll give you some details.

Ophelia: Xavier is pissed. These are the people who blew up the Phaedra story and ruined his career the first time.

Ophelia: I can't believe The Looking Glass scooped your story.

Ophelia: Though I had to giggle a little, because he actually said, "Take my wife's name out your mouth." But you know he has that accent, so it was adorable.

Ophelia: Not to mention, it made me swoon a little when he said, "My wife." I mean, I know I am and all, but … swoon. <heart eye emoji>

This is a pretty typical text thread for Ophelia. Except, of course, the content. I'm not sure what exactly she's talking about. Also not off-brand for Ophelia. Then, one more text comes in.

Gunther: We need you to return your paperwork so you can officially start. We'll be sending your first assignment over this week.

CHAPTER 27: CALLAGHAN

Hannah's staring at her phone, perplexed.

"Trouble?" I ask as I park down the street from her building.

"Ophelia blew up my phone, but I'm not sure what she's talking about." She's reading through her text messages again. Then, I see her eyes grow wide.

"What?"

Hannah shakes her head and gets out of the car. She grabs her suitcase out of the back before I can even attempt to do it for her and hustles down the sidewalk.

"Hannah, what is it? What happened?" I ask again.

She doesn't say anything until we're through her door. Then she's scrolling on her phone. The only thing moving on her is her thumb. It's like she's frozen.

If I didn't know better, I'd say she was freaking out about something. Hannah's never been one to get all wound up and frenetic. Steady hand is a better description. I'll wait until she tells me. I sit down on the couch, prepared to make myself comfortable.

Hannah finally remembers—or realizes—I'm there and points at me. "You."

I point to my own chest before throwing my hands in the air. "Me what?"

"You were in the BFL at the same time as Xavier."

I try not to wince. My stint in the BFL was not my finest moment, and I try never to think about it.

He never did live up to his potential.

"We only overlapped by a year or so. I was going out as he was coming in. Why? What's that have to do with anything?"

"Do you remember when the whole story with Phaedra Jones hit the news?"

"I mean, I was back here, so it wasn't like I had first-hand access to the British rags that reported on it day after day. But you know how they are with the royal family. They're like that with footballers too."

Hannah sits down, dropping her head into her hands.

"Why? What's this got to do with you?"

She picks up her phone and starts scrolling through again. "Ophelia told me I could report on their wedding. Xavier's pissed though."

"Understandably. The paparazzi ruined his career. He's banned from ever playing in the BFL again. You of all people should know the implications of that. I'm pretty sure he was on the cover of *The Looking Glass* like every day for months."

Hannah looks up from her phone, her face pale. Something's very wrong. "Mother fu—" Hannah drops her phone and rushes out of the room, down the hall, and to the bathroom. I stand up, unsure if I should follow her.

I mean, I should follow her and comfort her and all, but if she's puking, she might need a moment to herself first. She had turned all sorts of pale.

But when I go in there, she's not getting sick. She's sitting on the floor with her back to the tub, knees pulled up, and her face like stone. It takes me a minute to realize there are tears moistening her cheeks.

I slide down onto the floor next to her. It's a tight fit. "Han, what's wrong? What happened?"

She shakes her head like she doesn't want to talk.

"Han, you can tell me. What's going on?"

"I ... I'm finally on the verge of getting what I want. Or at least what I think I want."

"Yeah, the interview? Oh shit, did you get a message from them?" Obviously from her current state, it wasn't a good message.

"Yeah, in the middle of the messages from Ophelia."

"Okay, and? What's the problem?" Patience has never been a virtue of mine. I work on the theory that waiting is for the weak, and I plow through obstacles with dogged determination.

She looks at me, her eyes watery. "I've wanted this for so long, and every time I get close, it slips through my fingers. It's why I gave up trying. First I lost it when I got sick. Then when I finally finished school, I wasn't able to get an internship and barely anyone would even glance at my resume. But every time I have a glimmer of hope, my imagination starts running wild with it. And then when it doesn't come to fruition, I'm even more devastated. In some ways, it was easier not even trying because then I wouldn't get my hopes up, only to be disappointed, you know?"

I don't know. I can't imagine not giving everything one hundred percent, one hundred percent of the time. I mean, my life is totally out of balance, and I only have one thing in it, but I give it my all. She's staring at me, her eyes boring into my soul. I feel like she's not just talking about the internship and job. She's had a lot of disappointments in her life. She had to give up soccer when she got sick. I try to imagine what that must be like.

I can't picture it at all.

"That's not how I'm wired, so I don't really understand." My answer is honest, but I don't want it to seem like I don't care. "But if you're doing what's right for you, I'm sure it will all work out in the end."

I'm not sure it will, but I'm trying to be supportive. Or at least not a total douche.

"They offered me a job. They want me to start this week," she says finally.

"That's good, right? Didn't you say this is your dream job?"

Hannah shakes her head. "Not my dream job, but I thought it was a step in the right direction. Several steps actually. It'd get my foot—and maybe my whole leg—in the door for sure. Or at least I thought it was."

"So what's the problem?" I repeat.

She stands up. "Let's just say that there's a facet to this job I didn't consider. I was so busy trying to stick my foot in the door that I didn't realize I might be slamming it on someone else."

I manage to get to my feet in the cramped quarters. "You have to put you first. It's the only way you're going to get ahead. No one else is going to be looking out for you and your career, so do what you have to do."

"I'm not sure *I'm* wired that way."

"If you want to get ahead in the world of professional sports, you have to be, whether it's playing them or reporting on them. Because at the end of the day, you're going to be there by yourself. Sure, people might help you along the way, but it's only because they want something in return. Everyone wants something from you."

Hannah's expression changes. "Oh, Cally. Is that how you really feel? That people only want something from you?"

"It's not how I feel. It's how it is. There are many people who profit and benefit from my blood, sweat, and tears. There aren't many people who care about me." It feels so raw stating it aloud, but as I take stock of my life, it's the truth. I consider Justice one of my closest friends, but he makes a living off of me. Teammates are cordial because I help them win and help the team. Coach Dawes is one of the only past coaches who keep in touch, but I'm bragging rights for him since he recruited me and launched my career. A feather in his cap that gives him the clout to get better recruits and further his own ambitions. I wouldn't be surprised if he gets tapped to coach a USSL team soon.

We won't even get started on my parents or ex-wife.

"I care about you," she whispers.

"Do you?"

"Of course I do. I've always cared. But it was complicated. I almost died after we were together, and you were off living your dreams. It made me hate you for a while, even though I know you technically had nothing to do with it."

My chest clenches, thinking about Hannah being so sick. "I wish I had known." I pull her into a tight hug.

She laughs bitterly against my chest. "What would you have done? Left Nevada to come sit by my bedside?"

We both know the answer to that.

"And I wouldn't have let you give up your dream for me. We weren't anything. I mean, other than friends."

"Friends with benefits?" I'm kicking myself for not keeping in touch with her all these years. I didn't have a place for her in my life back then. I should have made one.

She looks up at me. "Friends with potential."

I consider that.

Hannah LaRosa has so much potential.

"Can I offer you a different perspective?" Hannah asks.

I nod.

"Maybe, people only treat you transactionally because you don't offer them any other way of interacting. You don't show them who you are. You don't open yourself up. The only commodity you give them is what you can offer to them as a soccer player. You don't let them see who you really are."

Her words hit the mark like an arrow.

How do I tell her I don't know who I am without soccer? "It's consumed so much space in my life that it pushed everything else out. It's all anyone wants from me because it's all I have."

"It's not all you have. It's the easiest thing you have."

These words land like a blow, causing me to wince as if I'd been struck. I step back, dropping my hands from her waist. Hannah may look calm and innocent, but she pulls no punches. "Easy? You think it's easy? Do you know how hard I work? Do you—"

Hannah puts her hands on my chest. "Easy. I don't mean that a professional sports career is easy. It's not at all. Less than one percent of D1 male soccer players ever sign with a professional team. You not only signed, but you've maintained it all these years. You've played all over the world. You're literally one of the best in the country. That's not only not easy, but it's nearly impossible. But it's easy to let that take over and be your whole personality."

"That's because it is my whole personality."

"But it's not. I'm sure there's more there, but it's hard work to look and find it. To cultivate and develop it. To work on yourself. Because, Callaghan Entay, you are so much more than soccer."

She is the first person to ever acknowledge that.

My God, I think I love this woman.

"Hey, are you guys gonna stay in there all night?" The moment is interrupted by Hannah's roommate knocking on the door. I didn't even realize anyone was here besides us.

Like always, when I'm with Hannah, nothing else exists.

That's bad. So very bad. I didn't work this hard for this long, making all those sacrifices to forget that there's a world outside her molten chocolate eyes and engaging smile.

Yet, still, I can picture lazy days far away from the soccer field spent with this woman.

I could see us lounging on the deck of a boat, like Bastian St. Ames dreams of. I don't even know how to sail. Or better yet, a house on the beach, overlooking the Atlantic Ocean. Maybe in Sea Girt or Avalon. We'd have coffee on the balcony in the mornings, watching the sunrise. Long bike rides with the salty air whipping past our faces. Pork roll for breakfast.

This is crazy. Maybe I've taken too many balls to the head.

Hannah smiles slightly at her roommate's interruption. "We're done." She pushes past me to open the door and slide out. She gives Carlos a hug as she walks by. "You remember Callaghan."

He looks me up and down. "Mr. Cally Entay? Of course, I do."

Hannah turns to me. "I'm surprised no one's ever used that in a piece about you."

"Because I've punched more than one guy who called me Cally." It's another thing the press has had a field day with. In my younger days, I had a slight proclivity toward bar fights. Mostly over my name. What the hell were my parents thinking when they named me? Did they not even consider that dumbass nickname that would follow me around my whole life?

"You don't seem to mind it when I call you that."

I lean in and kiss her gently. "That's because I love hearing my name from your lips."

"Aww, you guys are the cutest," Carlos says. He asks Hannah, "How was your trip?"

"Great!" She tips her head in my direction. "Obviously."

"I wanna see your pics," he demands.

We crowd around Hannah's phone as she swipes it open. There are a lot of great pictures and video clips that she should be able to use for her ClikClak account. Why hasn't she been posting?

"What did you get up to while I was gone?" Hannah asks, letting some video footage play. I don't think Carlos appreciates the footage of the big names in the clip, but he's being a good sport. No pun intended.

"I got my new backdrop and lights in. I set them up in the corner of my room. You've got to see it. It'll be a great place for you to film. Come look at it."

Hannah gives me a small wink and hands me her phone before walking down the hall after Carlos. Without really thinking, I continue scrolling through her footage of the weekend. There's a whole series from the photo shoot.

It's so weird seeing myself like this. It's going to take some getting used to, especially if I make it on a billboard somewhere. I scroll through the pictures of yesterday until a video pops up.

It's Hannah, recording herself walking along the street in Manhattan.

Word on the street is that Boston Buzzards goalkeeper Callaghan Entay is injured. This is not public knowledge, but once it gets out, will it affect his standing on the US Men's National Team?

Her words are like catching a cleat to the gut.
Or worse.
Because I trusted her.
Because I thought she was different.
Because she was using me, just like everyone else.

But not only is she using me, she's out to ruin my career.

CHAPTER 28: HANNAH

The door slamming is my first sign something's wrong.

A journalist, such as myself, has these stellar powers of observation.

I rush out to the living room to find it empty. Maybe Cally went out to the car to get something.

I wait a minute. Then two.

Then I look out my front window and down the street to see a red Volkswagen pulling into the spot where we'd parked.

Callaghan's gone.

What the hell?

I reach into my pocket for my phone, but it's not there. Where is it? Where'd he go?

My stomach clenches. This is not good. I don't know why, but Callaghan took off. Did I give everything away in my face? That I'm falling for him. Maybe he realized it and left rather than break my heart in person.

Or maybe calling him out on not giving more to people was too much. Maybe it hit too close to home. I can imagine that might be a hard pill to swallow.

But to leave without even saying goodbye?

I start to sweat and my hands begin to shake. How could he leave without saying anything? Is the prospect of being with me that awful?

Leaving is on brand for him, but I thought he'd changed.

Panic rising, I look around the living room to find my phone face down on the couch. As soon as I unlock the screen, I know exactly what happened. I see what Callaghan saw. On autoplay is the video I made while walking to get Cally his ibuprofen.

When I was mad.

When I recorded something I shouldn't have. Dammit, I should have deleted it as soon as I finished it. I was never going to post it. I was simply mad at him. At his cavalier attitude about the health of his kidneys. He didn't know what a trigger that was for me. But I would never post something like that. It's slimy and gross.

It's one thing to report sports news and another to spread rumors that could cost someone their career. Prior to today, I never saw myself crossing that line.

Now I've crossed it twice in one day.

What am I even doing?

Oh God, he thinks I'm going to put this video out there. He thinks I'm going to tell the world that he's injured and put doubt in the minds of the National Team staff that he can do his job.

I want to smack myself upside the head. Why would I even think about recording something like that? It was stupid and foolish. But I also wanted to vent and process the emotions I was having. Like writing an email with no intention of sending it.

It's therapeutic.

He doesn't know that I was never going to post that video.

I'm sure that doesn't matter to Callaghan, though. He saw what he saw, and he's going to think what he wants to think. Obviously, or he wouldn't have taken off.

Of course, that's what he does.

He leaves.

At least he's consistent.

I should have known better. I should have known I wasn't meant to have this. I wasn't meant to have this career. I wasn't meant to find love. I wasn't meant to have *him*.

I wonder whom I pissed off in a former life to be living out this kind of karma.

I must have been very bad.

My phone buzzes, making me jump. I fumble as I flip it over, hoping it's Callaghan.

It's not.

Ophelia: Xavier is pissed. I think he has PTSD from all the crap The Looking Glass *put him through before.*

As if I didn't feel like shit enough.

Me: I'll take care of it.

Ophelia: You're so sweet, but it's not your problem. Xavier says it's the norm, and I'll get used to it.

Ophelia: Ironic, considering he's the one all riled up about it.

Ophelia: I had 10 minutes of ClikClak fame, but Xavier's actually famous.

Ophelia: I mean for sports people.

Ophelia: It's not a big deal. They didn't report anything fake. They didn't even make anything up.

Ophelia: I'm mostly pissed they scooped your story.

I guess I did a good job at remaining anonymous in my videos for *The Looking Glass*. The small corner of my jaw and the voice filter was apparently enough.

I officially am the world's shittiest person.

How do I tell her it was me? She'll hate me, just like Cally does. And even if she doesn't hate me, she'll be mad. I doubt Xavier will forgive me anytime soon. The press did pretty much ruin his career, not once but twice. If Ophelia—with my help—hadn't saved it, he'd be done for good this time.

Through the tears that refuse to stay in my eyes, I stumble to my room and collapse on my bed. In such a short time, I've achieved my dreams only to have them ripped out of my hands moments later.

I doubt Callaghan will speak to me again.

He just confessed to me that people only use him for what he can do for them. And then he sees that video. It looks like I was using him.

Maybe I was.

Not intentionally, of course.

But I did have inside information because of my personal relationship that I considered sharing. I may have only considered it for a split second, but the thought crossed my mind, at least long enough to record that video.

How could I have been so impulsive and stupid?

Ophelia and Xavier will never trust me if they even want anything to do with me.

And let's face it, can I really work for an organization that trades on ruining other people's lives with salacious gossip? Just because it's about athletes doesn't mean it's what I want to do.

I want to be in sports. Broadcasting from the sidelines. Running analytics. Being there to witness great plays that go down in history.

I don't want to spread rumors about people.

If I turn down this job, there's no guarantee I'll get another one. I have no appreciable body of work other than ClikClak. I'm much older than the average sports reporter starting out. And let's face it, I'm a woman, and I'm not built like a supermodel.

That's four strikes.

I'm out.

"Hey—oh my God, what happened? Where's Cally Entay?" Carlos stops abruptly when he walks into my bedroom.

"I fucked up. I … I really … I can't …" I sputter through the sobs that are now overtaking my whole body. There is no way to articulate how badly I messed this up.

There will be no coming back from it.

I can't take the job for *The Looking Glass*. I can't be one of those people. But even if I don't take it, Callaghan will probably never give me the time of day to explain it to him.

He'll never trust me.

He thinks I'm just like everyone else in his life.

CHAPTER 29: CALLAGHAN

I f the team physician says you're out, you're out. I can't override him." Johnson crosses his arms over his chest. "You know better than to try and train anyway."

This is what I get for going to the athletic trainer about my shoulder. He and the PT promptly called in the team doctor, and now I'm benched. As if the past two weeks could get any worse.

They've got me out for six to eight weeks, depending on how I progress through physical therapy.

"Go home, Entay. Don't make me get Janssen involved," Kenley says as he walks into the training room. "You're working with PT and following their program. Until you're cleared, no working out here."

"It's been two weeks," I mutter as if the ligaments will magically knit themselves back together in record time simply because I want them to.

Kenley looks at his iPad. "And the notes say you're out for at least four more for rehab. Are you doing your program?"

"Of course I am. Don't be ridiculous." Like I wouldn't follow every instruction in order to get me back into training as fast as possible. That is, except for the instruction not to train.

They won't even let me run. You know, because the arms swinging back and forth and all. Who knew the shoulder joint did so much? All I'm cleared to do right now is lower extremity flexibility and leg workouts, as long as I wear a sling to protect my right arm. And they're all watching me like hawks.

Maybe because they know that, given the opportunity, I'd do something stupid like try to start working out. Which is exactly what I did when I left Hannah's apartment two weeks ago and ended up messing up my shoulder even more.

I sit down on the bench and stew. It's so freaking hard to watch everyone else training while I can't do anything. I take the sling off and throw it on the ground.

Xavier Henry walks by. "Bummer about the shoulder, mate. How's it feeling?"

I shrug. "Doing a little better. Thanks for asking. How's it going with you?"

He wipes the sweat from his brow with the back of his hand before taking a long drink. I'm jealous of his perspiration. "Doin' alright. We've got the wedding next week, so Ophelia's running around like a fart in a mitten for that. You're coming, right?"

I nod, even though it's the last thing I want to do.

"Turns out *The Looking Glass* story that talked about our wedding wasn't a leak. Not really. Ophelia's friend Hannah was on assignment from them. We'd told her she could use the story for her channel. We didn't realize she worked for that rag. If I'd known, I prolly wouldn't have given her the green light."

It's a good thing I'm sitting down, otherwise, a feather would have been able to knock me off my feet.

Hannah was working for *The Looking Glass*. *That* was her opportunity? It all hits me like a Mack truck. She wasn't just going to publish that video to her ClikClak. She was going to tell it to the world.

It's a good thing my right arm isn't working, otherwise, I'd be punching something right now.

As if alerted to my rising blood pressure and rage, Coach Janssen walks in and jerks his head in the direction of his office, indicating I should join him. I shove my hands into my pockets and drop my head as I follow like a petulant child.

This isn't going to be good.

I don't fucking care.

I can't believe Hannah.

"What do you think you're doing?" Coach doesn't waste time or mince words as he sits down behind his desk.

"I …" I can't even come up with an excuse for what I'm doing here, other than if I don't burn off some energy some way, I'm going to explode. I'm practically seeing red.

"It's time you go talk to Watson Ross." He's the sports psychologist who works with most of the pro teams in the Boston area. Coach takes out a business card, holding it out to me. "You have an appointment in an hour."

I stare at it without making a move to take it. "I'm fine," I say through clenched teeth.

"You're not fine, and we can all see it. You're about to implode on yourself. You're wound so tight it wouldn't surprise any of us if you gave yourself a heart attack or stroke." He's still holding out the card.

"It's just the shoulder. It came at a bad time." I can't meet his gaze.

"Talk to Watson. Trust me, you'll feel better. It's not an option. It's a requirement to return to play."

I snatch the card out of his hand without saying anything before I storm out of his office.

"Hey, Cally. Bummer about being benched." Brandon Nix is suddenly in my path as I make my way to the door. I do the only responsible thing and shoulder check him—with my left shoulder of course—and ignore the asshat. He's got to pick a fight everywhere he goes. In the locker room, at the bar, on the field. He can't control his mouth or temper, and it's cost all of us at one time or another.

My move takes him by surprise, and he stumbles back.

"Hey—what the fuck was that?" Nix comes charging after me. He's incapable of backing down from a fight, even when he's 100 percent in the wrong. Suddenly, TJ Doyle and CC are there, holding us back.

I've never wanted to hit someone so badly in all my life. "You're an asshole, and I've had my fill of assholes right now."

"I might be an asshole, but you're not one," Brandon retorts, bucking against the restraints.

"Actually, you kind of are, but never so openly aggressive. What crawled up your butt?"

I shake off CC.

"They want me to go talk to Watson. I'm benched until I do."

"You need to. You're a loose cannon."

I scoff. "You're one to talk."

"I'm not saying I have my shit together. We all know I don't. But you do. Or at least you used to. I get that you're injured, but we all get injured. The perfect Callaghan Entay isn't above getting hurt. You're not above it." Brandon walks away before I can retort.

Fuck. If Brandon Nix is calling me out, I must be in worse shape than I thought. He's right. Not that I'll ever admit that to him. I'm not above getting hurt. It's not as if this is a new occurrence for me. It happens all the time.

At least the physical hurt.

The emotional hurt—well, that is uncharted territory for me. I still can't believe Hannah was going to sell me out to further her career. If you'd told me Katherine was doing it, that I'd believe.

Not Hannah.

I thought she was different. I thought she cared about me as a person. Not Callaghan Entay, goaltender. I didn't even realize I was trusting her until she blew my trust right out of the water.

What gets me the most is I offered to help her. I told her to use my name and connections. She said no. She told me she wouldn't use me to get ahead.

She lied.

I didn't picture her as being a liar. That's a new development that I didn't see coming. I was totally blindsided.

Xavier's news was a one-two punch I didn't anticipate.

I replay our conversations over and over again, trying to look for some clue I may have missed. Some signal that she was going to shoot right when I was diving left.

There were none.

Except for maybe the whole sepsis thing. She initially told me it was all my fault. Her losing soccer and her chance at a career. Sure, Hannah recanted that, but she said it.

Maybe getting close to me was some elaborate revenge plan. And when my defenses were down, she struck. She had to have known what releasing a story like that would do, especially via *The Looking Glass*. Justice and Heaven would have been working overtime to spin that PR nightmare. I never imagined her to be that diabolical.

It'd be worse than another false paternity claim. So much worse.

Because there's nothing false about it. My shoulder's shit right now, and it may jeopardize my role on the National Team. Hell, it might even cost me my starting spot on the Buzzards if rehab isn't successful and I end up needing surgery.

The physical therapy team is optimistic that a conservative rehab course will prevent me from having to go under the knife. But that takes time and patience I don't have. Not to mention that there's no guarantee. If I end up needing surgery, I'll be out for months.

Kiss my career goodbye.

Once the rumors start, it's hard to get rid of that doubt. I'll be left playing defense that I'll be fine, rather than the offensive position that I'm the best player for the position.

Since I have nothing better to do with my time, I drive over to Watson Ross's office. I'm not sure why Coach thinks he can help me. It's not a sports issue. I'm not in a slump or have the yips or anything like that. I'm hurt and I was betrayed.

Pretty simple.

Coach already said I won't be allowed back until I've had at least one session on the couch. Maybe that's all it'll take. I'll show that I can be a team player and follow directions. Maybe they need me to be a good example for other players.

This isn't a completely new experience for me. I've met with psychologists over the years. Usually, it's for a screening that everyone has to participate in. I've never had to go to talk about my issues.

I don't have issues.

I eat, sleep, and breathe soccer. It doesn't leave much time for anything else. This is what I inform Watson Ross the minute he asks how I'm doing.

"Oh, I see how it is. Okay." He nods.

This guy looks like he's straight out of casting for "middle-aged hippie." He's got long dark hair and an unruly red beard, both streaked with a generous helping of gray. He's wearing loose-fitting cargo pants and flip-flops.

It's February in Massachusetts, for Christ's sake.

It's official. I'm at an all-time low.

CHAPTER 30: HANNAH

This is an all-time low, even for me.

That says a lot considering I ended up in the ICU and lost a kidney one time. This—this is somehow worse. So much worse.

Yet, nothing's changed. I'm exactly where I was in November when I first saw Callaghan Entay again. Literally. I'm at The Tower, working Ophelia and Xavier's wedding.

I tried to get out of working, but Ophelia wouldn't hear of it. She requested that I be their personal staff member, meaning I'm only responsible for taking care of the bride and groom. Even when I fessed up to being the person who leaked the story to *The Looking Glass*, she still wouldn't let me off the hook. She was upset that they'd scooped my story. When she found out it was actually me, it didn't seem to bother her anymore. And apparently, Xavier was relieved that it was good press rather than negative, so he's letting that transgression slide.

If only everyone could be so understanding.

Callaghan won't take my calls or respond to my texts. I suspect he blocked me. He had to know I'd never do anything to jeopardize his career, even if it meant getting ahead in my own.

My career that's going nowhere fast. Especially not since I turned down the job for *The Looking Glass*. I want to report sports, not gossip. Sure, I'd done some tongue-in-cheek posts for ClikClak, but that's not how I want to spend my life. I want to be at the game, not at the afterparty, waiting for someone to cheat on their significant other or get caught doing something illegal.

And I'd rather be serving prime rib than doing something that makes me feel like I've sold my soul to the devil. I was so excited by the thought of the possibility that I didn't think of the reality of what I was doing.

I sneak out of the kitchen to watch the ceremony. We're in a holding pattern until this part is finished, waiting to transform the Library from a ceremonial space to a dining and dancing space. Ophelia looks beautiful, naturally. She's beaming at Xavier, waiting for her at the end of the aisle. Xavier's best man is his brother Philip, who's in charge of the caged dove Ophelia had brought in.

Dave, my manager, nearly had a stroke when he saw it. After countless assurances from Philip that he was a trained bird professional and that no one would get sick from bird flu, Dave acquiesced.

Now let's all say a quick prayer that the health department doesn't make an unannounced appearance. If they do, we can always lie and say it's an emotional support dove.

I keep my gaze on the bride and groom, willing myself not to scan the sea of dark suits in the audience. I've spent days mentally preparing that he'd be here and what I'd say to him.

That is, if I could get him to talk to me.

If he's not here, the night will be so much easier for me, but I'd also be crushed that I don't get to see him.

The audience is clapping and Ophelia and Xavier are walking hand in hand down the aisle. They'll have cocktails and their receiving line in the bar area while we roll out and set up the tables. For us in the main room, it's an all-hands-on-deck operation that leaves me little time to think about anything—or anyone—else.

Now if I could just do this twenty-four, seven.

Forty-five minutes later, and we're ready for the festivities to start. It helps that there are fewer than a hundred people in attendance. Five tables are set up on either side of the dance floor with a head table for Ophelia and Xavier. That's my table for the night. Unfortunately for me, it's right up front and center, so everyone will see me coming and going.

If Callaghan's here, I won't be able to hide from him.

I get the nod from Dave to let Ophelia and Xavier know it's time to make their entrance.

The guests are ushered into their seats, and I can no longer restrain myself. I search the crowd until I spot him, leaning on the bar, drink in hand.

My breath catches in my throat.

He's staring at me. Now I fully understand the saying "If looks could kill."

There is no doubt in my mind that he hates me. The cold expression on his face says it all. I don't need to worry about what I'm going to say to him, because he's not going to listen. He's not going to give me the chance.

But as Ophelia and Xavier take their first dance, I can't help but look from the happy couple to him. They didn't even know each other a few months ago and now they're the picture of romance and love.

I've been pining away for Callaghan Entay for almost half my life, and what do I have to show for it?

He has every right not to return my feelings, but at the very least, he can give me five minutes to explain. I need him to know I didn't betray him. I need him to know that I was there for him, not for what he could do for me.

It may not matter to him—*I* may not matter to him—but he has to know one way or the other.

Before I can do that, though, I have to get through the rest of this evening, smiling and being pleasant and not letting anyone know my heart has been ripped from my chest and smashed into a thousand pieces.

Not to be dramatic or anything.

I put on my best professional demeanor and make sure Ophelia and Xavier have the best possible night they can. It's a lovely reception. Only one person seems to be miserable. One person besides me, that is.

I feel his gaze follow me as I move about the room, doing my duties. He's continually pulling out his phone and scrolling, frowning at the screen. I can only imagine what he's unhappy with this time, but at least I didn't have anything to do with it.

I've been posting drafts that I'd recorded earlier, but I've yet to make any new content for ClikClak since my last submission to *The Looking Glass*. If I didn't think it was absolutely vital for getting a job, I'd probably delete my whole account.

This social media thing isn't for the faint of heart and can cause a lot more problems than one realizes. It does things to one's brain. Chemical things that create the need for validation from total strangers. One starts to crave likes and views and follows, quickly abandoning important things like sleep to get those hits. And when the likes and views and follows slow down, the person grows desperate to post something—anything—that will gain traction.

I'm guessing this is very much how addiction feels.

Sure, social media is great at connecting people, but it's equally, if not more, divisive. It's easy to post something I'd never say to a person's face, just to get views. Never in a million years would I have told people about Callaghan's injury, yet in a moment of weakness, I was prepared to broadcast it to the world.

Social media should come with courses on responsibility and etiquette. I'm sure there'd be a lot less drama on ClikClak if everyone treated people how they would in real life.

It's just as easy to block someone, without giving them the chance to explain.

That's bullshit too.

The party is starting to wind down, and I see Callaghan heading toward the door. Oh no, he's not going to Irish exit on me. Not before he hears me out. I check in with the happy couple to make sure they don't need anything.

"You guys all set?" I can't tear my eyes off of Callaghan, who is getting closer and closer to the exit. "I, uh, have to excuse myself for a minute."

Xavier follows my line of sight. "Oh, thank heavens. Go talk to the bloke, will you? He's been downright miserable. I dunno what transpired but he needs an attitude adjustment, right quick."

Ophelia squeezes my hand. "Good luck, and don't hurry back."

Lucky for me, the bridal table is near the door, so I'm able to catch up to Callaghan without too much difficulty. From behind, I grab his left elbow and pull him into the bathroom, spinning him around and pressing my back to the door before he can leave.

"Resorting to kidnapping now? I should have realized how low you'd go for a story."

I recoil, his words landing the blow they were meant to. "Five minutes."

"Two." He crosses his arms over his chest.

Great. I don't even have time to think about what I'm going to say. "You didn't let me explain."

"There was nothing to say."

"Um, yeah. There was a lot to say. You didn't even give me the chance. You took off and blocked me."

"I didn't block you." His eyes are cold and bitter. That admission hurts worse.

"So you've seen my texts and calls. You've just ignored them." This makes me more livid than I ever thought possible. I envisioned that he was so hurt that he couldn't bear to be in contact with me.

But no, he just ignored me. Pretended I wasn't there, even though he could clearly see my attempts at apologies and explanations.

He simply chose not to see me anymore. Like I didn't matter. My blood starts to simmer.

"I told you, I have nothing to say to you."

"Then just listen, for Pete's sake. Yes, I made that video. I was upset. I should have deleted it immediately. Hell, I shouldn't have even recorded it. I was a little triggered about the whole kidney damage discussion and started having a panic attack. But as soon as I recorded it, I knew it wasn't my news to share. And I didn't share it. I didn't intend on sharing it. I was going to delete it, but you called and then I got back to the hotel, and you were in a towel and I got distracted. I sent tons of stuff over to *The Looking Glass* and didn't send that. I would never betray you like that."

"At least when Katherine was betraying me, she didn't try to hide it. Your whole purpose there was some sort of cloak-and-dagger bullshit, reporting for a piece-of-crap gossip magazine. You weren't even honest about that!" His voice is growing louder. I hope no one can hear him. The last thing I need is to have *this* be fodder for the gossip columns.

I drop my voice to a low whisper. "I told you I was there about possible work. The only thing I didn't tell you was the name of the organization. Hell, you didn't even stop to wonder why I was there in the first place. You were too busy mauling me and treating me like your arm candy to ever wonder why I showed up like that or why I didn't have a pass. But that shouldn't surprise either of us, now, should it? You don't think about anyone but yourself. It's a little ironic. You're all about people only wanting things from you, but have you considered that the only time you have relationships with people is because of what you get from them?"

It's his turn to recoil slightly. A small flinch, but I see it, so I continue. "I thought you were always singular in your focus on soccer."

"I am." His voice is steel.

Suddenly, it's clear to me. Why relationships don't work out for Callaghan. Why he has no one in his life. Why he has nothing but soccer. "No, you're not. You're selfish. You hide behind your sport and your career, but all you're doing is putting yourself first. You're not emotionally available. You're not open to anything outside of soccer. All relationships are give and take. Sure, you may surround yourself with takers, but maybe that's because that's how you're wired. You're a taker. You only want what will benefit you. You took what I had to offer you, and the moment it got a little hard, you were out of there."

Suddenly, I'm done. I don't want to fight him. I want to go home, eat an entire pint of ice cream, and cry for three days.

I was right all along. It's easier not to try because then you're never disappointed.

CHAPTER 31: CALLAGHAN

Hannah walks out without saying anything else. I stand there, stunned for a minute. How had she turned this on me? Like I'm the one at fault. Like I'm the one who betrayed her.

I can't wait to get Watson's take on this one.

Okay, so talking to Watson hasn't been that bad. He got me to admit that I don't know what I'm going to do if the shoulder keeps me permanently sidelined. He wants me to take a career aptitude test to figure out what I'd be good at.

He's very into making plans that have nothing to do with soccer.

It's weird. He hardly ever talks about soccer with me.

The next morning, I find myself back on his couch. Well, chair actually. He does have a couch, but it's not at all comfortable. He's got a rocking chair I find much more soothing and therapeutic. Without even needing the lead-in questions to prime the pump, I launch into a recounting of last night's events.

"And what do you think about what she said?" Watson tents his fingers beneath his chin.

"What do I think? Can you believe her audacity?" I still can't believe it myself.

"Totally. But what part do you find the most incredulous? That she wanted to explain that she made a mistake in a vulnerable moment? Or that she never sent the video and had no intention of doing so? Did that story ever hit the news?"

I blink. "Um, no."

"But you're out on the injured list. Is it because of Hannah?"

I thought I told Watson what happened. He should pay closer attention. "Well, no. I tried to work out and ended up tweaking it more. Kenley was there and saw me do it."

"So it never broke on *The Looking Glass*? It's been like two weeks since this happened. Did I miss the story?" He raises an eyebrow slightly.

"No, but that's not the point. How can I trust her? Actions speak louder than words."

"Yes, indeed they do. So your job before our next session is to think about Hannah's actions. In the past as well as now. Are they in opposition to her words? And then apply that critical eye to yourself."

After my appointment, Watson's words race around my head. Hannah's actions. Going all the way back to college, she helped me pass a class. She encouraged me in the weight room and on the field. She snuck out so my friends didn't make fun of me for sleeping with her.

As if. It still burns me that she could have thought that.

And then … she almost died. She didn't reach out. She didn't make me feel guilty for leaving. For ghosting her and all my friends.

Her first contact with me in November, four short months ago, was to try to help Xavier Henry, whom, by all reports, she didn't even know. She said it would help the Buzzards too.

She was right.

She had no reason to want to help either one of us, but she did nonetheless.

Then, she helped Ophelia convince Bob Miller to get Xavier out of his contract with the Terrors and hire him for the Buzzards. Hannah reported on this on her ClikClak channel, but it didn't go far. Good news rarely spreads as fast as bad news.

Then, in New York, she stepped right in and helped me get away from Katherine with no questions asked, even though she was there trying to get a job. The job she'd had to put on hold when she almost died.

I've been watching the content on *The Looking Glass's* social media. I can tell the videos from the event that Hannah sent in, and they were all relatively innocuous. Nothing was damaging, even though it was interesting information. There's been nothing from her since.

On the other hand, I ghosted my friends and the girl I was interested in as soon as my career started to take off. I don't make time for anyone outside of the soccer team, and even then, that's in the context of practice and games.

My ex-wife told me I was so emotionally unavailable that she had to have a side piece to meet her needs.

When Hannah reached out, I immediately criticized her, instead of listening to an old friend. I barged into her place of work to demand that she spill her secrets to me because I wanted to know. I never considered whether I had a right to know.

And then I basically coerced her into being my date so I didn't have to deal with Katherine.

She did it all.

She stayed with me for two days, even though she was basically on a job audition. She even saved me from being exposed by taking the tape off my shoulder.

And I wouldn't even give her five minutes to explain.

God, she was right. I'm the most selfish bastard that ever lived.

For the first time in my life, I don't have soccer to blame. I can't use it as the scapegoat—the crutch—for this. Nope, this is all on me.

This realization slams into me. Intense, visceral awareness dawns on me. My whole life, I've acted this way. Acted in my own self-interest but called everyone out for *their* behavior.

As if that was the problem all along.

I could be just as spoiled and entitled as my mother. As Katherine. But even worse, I hurt Hannah in the process.

Not just now, but back then too.

She wasn't supposed to be a one-night stand.

Then or now.

But I was too busy focusing on my career—and myself—to do the work to keep her. Would it have been that hard to keep in contact with her when I moved to Nevada? It wasn't like the olden days when I would have had to mail an actual letter.

I could have texted her. I could have kept my MySpace. I could have done the bare minimum to let her know that she meant more to me. But I didn't. Because all I thought about was playing soccer.

God, even when she was freaking out or struggling with things, I always managed to turn it around to be about me. Like in the hotel when she was telling me about her illness, and I decided it would be a good time to have sex. Or when we got back to her apartment, and she was obviously upset. She'd been asking me about Xavier and the BFL, and then somehow we were talking about me and how people use me.

Not to mention, I encouraged her to put herself and her career first, even if it meant screwing others over. But then, I punished her for doing just that. Not even doing it. *Thinking* about doing it.

I had the nerve to be angry with her.

The question I should be asking is why does she want to be with me? What do I have to offer her? She's not in it for the status, that's for sure. She didn't want my help.

She didn't even want to use me. If she had, she'd be on top with the story about my shoulder, breaking it before the Buzzards even knew what was going on.

God, I feel like punching something. Unfortunately, it's relatively difficult to punch yourself in the face, though Lord knows I deserve it. I pick up my phone to call her but drop it before I can pull up her number.

What would I even say?

I need to figure that out before I make things worse.

Not that they can get much worse.

"Thanks for coming in, Cal." Coach gestures for me to sit down. Today's the first day of practice, and I'm still sidelined for a minimum of three more weeks. Needless to say, the last five days since my big revelation have been like a living hell.

The entire foundation of who I am has been shook.

Not to mention, I spent at least three of those days at the bottom of a bottle of whiskey, where all the best decisions get made. It was a good place to mentally replay every conversation I've ever had and realize I'm a shitty human being.

There were several drunken texts. At least they were only to Watson Ross, who had a play-by-play of my downward spiral. He probably shouldn't give his number to patients.

I'm still hungover and getting called into Coach's office isn't helping.

"I wanted to be upfront with you and let you know CC will be starting in the scrimmage match in four weeks."

"Even if I'm cleared?" It would be tight, but possible.

"Even if you're cleared." Coach folds his arms across his chest. I'm sure he expects me to pitch a fit. Yell and scream, and start throwing things. Because let's face it, it wouldn't be unheard of from me.

Instead, I take a beat and consider the situation. Consider how it affects the team as a whole, not just Callaghan Entay. I nod. "It's a smart move. There's no guarantee I'll be back, and even if I am, I'll need time to get back into shape."

"Plus, there's the matter of the National Team."

I grimace. It's like waiting for the other shoe to drop. We're too far out to announce starting lineups, but this doesn't bode well for me. "If I still have a place there."

"I have it on good authority that you do."

I don't know where he's getting his information, but I should trust him. Bjorn Janssen takes care of his players. "If—and that's a big if—it's still the case, then I'll be with the National Team for most of July. Perhaps a bit in June too. It'll help CC to get more starts in goal so he's prepared for then."

"Exactly what I was thinking. I want you as healed and in the best condition you can be for Paris." He pauses, considering his words for a beat. "In the meantime, let's discuss what your role with the Buzzards will be."

"You mean other than sitting around and sulking? But I'm so good at that."

"You are, indeed." Coach laughs.

"But I could work with CC. I mean, with CC and Max," I add quickly, careful not to step on the goalkeeper coach's toes. "CC didn't get much playing time last year, so I could offer him a perspective on some of what I see from in the goal."

Coach Janssen bobs his head in agreement. "That would be a wise use of your time, and it would undoubtedly be of benefit to both CC and the Buzzards. I'm sure Max won't mind taking you under his wing. Who knows? That may be you in a few years."

I feel better after my talk with Coach. From an objective point of view, everything makes sense. And in the long run, it's probably better for me too. As the malted remnants of barley and rye have been floating around my brain, it's occurred to me that I'm not ready to part with soccer.

Big shocker, right?

But I can't play forever, and the one thing I can see myself doing is coaching. I think working with Watson made me realize that. That I do have something to give back. That I can do something else, besides play. Another thing I've been considering as a possibility if coaching isn't the right fit is working for the organization in some manner. Maybe even doing commentary.

That thought immediately pulls my mind back to Hannah. While I may have been working on figuring out my career future, I still don't know how I can even begin to go about redeeming myself to her.

It's not like flowers are going to do it.

No, I've got to think bigger. I've got to do better.

I've got to *be* better.

CHAPTER 32: CALLAGHAN

Growing as a person takes a lot of work. I'm much more used to working on my physical self than my emotional self. Lucky for me, I've got spare time. I'm doing my rehab religiously, and the shoulder is improving. My PT has me out for two more weeks, which means I'll get to start training again the first week in April. In the meantime, I'm going to practices and working with CC and Max. But I don't have the grueling workout schedule I normally would have at this point in the year.

It's kind of nice. I can't believe I'm admitting that. Three months ago, I could never have imagined a life that wasn't one hundred percent soccer, one hundred percent of the time.

This is the longest I've ever been sidelined in my career. It's probably the universe's way of teaching me about balance. If you'd asked me before what it was, I'd say it had to do with not falling over, and that I had very good skills in that area.

But what I didn't realize was my life was totally out of balance. It was all soccer and nothing else. And while I lamented that fact, I did nothing to change it.

To even the scales so to speak. Now that my hand has been forced, I can see what I've been missing out on all these years.

One of the best parts about having a little more time is getting tapped to do public appearances for the Buzzards. Dare I say, they've actually been fun. I've done some press interviews, served coffee at a Dunkin' Donuts drive-through, and even donated a pint of blood at an American Red Cross bloodmobile. That's something I'd never have been able to do while I was actively training.

I wasn't even supposed to donate that day, but after reading the promotional materials, I knew I had to. There was a story of a guy whose car was broadsided by a dump truck, and he lost 60 percent of his blood. He received over thirty-six transfusions while in the hospital. He's now an Ironman triathlete.

Though his story inspired me, I couldn't help but think about Hannah while I was on the table with needles in my arm. What she must have gone through when she was sick. I've looked up sepsis. It's nasty. And scary. It doesn't discriminate between young or old, sick or healthy. Hannah's lucky to have survived.

I still can't think of a way to make it up to her. I've never been close enough to someone to be able to buy a thoughtful gift. My mother sends me a list every year for her and my dad, with no thinking involved. Would Hannah think a t-shirt that says "Girls with one kidney have more fun" is amusing or offensive?

I'm guessing if I have to ask that question, it's probably not a good gift.

See? I am growing.

My phone chimes with an email alert. It's the itinerary for tomorrow. I'll be appearing and signing at a health and wellness expo to benefit youth sports programs in Jamaica Plain and Allston. I'm on a panel with players from the Red Sox, the Patriots, the Celtics, and the Bruins.

I'm actually looking forward to it. I might even smile. There's bound to be news coverage. Hannah would probably love it.

No probably about it. This is right up her alley.

I wonder if she even knows about it. I'd check her social media, but she's blocked me everywhere. There's got to be a way to find out.

Me: Can you do me a favor? Please?

Heaven: This must be big. You used the word please.

Apparently, my reputation for being a douche precedes me.

Me: It's not huge. I'm just trying to be a more decent human being.

Heaven: Shoot. But only because you're being nice.

Heaven: Just kidding. You literally pay me to do things.

Me: I thought Justice paid you.

Heaven: I take a cut of his cut. I do that for all his PITA clients.

That's deserved.

Me: Touché. Can you check Hannah LaRosa's ClikClak?

Heaven: NP. What am I looking for?

Me: Is she still on? Is she still posting? Has she said anything about the expo?

Heaven: Too scared to look to see if she's made more videos about you?

Me: She blocked me.

Heaven: WHAT? You guys were so cute. What did you do?

Heaven: Never mind. Not my business. Why don't you just create another profile and look for yourself?

I blink, processing the text.

Me: You can do that?

Heaven: Yes, Boomer, you can have more than one account.

For the record, I'm solidly a millennial. I'm just a millennial that hasn't had tons of time for this stuff.

But no, I had no idea you could have multiple ClikClak accounts. Within about three minutes, I'm the proud owner of the profile @mastermind1313. I navigate to Hannah's account. There are still a bunch of dog park posts. There's still sports news. None about me or any of the Buzzards.

My mouth goes dry when I watch her most current post.

Good evening, sports fans. How does that sound? How about this is Hannah LaRosa, reporting live for WYBM? That's right! You're looking at the new weekend field sports reporter for WYBM in Binghamton, New York. If you're wondering where that is, don't worry, so am I. Just kidding. I'll be reporting on high school athletics as well as covering the Binghamton University Bearcats as they continue their rise to domination in America East. I just wanted to thank all of my followers here on ClikClak, which helped me land my dream job. They told me they loved my content and can't wait for me to bring it to WYBM. Tune in at six and eleven p.m. on Saturdays and Sundays to catch me live!

I should be happy for her. She's getting what she wants, what she's always dreamed of. Sure, it's a local station, but that'll give her street cred. Everyone has to start somewhere.

But Binghamton, New York? That's like five hours away. We have local stations here. Hell, I'll be working with a team of them tomorrow at the fundraiser.

I'll be working with a team of them tomorrow.

I want to smack myself on the head. How could I be so dense? It was staring me in the face all this time. I'm going to need to act quickly if it's going to work.

Time to assemble a ragtag team to make one woman's dreams come true.

CHAPTER 33: HANNAH

I can't believe you're leaving me," Carlos pouts.

"Um, this was your idea in the first place. Literally."

"I know, but I didn't expect—"

I laugh. "What? That it would work?" My ClikClak following is over three-hundred thousand at this point and growing by the day. I think the only national event I'll get hired to call will be the Puppy Bowl, but it's a start.

I mean, WYBM basically told me that my content was why they wanted me. They saw what I would look like on camera and how I would sound. Carlos's plan was a success.

It does, however, mean I'm moving to Binghamton, New York. That's not super ideal, but there is a bright side. There will be no chance encounters with Callaghan Entay.

Hell, he doesn't even know I'm leaving. I blocked him on everything, so he can't get in contact with me. Not that he would try. No, he's too busy being high and mighty, only thinking about himself.

"I still think you should come with me. Do you know I have to do my own makeup and wardrobe when I'm on air?" They do have a team of hairstylists, but I'm left to figure everything out for myself.

"Girl, you can't afford my services."

He's right. His ClikClak has exploded as well, and he's getting sponsored deals left and right. His idea was a rousing success. Now if he'd only come up with it a few months earlier, I could have avoided getting entangled with Callaghan Entay again and spared myself a ton of heartache.

It sucks to have feelings for someone who doesn't deserve them. He never has and he never will. But I can't seem to stop myself from feeling them any more than I can stop myself from breathing.

I look around the apartment. I have a lot of packing left to do before I pick up the U-Haul on Monday. I've hired a few strong bodies to help me load up the big stuff. Once I get the truck packed, I'm on the road.

My sister and her husband are meeting me in New York since it coincides with the April break they have as schoolteachers. Between the three of us, I should be able to get settled before I start work in a week.

My life is finally coming together.

Bang. Bang. Bang.

The knocking on the door makes both Carlos and me jump. "Expecting someone?" he asks.

I shake my head. "You?"

Carlos says, "Maybe it's your man, trying to make amends."

"I don't have a man. Go look through the peephole. Maybe it's for you."

"Hannah LaRosa? Are you in there?" I don't recognize the voice.

"Shit, what if it's the wrong apartment?" Another voice responds.

"It's 11 Franklin Street, right? Go downstairs and check the mailbox."

"I'm sure. I read it on the way in."

"Can you even read? You go check the mailbox."

"I read to your momma every night when she's going down on me."

Carlos and I stare at each other as we hear what sounds like a tussle on the other side of the door. There's grunting and foot scuffing and a loud thud as someone apparently slams into the wall.

That does it. I pull open the door and yell, "Listen, you knuckleheads, if I lose my share of the security deposit, I will hunt you down and make you pay for it."

If you'd have told me we were about to be robbed by a group of Irish mobsters from Southie, I would have believed it. If you had told me it was a group of neighborhood teens high on pot, I'd have believed that too.

But I do not believe my own eyes as I stare at Brandon Nix holding Landon Stubbs in a headlock outside my door. Why would two players from the Boston Buzzards be here?

"Are you two even serious right now?" I put my hands on my hips, feeling like a mother with petulant children. I imagine this must be how Coach Janssen feels quite often if their conversation outside my door is any indication.

No wonder Callaghan pushed so hard for high standards. These yahoos could blow everything in a heartbeat.

They both straighten up. Landon looks me up and down. "You're Hannah, right? From ClikClak?"

I nod. Why are they here and how did they find me? "What do you want?"

"We want you to come and do some videos for us. We're soccer players. For the Boston Buzzards," Brandon adds helpfully.

"I know who you are, Brandon Nix. I also know your temper probably cost the Buzzards the semifinal game. If you hadn't pulled that penalty in the box, or if you had at least made your kick during the shootout, the year could have ended quite differently for your team."

His mouth opens and closes. Landon takes this opportunity to guffaw at his teammate's expense. Okay, probably not the nicest thing to say in the world, but I'm out of patience with cocky footballers.

"Why should I help you out?" I fold my arms over my chest and lean against the doorway as if I don't have a care in the world.

"We want to help you out. There's this thing. This expo. And there's a signing, with like, lots of big names. It's to benefit youth sports programs in impoverished neighborhoods. Don't you think all kids should get to play sports, even if their parents can't afford the fancy leagues?" Landon Stubbs tells me.

I know the sacrifices my own parents made to get me to D1 status. There are a lot of kids who might have that talent but not the means. "Of course I do."

"So we think you should come with us and do a series of ClikClak videos," Landon adds.

"Maybe even live ones to get people to come down and raise more money," Brandon chimes in. "Think of all the poor kids with no dads who need our help."

God, he's a PR disaster in the making.

"Can't I just give you a donation?" Not that I have any money to spare, but if it gets these guys out of my doorway, it'll be money well spent.

"No, we need you," Landon says. If I didn't know better, I'd think that was a hint of desperation in his voice.

"Oh, what I wouldn't give to have two men begging me like this." Carlos rests his head on my shoulder. "Un un un. The things fantasies are made of."

"You can have them both. I'm all done with soccer players." I nudge him off me and turn to go back inside.

"Wait!" Brandon's hand shoots out, grabbing my upper arm.

I look from his hand to his face. "You have about two seconds to take your paws off me before I drop-kick your teeth in," I say in a low voice.

He pulls his hand back as if it were on fire. "Sorry. I didn't mean to—"

Landon jumps in. "What this idiot is trying to say is will you please come to the event with us? It's an

opportunity for you that you can't pass up. Trust me."
There's no doubt about it. He's desperate.

Why?

Which is what I ask them.

"Listen—at the risk of getting my teeth kicked in—I think you need to take a leap of faith and come with us. You know me. I'm an asshole, but I'm an honest asshole. This is going to be good for you. And if it's not, I promise you an exclusive story on me, and you can make me look as bad as you want. I won't complain."

Oh, that's tempting. Very tempting. He's got viral disaster written all over him.

"Bring your friend, if you don't trust us. I swear, we're safe," Landon offers, tipping his head toward Carlos. I'm pretty sure Carlos would rather vote for Donald Trump than go to a sporting event. However, he must see something he likes because he's agreeing.

"It could be fun."

I look at my traitorous roommate. "I see how it is. Fine. I'll go."

"Do you want to fix your face and stuff?" Brandon asks. "You might want to."

"Damn, bro. Why you gotta be brutal? I think what he means is that you look like you've been working out, and do you need a minute or two to freshen up?"

I haven't been working out. I've been packing, but the details aren't important. Tweedle Dee and Tweedle Dum have informed me that I look like crap, so I do as suggested and brush my hair and throw some makeup on.

Now, let's see what's so important.

CHAPTER 34: HANNAH

When I was recuperating, I watched a lot of sports with my dad. But my mom always watched old movies. One of her favorites was a musical called *Kiss Me Kate!* It's a '50s version of Shakespeare's *The Taming of the Shrew*, set to music by Cole Porter. In it, the main character, an actress, is held hostage by two gangsters, who prevent her from leaving the theater while providing comic relief for the movie.

I sort of feel like that now.

Even their names—Landon and Brandon—carry a ridiculous quality. Carlos is having a grand old time with them. It's fine. He can.

I'm in the back seat trying to figure out what the hell is really going on. Callaghan's got to be behind this, right? There's no other reasonable explanation. My phone dings.

Ophelia: Are you on your way yet?

She's famous for jumping in midway through a conversation, even though the other person wasn't present for the first half.

Me: On my way where?

Ophelia: To the Sports and Health Expo. We sent some players to pick you up.

Okay, this is maybe making a little more sense. As much as anything with Ophelia makes sense. I mean, it does in the end, but you have to trust her process. Even when that process is convoluted.

Me: Why?

Ophelia: There are tons of famous sports player people here.

Me: You mean athletes?

Ophelia: <laughing emoji> Those people. You will get tons of content for your channel. And if you blow up big enough, you don't have to move to Binghamton.

Ophelia: It's like really far away. And it'll be too hard to meet for coffee if you're that far away.

Ophelia: Also, I need you to explain soccer to me more.

Ophelia: Apparently I need to learn how to be a WAG. <heart eye emoji>

Oh, this is the sweetest thing ever.

This is Ophelia and Xavier trying to help me out for helping them out. Xavier actually told me he was impressed with the character it took for me to quietly do the right thing and make sacrifices careerwise rather than compromise myself. It was the most he ever said to me at one time. Well, he said it in a text, and it was definitely over the word count because he's not a serial texter like his wife.

Attending this event and making content there is a good idea. While I took the job in Binghamton because it didn't require me selling my soul like working for *The Looking Glass* did, it's still a part-time gig, and the pay isn't great.

And it's still not my dream.

So, if I can use the connections I have to maybe pick up some sponsor deals on ClikClak, then so be it, especially when those connections kidnap me to make the videos in the first place.

It only takes about fifteen minutes to get to Hynes Convention Center, where the expo is being held. I use every single one of those minutes furiously jotting notes down in my trusty notebook for things I can make videos about. I've got tons of ideas. We park in the garage and then walk down Dalton Street to Boylston.

Okay, so I'll miss this when I move. There's nothing like the energy of Downtown Boston, especially Back Bay. There used to be a really fun restaurant across from Hynes that had a drink called a cactus bowl. It was as big as my head.

I'm guessing they don't have anything in Binghamton like that.

I pull out my phone and start recording.

I'm heading into Hynes Convention Center for the Health and Wellness Expo. Proceeds from this event go to help support youth sports in Jamaica Plain and other underfunded areas of the greater Boston community. This is a cause near and dear to my heart. Believe it or not, at one time, I was a D1 athlete. I grew up on recreational and travel teams, eventually parlaying that into a full scholarship for a

Division 1 college. Those sports get expensive fast! Let's help out some kids fund their dreams to play!

I don't need to give too much detail, but some personal touches can't hurt. I stop walking while I add captions, a title, and my hashtags before uploading it to ClikClak. Brandon keeps walking, but Landon stops to wait for me.

"You don't have to wait. You delivered me. I'm sure I'll find Ophelia somewhere. Plus, I want to wander around and get ideas for content. But thanks anyway. That's sweet of you."

Landon looks at Carlos, whose facial expression can best be described as "deer in headlights." This is so not his zone. "Um, I have strict marching orders to get you to the signing area."

"Signing area? Who's signing?" I look around for some clues. There are five major sports teams in the Boston area, so there are a lot of possibilities. "Is Ophelia with Xavier? Is he signing?"

He's an odd choice for the Buzzards, considering he only officially joined the team in recent months. They've only played one game. A win over the Sacramento Saints. I didn't watch it. We walk through the main lobby before turning into the large exhibit hall.

It's an absolute bustle of noise and energy. I take video footage to edit later. I have a feeling I won't be experiencing anything like this again anytime soon. We follow the signs that say "Signings This Way." Maybe, if everything goes well at WYBM, in a few years I can get a job for a Boston station and come back here.

Hopefully, by then I'll have finally forgotten all about Callaghan Entay.

And there he is, right in front of me.

As if thinking of him conjured him to life, right in front of my eyes.

To be accurate, he's sitting at a table between Dinaly Maxstud from the New England Patriots and four-time golden glover Sam Travers from the Red Sox. Doug Ellersby from the Celtics and Jean-Luc Patrice of the Bruins round out this all-star quintet.

Part of my brain is short-circuiting with the absolute sports talent in this room. The other is raging that *he's* part of that group. And my heart—alas, she's shattering into a thousand pieces all over again.

He'll never not take my breath away.

I want to look around for Ophelia, but I can't tear my gaze off him. That magnet pull is as strong as ever. I'm not sure moving three hundred miles away will be far enough. Maybe I should see if there are any sports reporting jobs open in Alaska.

Instead, I do the mature, responsible thing.

I turn around and attempt to leave.

Except I crash into the brick wall otherwise known as Brandon Nix.

"Um, where you going?" He puts his hands on his hips, his stance wide.

"I'm leaving. I don't want to be here." I start to move, but he moves with me, blocking my way.

"Here's the thing," he starts. "I don't know you at all."

"Then why are you involved in this?" We're continuing to do our bob and weave. Unfortunately for me, my soccer days are in the past, and Brandon's one of the best at cutting and weaving.

"Because I asked for his help." Callaghan's voice is close behind me. I've nowhere to go. They've essentially got me boxed in.

"This is you? Ophelia didn't do this?" Rage rockets through me. "What the hell?"

"I asked for her help too. I didn't want you to figure it out beforehand."

I'm so confused as to what's going on. What is Callaghan up to? Why is he enlisting all these people? Better yet, why are they helping him? I fire off those questions in that order.

Callaghan smiles. "Geez, I thought a journalist knows better than to ask all their questions at once. Let me see if I can get them all." He starts ticking off on his fingers. "Number one, this is a fantastic opportunity for you to cover this event and make great content that will benefit you directly. You're in a room with sports greats, and you have unlimited access. They're all on board."

He turns to look at the panel, and if I'm not mistaken, Sam Travers gives him a thumbs-up. Callaghan holds up two more fingers. "Number two and three. I think those are best answered together. I enlisted people because I knew you'd never come for just me. And the reason they're helping me is twofold. First, because I rarely ask anyone for help. Second, and most important, because you've shown up for the Buzzards and Ophelia and Xavier specifically and helped them out of the goodness of your heart. They want to return the favor."

I am too stunned to speak.

CHAPTER 35: CALLAGHAN

O kay, she's not arguing back and she's not trying to run away anymore, so that's a good sign. Or at least a small window to plead my case. I continue, "Even if this does nothing for your career, I figured you'd appreciate an opportunity like this, just as the fan you are."

"But what are you doing?" she asks again.

I look at my feet for a beat before I answer. "I'm trying to make it up to you. I was wrong. So wrong for acting the way I did. For not listening. Hell, I even told you to be selfish and put your career first, and then I held it against you for doing just that."

Watson Ross would be so proud of me.

"And I know you're leaving, and I can't stop you because you're following your dream. I've caused you enough derailments and detours. I can't do that anymore. But I can give you a send-off that you'll never forget. Maybe it'll help lead to bigger and better things down the line."

I wish I didn't have to have this big confession in a room full of people, but at least the signing hasn't started yet. The majority of the crowds are still outside. I've probably got about two minutes. Max. Here goes.

"Hannah, I want you to be happy. I want you to be fulfilled. I want your biggest dreams to come true. So, even though you hate me, start right now. Get the interviews. Make the videos. Do what you were born to do. Don't let some petty feelings about a guy who was too stupid and selfish for his own good get in the way."

"If he tells her 'you complete me,' I'm going to puke." Brandon has to get his two cents in.

I ignore the asshat and continue. "I don't want to be transactional. Not with you. I want to give you everything, expecting nothing in return. I want you to have your chance to live out your dreams, checking your career goals off one by one. I want you to be happy and, most importantly, healthy." I take her hands in mine. "And I want you to know if you ever need a kidney, you can have mine. Even if it's July and I'm in Paris, you can have it. I gave blood and found out I'm type O negative, so I can donate to any blood type."

"I don't want your kidney."

She hasn't pulled her hands from mine. I'll take that as a good sign.

"It's yours if you need it. To be honest, I'm still selfish and hoping you don't need it during the middle of the Global Games because, not to sound like a douche, I still want to take the National Team all the way. But if you really need it, I'll fly back."

Hannah's mouth opens and then closes as she takes in her surroundings. "I wouldn't let you do that for me," she finally says.

"The offer's there, any time you need it."

"Let's hope I never do."

"Okay then. Now are you going to get going on making your content? Also, a team from WCVB will be here, and if you want, they're prepared for you to walk around with their reporter and crew. Figure it can't hurt to start making network connections, especially if you ever want to move back here someday. Let's face it, Boston has a lot better sports teams than anywhere in New York."

That statement causes the room to erupt in applause, along with some "Yankees suck" chants.

Hannah starts laughing. She rises up on her toes and leans in to whisper in my ear, "This is good, but what will you give me for my silence that you used to regularly wear a Yankees baseball hat when you were in college?"

I have to laugh too, though, in this room, that factoid *may* actually put my life in danger. "You can have my heart and undying love and devotion."

I didn't actually mean to say that, if only so I didn't scare her away. But the words are out, and I can't take them back. "Actually you have that anyway. You always will."

Hannah steps back and looks at me long and hard for a moment. A small smile dances across her lips before she says, "I've got work to do, and so do you. Thanks for the opportunity today. I appreciate it."

And with that, she steps away from me. One of the event coordinators is ushering me to my seat as the doors are about to open, and hundreds of fans are lined up.

The next two hours are organized chaos and frenetic energy. There are squealing sports fanatics, crying kids, and grown men weeping like babies. Picture after picture, signature after signature. They keep saying they're going to have to shut the line down, but our agents, as a collective group, agree to add another hour to our scheduled session. There are too many fans, and we don't want to let any of them down. We're going to grab a bite to eat afterward.

I'm sure I'll get ribbed endlessly about the stunt I pulled for Hannah, but it was worth it. She was smiling as she went out to explore with the crew from WCVB.

I'll have to check her ClikClak later to see what kind of content she was able to produce. I hope it goes viral and gets her lots of visibility. After all, that was the plan.

But as I get up to leave, there she is, standing before me.

"You came back," I say. Then I realize she's probably looking to talk to some of the other guys at the signing. She's not here for me.

"Um … I got so excited I forgot about Carlos. Have you seen him?"

Heaven walks up. "Landon gave him a ride home. He asked me to tell you. Cal, are you ready? We have reservations at The Parish Cafe."

Right.

I look at Hannah. This could be it. The last time I see her in person. I want to take her into my arms and never let her go. I want to tell her that knowing her has made me a better man. I want to tell her that my life will never be balanced unless she's in it.

But I can't do that.

I can't make this about me and what I want. As long as she's happy, that's all that matters.

Even if letting her go rips my heart out. As long as she's happy.

CHAPTER 36: HANNAH

Today has been a dream come true. This is what I've wanted my whole life. To be immersed in the world of sports. The only thing that could have made it better would be to have actually been at a game.

All because of Callaghan Entay.

I'm still trying to wrap my mind around that one.

I can't figure it out. Why would he do this for me? He called in a lot of favors. I think about the business card in my pocket. The cameraman indicated that there might be an opening at New England Sports Network in the near future. NESN would be huge, as it's owned by the Red Sox and the Celtics.

It's a long shot, but both the field reporter and the cameraman said they'd keep in touch. We did have a lot of fun, and I can't wait to work through and edit the footage. I'll have content for weeks.

It seems, after a mere twelve-year delay, my life is finally coming together. Of course, I had to put myself out there. It didn't come to me, and it didn't happen without risks. I'd been so scared of the feelings of letdown and disappointment that I stopped trying.

This feeling is so much better.

And who knows? Maybe I'll be back in Boston soon.

There's just one thing.

I watch Callaghan walk out of the room, flanked by Justice and Heaven. He's smiling and Justice claps him on the back. Without stopping to think about what I'm doing, or whether I *should* be doing it, I break into a full run after them.

I'm ready for one more risk.

The crowds are thick, and people keep stepping in front of me. I'm bobbing and weaving, cutting right and left. Good thing my body has some muscle memory from years spent on the pitch. As I try to dodge around a kid, I lose my footing, stumbling backward.

I hear the "Oh shit" before I feel something hard slam into my upper back. That's immediately followed by a large crash and the shattering of glass. I continue to fall backward, slamming into someone. I'm wet and covered in splintered glass.

The hall has gone silent and it feels like every eye in the place is on me. As a server, this is one of my worst nightmares.

As a guest, it's not much better.

I'm on the ground, lying on top of someone, and I can't figure out how to move without sticking my hand in shards of broken glass. I don't think I'm bleeding yet, and I don't really want to be. "I'm sorry. I'm so sorry," I repeat to the poor person underneath me who does not get paid enough to deal with this kind of thing.

I try to roll over when I feel hands underneath my arms, hauling me to my feet.

"I can only hope someone got that on camera, so I have something to embarrass you with for once." Callaghan's eyes are filled with concern. "Are you okay?"

I look over my shoulder at the poor server I crushed and try to help him. He shakes me off and walks away, muttering under his breath. I know exactly where he's coming from. Now, there's nothing left to do but turn back to Callaghan.

"I'm fine. Embarrassed. Wet. I may have glass in my ass. So, you know, just great." I start to laugh because there don't seem like any other good options at this point. "I was trying to catch up to you. My spin move apparently needs a little work."

"You were coming after me?" His eyes brighten. "Why?"

"Because, no matter how much I might want to, I can't stay away from you."

"I don't want you to stay away."

"You're not mad at me anymore?"

"The only person I'm mad at is myself. I've made so many mistakes along the way, and all of them cost me you. I thought being sidelined was the worst thing that could happen to me. It sucks, sure, but I've also learned that there's something much worse out there, and that was losing you."

It's all I can do not to fan myself or swoon. Cally's never been able to feed me a line to catch me, but this ... hook, line, *and* sinker.

"Hannah, I've never known how to have anything in my life other than soccer. I'm trying to learn how to have more than that because I've missed out on so much. I've missed out on years with you, and I don't want to miss one more single second. I'm in love with you, Hannah. If you don't feel the same way, just tell me now, and I'll never bother you again. But I hope you realize that you belong with me."

Okay, so maybe some tears start forming in my eyes. I inhale deeply before I start, willing myself to say what I have to without blubbering like an idiot.

"It's hard for me to put myself out there. My defense against almost losing everything is to not make myself vulnerable. It kept me stagnant and in a holding pattern for a decade. I don't want to be stagnant. I want the big rewards, which means taking the big risks. And you, Callaghan Entay, are a huge risk."

I watch as his expression goes from hopeful to crestfallen in an instant. I continue, "But you are also the biggest, best reward I could possibly think of. And you're a risk I'm absolutely willing to take because I don't want to spend one more minute without you."

That's the last thing I'm able to say because his lips are on mine. Our bodies pressed together, hands desperately holding on as if this perfect moment was a mirage that could disappear instantly.

But as Callaghan's hands move up to my hair, he discovers that it's peppered with glass remnants.

Also, people are clapping, and we're being filmed. If no one got my spectacular wipeout, at least there will be this footage to live on the internet forever.

This one is just fine by me.

Justice and Heaven work to clear a path for us so we can leave without being mobbed. I created quite the scene.

"I probably need a shower," I admit.

"You're probably going to need help getting cleaned up." Callaghan's grinning like a devil.

"You're probably right."

Callaghan puts his arm around me and turns me toward the door.

"Hey, you can lift your arm without making that face," I note. "Is your shoulder feeling better?"

"It is, and I'll be released without restriction next week. The coach for the National Team said he was just happy at the timing of my injury, and he's not changing anything as of right now. I'm still starting, and we have a match in two weeks."

"You've still got to prove yourself out on the pitch this season though. You can't get sloppy or lazy now. The entire country is depending on you."

Callaghan laughs as we make it through the side door. "God, Hannah, are you ever going to stop busting my balls?"

"Don't worry. If I hurt their feelings, I'll make sure to kiss them and make them feel better."

Callaghan stops dead in his tracks. "Damn, woman. You keep talking like that and you're not going to make it to the shower."

I laugh. "That's what I'm counting on."

EPILOGUE: HANNAH

Hours later and my ears are still ringing from the noise in the stadium. Even with sound-dampening earplugs, I worry that I did some damage. It was worth it, though, to see Callaghan take his place in the goal for Team USA.

It would have been even better if they'd won the game, but they made it to the round of eight in the Global Games. Not many analysts had them advancing this far, especially considering the tough first-round matchups against Morocco and the Netherlands. They were in a tough bracket but made it through, in large part, because of my man.

It was amazing to watch him play in this venue, on the world stage. While part of me was envious of the sideline reporters, I enjoyed my role as number one supporter even better.

Whether or not the US won today, I'm going to be flying home later today. So, while I'm disappointed they didn't go all the way, I'm also a tiny bit relieved that I won't be missing anything.

For losing, it's actually a win-win situation.

The door to our suite opens, and I'm ready, waiting for Cally. I'm wearing his favorite thing—his jersey with nothing else.

"Well, that's going to help the sting a little." He gives me a weary smile as he walks through the door, dropping his bag.

"Here, let me help you unpack." I turn around and bend over from the waist, starting to unzip his bag, his jersey riding up and exposing my bare lower half.

"My God, Hannah, can you do this every time I lose?" He steps in behind me, his hands pulling my pelvis flush with his. "Or maybe not, because then I'd purposely let the other team score just to throw the game."

I straighten and he kisses my neck, which he knows I can't resist. I spin around and as I do, he grabs the hem of my shirt and pulls it over my head in one swift move.

"I will never ever tire of this sight. You're stunning. These hips. Your thighs. And your breasts are the most incredible things I've ever seen." His hands punctuate each part, with his lips coming to my breasts.

"Okay, maybe we could make this part of your post-game ritual," I pant.

"For caps or all games?" he asks, referring to his international career for the National Team.

I pull back and look at him. "Do you think I only want you to rock my world when you've had a cap? Don't be ridiculous."

"Then I will plan on rocking your world for as long as you'll let me, whether I've played that day or not."

"Deal."

After, as Callaghan is sprawled naked and lightly snoring, I look around the suite where we've been for the past week. This has been the most amazing experience, but in three days I'll have another one to look forward to.

I'll be running the social media—ClikClak mostly—for the Patriots. It's not sportscasting, but in some ways, it's so much better. I get to highlight athletes, feature awesome plays, tell fan stories, and basically eat, sleep, and live sports.

Obviously, I didn't move to Binghamton. Wild horses couldn't have torn me away from Callaghan after the Health and Wellness Expo. Since I'd let my lease go, I had no choice but to move in with him.

Yes, it was fast. But it was also practical.

He spent long days training and playing. He had several trips for games for the National Team. Our time together was limited, and I didn't want to waste time commuting. Callaghan is working on balance, but he doesn't have it mastered quite yet. The past four months have been a huge point in his career, and I got a front-row seat for all of it.

Meanwhile, I took some sponsored deals for ClikClak and continued looking for something in the field of sports reporting. My relationship with Cally did make things a bit more complicated, and most of the places I interviewed with were appreciative when I disclosed that I was dating Callaghan Entay.

It also meant that I didn't get those jobs. But I was determined that I would have it all, and when the opportunity for the Patriots opened up, it was like it had been made for me.

With the Patriots in Foxborough as well, the commute was nothing. I had close to a half-million followers on my private ClikClak account, so I knew how to grow this new area for the Pats.

And they didn't care that I was shacking up with a professional soccer player. I can have my cake and eat it too.

Mmm … cake. I should order from room service one more time before I have to pack to head to the airport. I remember there being a McDonald's at Charles de Gaulle, but not much else, and I'm not having my last meal in France be the Golden Arches.

When I get out of the shower, I find Callaghan furiously typing on his phone. He looks up, smiling. "Heaven changed my flight, and I'm coming home with you."

"You don't want to stay and watch more of the tournament?"

"Nah. I'd rather be there for your first day at work. I want to hear all about it. Maybe I'll even pack your lunchbox."

Okay, so maybe Callaghan is figuring out this balance thing.

"Not to mention," he continues, "I've got to get back to the Buzzards. They're falling apart without me. Have you seen the latest from Brandon? It's all over the news."

I pick my phone up from the nightstand and do a quick search. It doesn't take long to figure out what his—latest—controversy is. The hothead started screaming at a ref during a game. Not just any ref. A female one.

"I didn't think it was possible for him to be more of a PR disaster than he already was."

"It's Brandon Nix. Don't put anything past him. But he has a foot of gold and is faster than the wind, so everyone puts up with his shit. He's our top scorer this year."

"And your top penalty drawer. Talent doesn't give you an excuse to be a jackhole. I didn't let you pass on that."

Callaghan pulls me close. "Maybe all Brandon needs is the love of a good woman to straighten him out."

"There is no woman I hate enough in the world to saddle with that mess. Plus, my love isn't what straightened you out. If that were the case, you would have straightened out in college."

I try not to dwell on all those wasted years. No sense in spending energy on things you can't change.

"You know, I was working the night the Buzzards had their reception at The Tower. I saw you, but you didn't see me. My first instinct was to run. I thought about jumping out a second-story bathroom window rather than having to see you again."

"Really? Why?"

"Because I knew if I ever was around you again, I'd never be able to walk away."

Callaghan tucks my hair behind my ear, his hand caressing my jaw on the way down. "I'm glad you didn't jump out that window."

"I'm glad too." Glad doesn't even come close.

"I'm glad you gave me a second chance."

"If I know one thing, it's that you're a keeper." I laugh at my own pun.

"And if I know one thing, it's that you belong with me. Forever and always."

Forever and always.

I like the sound of that. He really is a keeper.

THE END

ACKNOWLEDGMENTS

To my readers: Thank you for being patient in waiting for the next installment of the Boston Buzzards. This was a difficult year for me personally, and I appreciate the grace and faith you've shown me.

To Katherine Gilreath: You were the winner and correctly guessed the title of this book! Thank you for letting me use your name.

To Alex Raby: Thank you for the Hoosier daddy line. <chef's kiss>

To my beta readers, Laura Heffernan and Juliana Miner. Thank you for dropping everything and your feedback. I was super stuck, and you both helped me cross the finish line.

To Michele: I'll never have enough words to thank you for being my person.

To Jessica Klein: Your work on the figures for the cover of this series is perfect.

To my editors, Tami Lund and Regina Dowling: Thank you, thank you, thank you for taking this book to the next level.

To my dad who didn't get to see my 20th book come to life. Thank you for the sense of humor. I miss you more than I can say.

ABOUT THE AUTHOR

Armed with quick wit, relatable character, themes of resilience, and always a happy ending, award-winning and *USA Today* Bestselling author Kathryn R. Biel writes comfort reads. Balancing drama and angst with laughter and love, Kathryn weaves stories that will whisk you away for a few hours and have you rooting for the underdog, whether it's through sports romance, romantic comedy, or lighter women's fiction. By day, Kathryn is a pediatric physical therapist and Chief Domestic Officer of the Biel household. By night, when not writing, Kathryn can be found at the dance studio, knitting, watching sports with her husband and son, cuddling with her four cats, embarrassing herself on TikTok, and doing absolutely anything to avoid cleaning her house.

Kathryn is the author of 20 books, including the award-winning *Live for This*, *Made for Me*, and *The UnBRCAble Women Series (Ready for Whatever, Seize the Day,* and *Underneath It All)*.

Sign up for Kathryn's newsletter!

Scan now to instantly receive FREE exclusive bonus content!

Stand Alone Books:

Good Intentions
Hold Her Down
I'm Still Here
Jump, Jive, and Wail
Killing Me Softly
Live for This
Once in a Lifetime
Paradise by the Dashboard Light

Boston Buzzards:
XOXO
You Belong with Me
Zero to Hero (2024)

A New Beginnings Series:
Completions and Connections: A New Beginnings Novella
Made for Me
New Attitude
Queen of Hearts

The UnBRCAble Women Series:
Ready for Whatever
Seize the Day
Underneath It All

Center Stage Love Stories:
Act One: *Take a Chance on Me*
Act Two: *Vision of Love*
Act Three: *Whatever It Takes*

If you've enjoyed this book, please help the author out by leaving a review on **your** favorite retailer and **Goodreads**. A few minutes of your time makes a huge difference!

Milton Keynes UK
Ingram Content Group UK Ltd.
UKHW020244221123
432980UK00016B/1015